PENGUIN BOOKS

MIRAMAR MORNING

Denis Edwards is an Auckland writer. He is the author of six books, is an award-winning journalist and has written three plays. He is a past president of the New Zealand Writers Guild.

Also by Denis Edwards

BOOKS
Vows: Priests and Nuns Speak Out
Killer Moves
Miramar Dog
Eden
Rebound
Connor is Free

PLAYS
The Public Good
Angelo's Song
Peace

MIRAMAR MORNING

DENIS EDWARDS

PENGUIN BOOKS

PENGUIN BOOKS
Published by the Penguin Group
Penguin Group (NZ), cnr Airborne and Rosedale Roads, Albany,
Auckland 1310, New Zealand (a division of Pearson New Zealand Ltd)
Penguin Group (USA) Inc., 375 Hudson Street,
New York, New York 10014, USA
Penguin Group (Canada), 10 Alcorn Avenue, Toronto,
Ontario, Canada M4V 3B2 (a division of Pearson Penguin Canada Inc.)
Penguin Books Ltd, 80 Strand, London, WC2R 0RL, England
Penguin Ireland, 25 St Stephen's Green,
Dublin 2, Ireland (a division of Penguin Books Ltd)
Penguin Group (Australia), 250 Camberwell Road, Camberwell,
Victoria 3124, Australia (a division of Pearson Australia Group Pty Ltd)
Penguin Books India Pvt Ltd, 11, Community Centre,
Panchsheel Park, New Delhi - 110 017, India
Penguin Books (South Africa) (Pty) Ltd, 24 Sturdee Avenue,
Rosebank, Johannesburg 2196, South Africa

Penguin Books Ltd, Registered Offices: 80 Strand, London, WC2R 0RL,
England

First published by Penguin Group (NZ), 2005
1 3 5 7 9 10 8 6 4 2

Copyright © Denis Edwards, 2005

The right of Denis Edwards to be identified as the author of this work in
terms of section 96 of the Copyright Act 1994 is hereby asserted.

Thanks to Carole and Yunus Faraji for the use of their front yard
and house for the cover photograph.

Designed and typeset by Egan-Reid Ltd
Printed in Australia by McPherson's Printing Group

All rights reserved. Without limiting the rights under copyright reserved
above, no part of this publication may be reproduced, stored in or introduced
into a retrieval system, or transmitted, in any form or by any means
(electronic, mechanical, photocopying, recording or otherwise), without the
prior written permission of both the copyright owner and the above
publisher of this book.

ISBN 0 14 301980 5
A catalogue record for this book is available
from the National Library of New Zealand.

www.penguin.co.nz

To

*John and Giselle Edwards
in Melbourne*

*Dennis Minehan
in Cooma*

The much-loved Australian connection

Characters

1972

Frank Jones – involved in the Annandale parcel bombing

Helen Murphy – an Auckland lawyer and sister of one of the bombing victims

Archie Fallon – a retired judge and former partner in Helen's law firm

Beverley Martinelli – doctor; a cancer specialist and friend of Helen Murphy

Fred Lashing – detective sergeant assigned to the Auckland bomb case

Thompson, McKenzie, Gilfedder, McGibbons, Fredericks – lawyers at Helen's firm

Felicity Castles-O'Brien – lawyer at a small firm and a friend of Helen's

Des Laughlan – an Auckland private detective

Jack Gravity – a Wellington petty criminal who makes a disturbing discovery

Colleen Jones – secretary and receptionist at Helen's law firm

Mack Bresnahan – fitter and turner at the Wellington City Council workshops, lives near the corner of Nevay and Fortification roads, Miramar

Gwen Bresnahan – Mack Bresnahan's wife

Maher – a Wellington policeman

1947

Pat Feeney – police inspector, Catholic, officer in charge of the Marie West murder investigation

Marie West – Catholic, found strangled on the lower slopes of Wellington's Mt Victoria

Bill West – Catholic, Marie's father, rumoured to work for John Augustine O'Malley

John Augustine O'Malley – Catholic, a successful Wellington bookmaker

Murray McCarthy – Catholic, a Wellington detective, specialising in gambling and vice

Dr Phillip St John Mortimer Price ('Filthy Phil') – Anglican, a Wellington pathologist

Jimmy Byrne – a Wellington policeman and a Feeney confidante

Eric Henry Compton – Presbyterian and Freemason, chief superintendent, Wellington police

The Bishop – Catholic Bishop of the Wellington diocese

Jamie Johnston and Corbett Wilson – Catholics, lawyers and advisers to the Bishop

Xavier Simeon Weir – disbarred lawyer, lapsed Catholic, Murray McCarthy's legal adviser

Moira Ormrod – owner of the house at Ararura Road in Karori

Hubert Jefferson – journalist and *Truth* columnist

chapter one

Sydney, 1972

Frank Jones could see the police standing around up there ahead of him. So far it was all right. He wasn't feeling tense or anxious or any of those things. He was calm. Why wouldn't he be? They were just standing there – not taking any notice of him. Still, they hadn't seen him yet and he hadn't done anything to attract their attention. He was just another guy in a car. He could turn around and take off and they wouldn't know anything about it. It would cause trouble later but the option was definitely there. He swallowed. He had only a few seconds now before that choice was gone and he'd have to go through with it. One good thing was that he couldn't see the bodies. If they'd been lying around all over the front garden that would have thrown him from his supposed focus on driving the police car quietly and carefully, but not too slowly, right up to the police cordon.

The woman from headquarters had talked to him about this moment. 'We don't want any of the nonsense you see on television – no jumping out of the car, yelling orders and taking charge of everything. Are you clear about that? None of it! All right?'

'Just drive the car up?'

'That's it. Calm, slow, measured.'

'Walk up like I was on a Sunday stroll? I'll end up looking like a bit of an idiot.'

'You will not look like an idiot. You are not an idiot.'

'Thank you,' Frank muttered.

'You are a valuable member of the team. Keep remembering

that. You are not a dork. You are a policeman who is really going to go places.'

He knew what to say when he hit the cordons, didn't he?

Yes, he bloody did know, thank you very much.

There'd be the uniformed coppers guarding the lines. He'd get the cold looks turning into glares; the snippy 'Who are you?' and 'No one's allowed through here.'

'They might put "sir" on the end of it; they might not,' the woman from headquarters went on. 'Show them this badge and you'll get sent straight through. The reporters and cameraman will see the uniformed fuzz backing off. They'll assume someone important has turned up. They'll make a run at you. That's what we want. You remember what to say, don't you?'

Of course he frigging remembered what to say. This was borderline insulting: Christ, it wasn't like this was Shakespeare and he had to remember pages of the stuff. Now, here they were, shoving out their microphones and cameras and all the rest of it. Let the words fall out. Here they go.

'I'm not able to say anything now but there'll certainly be a full briefing as soon as we have anything to tell you. No, I don't know exactly when that will be.'

They were getting it all into their notebooks, tape recorders, microphones and lenses. They seemed happy. He had to admit that was impressive. Maybe that woman in the New South Wales police's public relations department did actually know what she was doing.

Lining up Frank Jones for the Crime Scene Walk-in had been another win in the prolonged boxing match between the public relations staff and the front-line police, whom they regarded as a crude army of studs strutting around the place braying about how Real Cops do this and Real Cops do that.

The word had gone out. No Real Cops were to go anywhere near a camera until further notice. That notice was going to be a long time coming, after the fiasco at the Harvey shootings. The reporters hadn't appreciated being called 'parasitic cocksucking bastards', being told, 'Your name changes from Mike to Mary as soon as you hit the prison showers.'

The reporters agreed this might be true but they couldn't put it on air.

A decision had been made: 'We need a pretty face, and one that'll do exactly what it's told.'

Frank became the police's pretty face. Okay, not exactly pretty, but definitely good-looking, and not even close to the bad-breath body-odour types with the cheap haircuts, curled lips and angry eyes in police interrogation rooms on television.

Frank had thought about refusing, but knew what would be waiting if he did: a lot of flak. He could be fined or demoted. That's the last thing he needed, what with owing a bit of money around town. Roll with the punches, he'd told himself. Be bigger than that. Rise above it. He'd thought he was getting there until he saw a woman with a carload of children running an amber light on the Parramatta road. There was an extraordinarily bad moment there when he nearly snapped, whipped out his .32 to blow her away. But he held on, and the moment passed.

He'd done the right thing and he was a better man for it.

If he could do that, he could get through this. Get those shoulders straight and the head in the air. Be the model of the ruggedly handsome Sydney detective: all square jaw, strong, wide shoulders and a halfway decent suit. The trousers were safely zipped up: he'd checked before he got out of the car. The moustache and the muttonchops were just so. He had the appropriately deep voice – a lightly twanging Australian accent, not too western suburbs – for the little speech about not being able to say anything.

He got past the media and up to the house.

A white-faced constable was at the door. As Frank made to walk inside, the constable muttered, 'Jeez mate. Rather you than me,' and turned away to try and cope with whatever horror he'd just seen.

Oh yes, there was something else the public relations woman had told him: 'For God's sake, don't throw up where the cameras can see you. Get inside the door and close it behind you. Feel free to toss your lunch all over the place then. No one will give a shit except the crime scene detectives – they're always bleating about contamination. Ignore them. They won't be helping get the Commissioner on top news shows. If it really comes down to it, we'll win that one.'

Still, it was a bit off-putting seeing the two uniformed policemen vomiting in the bathroom – one into the basin and the other into the toilet.

Frank stopped at the kitchen door.

Jesus!

Mother of God!

The bombs lecture at Police College hadn't come close to preparing him for this. Obviously the two of them had been sitting at the kitchen table. The man now stopped at the neck. Just stopped. Frank's guess was that his head was in the spray of red and blue oozing down the French doors behind him, along with some of the porridge he'd been eating.

The woman was a worse mess. She was a human being from her feet to just below her waist. Everything from there on up was on the wall, mixed with the remains of a dog that must have been sitting on her lap. He could see a tail and a small white back leg. If he'd had to place a bet he'd have said it was a Bitchin or Bicho or one of those little white fluffy dogs. There were a few lumps of its coat and head on the wall in among bits of her upper body. It was going to take some serious work sorting out what was who in the thick ooze forming lines down the wall, and the small lumps of flesh dropping to the floor.

Well the Walk-in was out of the way. Frank reckoned he could leg it back to the squad car now. This was definitely for the oafs who liked this crap. He looked up. They were pulling a tarpaulin over the hole where the roof used to be – keeping out the weather and the news helicopters.

On the other side of the room a short, overweight, plainclothes policeman hid a smirk under a ratty moustache. He was enjoying watching Frank struggling against vomiting or fainting. He could have done with that; he needed some entertainment. This was going to be a tough investigation and he could do with some lighter moments.

Someone tapped him on the shoulder.

What?

'Excuse me, sir, there's this.'

A tough-looking uniformed sergeant was beside him. The sergeant's scarred face, with its many-times broken nose, was one the public relations people did *not* want on television, except perhaps in a deeply touching 'homely Aussie battler laments a lost mate' scenario.

'We mighta got lucky,' the sergeant said.

He was holding a fragment of a blue plastic envelope. Its edges were burnt. 'I'd say that's what the bugger got delivered in.' The sergeant's thick finger pointed at what was left of the sender's address: . . . New Zealand.

'Looks like a Kiwi's playing silly buggers.'

It didn't take a big brain to work out that the bomb had come from across the Tasman. If one of the victims was a sheep-shagger that was bad. Any case with an international component meant endless hours of liaising with Uncle Tom Cobleigh and all that slowed everything right down.

The chances of a quick result, a shit-kicking loser hobbling into court under a blanket, a brilliant press conference and beer and fish and chips all round in the Commissioner's office by the end of the week were sinking like a sack full of little kittens and big bricks. There was only one way to describe it.

It was a bloody tragedy.

chapter two

Auckland, 1972

Helen Murphy eased herself up from kneeling beside her mother's grave. That little stab of pain in her calves and ankles was something new. She was only forty-one; that sort of thing wasn't supposed to happen for years.

Still, it wasn't as if she couldn't cope with fighting pain. She had the genes – look at her mother. Her whole adult life had gone in battles with asthma and assorted other health problems. When she wasn't fighting her body she'd been in strident wars with the other wrecks and ruins in her life: husband, children, teachers, police, truancy and probation officers and a circus parade of unhappy bosses – her own, her children's and her husband's. So far as Helen could see, her mother had fought them all to a more or less honourable draw.

'That's the exact spirit you need, and you need it now,' Helen spoke quietly, to her mother's gravestone but for herself. 'Whatever fight you had in you, I need it now, because you were never up against anything like this.'

A murderer was out there, almost certainly in Wellington, and ready to strike at her. He'd already got Jennifer, her younger sister, while she was sitting at her house in Sydney's Annandale. She'd opened the parcel that had blown her and Freddie to pieces. Helen was next, and it probably wouldn't be long.

The pain in her leg eased. She was nearly six feet tall and a doctor had told her tall people had a higher risk of leg injuries. She remembered back to the days when modelling agencies were pestering her to sign with them. Her friend Wendy Mayes had followed up an ad in the paper and disappeared. A couple of months later the man who had placed the ad saw one of the police surrounding his house slip away for a pee. That was his chance. He sprinted down the road and leapt from the Island Bay cliffs. A few days later his body washed up on the coast. The police would spend the next six months hunting for Wendy's body without finding it.

Concentrate on the present, or you won't have a future! Helen admonished herself.

Above and behind her the clouds were pushing in low and hard from the Tasman Sea, over the brooding Waitakere Ranges and out over Henderson and Glen Eden. They sliced deep into the late afternoon to turn it dark before it was time.

Her mother had been dead for nearly seven years now: Helen's goodbyes were all said. The tears were gone. If she were honest, some of them had been for herself: at her disappointment that her mother had not lived to see Helen slip clear of the chains holding the Murphy family locked in anger, suspicion, self-pity and fear. Too many had fallen to alcohol, boredom and failure. The boys had turned to violence, headed for prisons and mental hospitals. The girls would occasionally 'go up north for a while', to maternity hospitals out of Wellington. Through it all the nuns and priests slaved to steer the family up from being the scorn of Miramar's Protestants to the heights of mere anonymity.

Normally by now Helen would have been in her car and on her way home to the distant eastern suburbs. Today was different. She stood still, not wanting to leave. Why? She didn't know, not for sure. Was she hoping her mother's faith and strength would seep through the earth and into her?

Once she'd have looked to Terry to help, but he'd died in January in an accident on the Bombay Hills. Helen hadn't looked for anyone since then. Eventually she would find another man, but not yet. The emptiness of Terry's loss was still too raw.

Helen's mother had spent many hours sobbing in front of the big crucifix in the living-room, pleading that Helen and Jennifer stopped at giving handjobs. She did this in front of the mortally embarrassed sisters, ignoring their begging for her to stop. If they didn't, and the result was a Blessed Event, she tearily beseeched God to make the boy marry them before their brothers found out and crippled him. That would free her girls of any nonsense about careers, they would settle quietly into a life of child-rearing and stress-managing sherry, the mix that helped Mother through her life sentence. Should God be merciful and allow them to avoid the Blessed Event, she begged Him to allow her daughters to become nurses, typists or even assistant heads of a department at Kirkcaldie & Stains Lambton Quay store. Any of these would be a sign from Heaven that the terrible burden of the Murphy chromosomes had been watered down enough to free them from the shadow of prison, mental hospital and maternity ward.

A year after her mother died, Helen qualified for the Auckland University law school. Now she was a lawyer: the only one in the family with a degree, and a job that didn't require her to put things on shelves or lift anything heavy.

Even cold in her grave her mother was trying to be as encouraging as she'd been in real life, Helen was sure. Except that it had always come salted with discouragement. Aim as high as you can, but not too high, because it's devastating when you fail.

Her poor mother. If she'd hung on another few years she would have been proud of her daughter the lawyer.

But she'd died visiting Helen in Auckland, and Helen and Jennifer had decided to have the funeral there. Why not? The family was scattered and they didn't know where to find most of them. Besides, it was better than going back to Wellington for the locals to gaze down at the coffin and give thanks to God for his mercy in letting another Murphy exit a horrible life. Helen and Jennifer were the only ones at the funeral and the next day Jennifer flew back to Sydney. New Zealand was her past, and was staying there. She had never been back.

Helen had a good idea of who had sent the bomb and why. What was she going to do if one arrived for her? So far she knew only one thing: she wasn't going to tell the police.

Too much had gone on back in the winter of 1947. She had to fight this on her own and she had to be strong. Finding a weakness – any weakness, even as small as a twinge in a leg – was frightening.

The wind coming down from Henderson riffled the flowers on the graves. The headlights of the cars speeding up Great North Road were flicking on, the yellow and white light spearing into the grey-turning-black evening.

A sudden noise frightened her. A small digger on little rubber wheels had come from nowhere and was pulling up beside her. A tanned, gnarled little man climbed down from the driver's seat. On this cold day he was wearing a thin jersey and faded old rugby shorts. His rheumy blue eyes looked at her.

'I'm sorry ter interrupt yer.'

His roll-your-own cigarette seemed to have a life of its own, bobbing and rolling across his mouth. Helen's fright was lost in her fascination with its stately rhythm from one side of his face to the other. It reminded her of walking on a rolling ship's deck when the sea was rough.

'It's just that when you're finished,' he nodded respectfully at the grave, 'there's a wee bit of pressure on for me ter . . . yer know . . . get things ready fer later on. It's Jews, yer see, and they don't like ter mess about waiting for the burial, them Jews. Their grave's right next door to this one.'

'Jews' came out as 'Chews'.

The gravedigger, trying not to be too obvious about freeing up his balls from his obviously too-tight underpants, wore what he hoped was an empathetic expression. Helen gave him a thin smile, took a last look at the grave and crossed herself – this was the the only time she did that.

She picked her way down the hill towards the carpark. Oh Christ. The heel on her left shoe had come adrift, forcing her into an awkward stumble. She didn't look back up to her mother's grave. She didn't want to see the digger's wheels reversing over her flowers. When she reached the carpark the tears came and nothing could stop them sliding down her face and being lost in the corners of her mouth.

chapter three

Wellington, July 1947

'Jesus bloody Christ!'

Inspector Pat Feeney grumbled to himself as he slowly climbed out of the Humber police car. He looked across to Cook Strait and the dark, threatening clouds filling in above it. If that wasn't a roaring, cold, wet bloody southerly storm lathering up to shave every leaf from every tree in Wellington, he was still home, tucked up nice and warm in bed.

Well, he wasn't.

He was out there at six on a frigging cold morning. If he'd done what his mother wanted and trained for the priesthood, he wouldn't be scrambling up through the bush just above the houses on Mt Victoria to look at a young murder victim. But he'd become a policeman, and this was what policemen did.

He was going through the little mental exercise he always used to prepare himself to look at a body. He would remember the very worst, and know that he had survived it, so he would survive whatever was up there. For him it was the woman in Seatoun. Terrified of being robbed, she'd made herself a prisoner in her house. When she had died her cats had had no escape and they had stopped being pets and become predators. By the time the police finally broke into her house they were finished with the softest flesh – the cheeks of her face – and were in her stomach. Nothing could be that bad again.

It wasn't as if he had to stay in the police, not now. There was enough in the superannuation to keep him, and the twins were close to leaving home. His wife had her own existence. As far as he could see, the only ones wanting him to stay in the police were Wellington's Catholics.

Feeney shook his head. Bloody religion and religious politics! They'd had millions killed, millions more lives wrecked and hopes destroyed. The girl up there was almost certainly one of them. Would he end up being another?

He could worry about that later. Meanwhile, he was being paid to go and look at the body. He had to get on with finding out who did it. He could stop the whining and get on with it. He back-heeled the Humber's door shut behind him and pulled his coat up around his neck. It was a waste of effort: the cold cut through it as if it didn't exist.

A young policeman saw him and stood to attention. Detective Inspector Feeney was important. He headed the big murder and robbery cases and had a big say in who did and didn't make a detective.

Feeney had been on holiday when the last murder case broke. Frank Wilkins had been pulled out of Evans Bay with his head smashed in and a chestful of bullets. As soon as he'd heard, Feeney knew where that case was going. Wilkins had spent almost all his life around Wellington's Catholic-dominated bookmakers. Feeney knew the Freemasons in the police would be sniggering into their little briefcases over his death. They'd Catholic coppers hunting the Catholic bookies responsible and they wouldn't have to do anything. They could stand back, let them eat each other.

Still, assuming this latest body was Marie West, this might not be any better. Marie's father, Bill West, worked for John Augustine O'Malley, the bookmaker Frank Wilkins had hung around with the most.

Christ, all roads led to the freaking Roman Catholic church. Would God mind telling him how was he supposed to protect the Catholics when they were happily slaughtering their way across Wellington?

Feeney let the photographers go up the track ahead of him. They were younger and fitter. Besides, the coming storm would destroy the scene – they needed to hurry.

He'd bet good money it wouldn't be long before he'd be summoned by the Bishop, 'hoping to get a quick word'. Another softly manipulative reminder of the sufferings of the faithful. Well, he'd had enough of them. What he wanted was a long spell away from it all – the rest of his life would be about right.

He could hunch up against the weather all he liked: he'd never be a small target for the wind and the rain. He was too tall and too powerfully built. Feeney's strong, coarse face would never let anyone call him handsome, especially not with his loose jowls and dark bulging eyes. A day without shaving meant an instant beard.

It would have been a wonderful look for a priest roaring against the sinners and fornicators.

Ah yes, his mother. Widowed years ago, she was eighty-six now. Her mind had evaporated but her body fought on. For everyone else it was a wrenching, enduring tragedy; for her it was a happily ignorant bliss.

The Humber would be all right where it was. That young copper over there could keep an eye on it.

Who was this?

A man of about forty was sitting on the kerb, ignoring the water running over his shoes. His face flicked through white to grey and back again. That'd be the poor sod that'd found the body. Best get him out of there and into a warm police station. Get his statement fast in case he dropped dead from a stroke or a heart attack. At the same time it might be worth a quiet question as to what he was doing on Mt Victoria at five in the morning.

Pat Feeney heard something behind him.

'Shit.'

Murray McCarthy was getting out of his car. He was the last person Feeney wanted anywhere near this. McCarthy was one of his worst problems, partly because the detective was also Catholic. He was a mad bull, living to antagonise people and not caring who, when or how often. Feeney always ended up having to protect or defend the bastard. He could run the Bishop's little speech over by rote: 'Yes, Murray is a problem, but always remember, he's one of ours.' Feeney's restraint with McCarthy – when what he really wanted was to throw him to the lions – was rewarded, usually in slices of information flowing out of the influential circle around the Bishop.

Well, information or not, he'd had enough. Sure, the Catholics might be under siege. Yes, the Bishop and the others could grant favours. But being a Catholic didn't mean you were above the law. McCarthy was going to have to go.

Feeney had been ready to move after the Filthy Phil business, but the stupid bloody Freemasons didn't have the brains to keep their bloody mouths shut. If they'd stopped screaming for McCarthy's head, Feeney would have given it to them. But because they'd made such a noise he'd been forced to protect the oaf against them.

Now McCarthy had turned up here, his strangely small face above that great oxen body glowing at the chance to gaze down on more death.

The young policeman beside Feeney raised his voice, trying to get his attention.

'This is Mr Fraser. He found the body, sir.'

Fraser stood up, wobbling slightly. Feeney and the young policeman had to grab his arms to keep him standing.

'She's up there. She's up there!' Fraser could barely force the words up through his dry throat. His eyes were wide open and red. He wouldn't be able to take much more. Feeney gently eased him down the hill, being careful to turn a neutral expression to McCarthy.

'Get Mr Fraser back to Central.'

Feeney made sure his voice was all authority. McCarthy's lip lifted in a sneer. He did not take witnesses back to Central. Junior officers did that. McCarthy wanted to be at the centre: by the body, endlessly questioning a rape victim or shoving his face close to enough to a suspect to smell his toothpaste before beating a confession out of him.

McCarthy turned to the uniformed policeman. 'Hampson, get Mr – what's yer name?'

'Fraser. Bob Fraser.'

'Fraser. Good on yer! Get him back to Central. Give him plenty of tea. Get some sandwiches for him and then get his statement.'

21

'Yes, sir.'

Feeney glared at McCarthy. It was outright insubordination. He'd pay for that, starting with being kept off this case. That would be a humiliating slight. It was also pretty bloody weak. Maybe McCarthy wouldn't even care. Why not do something direct and do it right now? Because other officers were watching and they were supposed to be senior officers setting some sort of example, that's why.

Feeney turned and began the climb up the muddy slope. At least there was one good thing. Feeney wasn't the only one taking a cold look at McCarthy. The whispers linking McCarthy to O'Malley's bookmaking were becoming too strong to ignore.

For God's sake, keep your bloody mind on the job, Feeney snapped to himself, grabbing at a manuka tree to stop himself falling. He shoved a thick clump of brush aside and stopped. He was almost on top of two more policemen. One of them thrust out a hand to stop him, dropping it when he saw it was Feeney. The body was only a couple of yards further on. Yes, it was Marie West, and she was going to be seventeen and a half for all time. She was well and truly dead.

chapter four

Auckland, 1972

It was six-thirty in the evening. Helen had been around the fourteenth floor three times now, checking everywhere: every office, the toilets, the photocopier room and the little lunchroom. She was definitely alone. Good. That left just her and the parcel bomb sitting quiet and malevolent on her desk. He must have sent them hoping they would arrive on the same day, only he couldn't have anticipated a two-day walkout by Auckland postmen. That allowed the Sydney one to arrive first.

Helen had whispered a heartfelt thanks to all the gods for the two wires that had peeped out from the little rip at the bottom of the cardboard box. And she'd crossed herself for the little bit of time she'd managed to spend in the library reading about parcel bombs. This thing fitted the profile. There was the extra taping across the top to stop it detonating before someone made a determined effort to open it. It was also quite heavy, just as the books said it would be.

Helen had planned, if a bomb arrived for her, to say nothing. She'd carry the wretched thing to her car, drive out to Hobsonville and slide it into the upper Waitemata Harbour's mud and silt. Let time and the tide bury it. By the time it had corroded enough to explode, the thing would have been under three feet of sand.

That plan died when the receptionist noticed the wires. Margaret had carried it to Helen's office, struggling to get it to her desk without dropping it. Helen couldn't miss Margaret's wide-eyed look, but the secretary said nothing.

Christ!

Instantly Helen could see what was going to happen. Sooner or later, and probably sooner, Margaret would say something to someone. Eventually that titbit would reach someone who would think 'Bomb!' A millisecond later it would be: 'Get the police, the army bomb disposal unit, the fire service and anyone else who ever wore a uniform up here now!'

Helen had been able to buy a little time. Margaret had a brother in hospital. Why not go and see him? she suggested. You have done enough overtime and you have helped us more than once. Have an afternoon off. Margaret had hesitated, but then she'd decided such opportunities didn't come along that often. She'd arranged someone to look after reception and she'd been on her way. That meant Helen had until the morning before word began getting around. Now she was trapped into doing the one thing she didn't want to do. She was going to have to tell the police.

Shit.

Right from the moment she'd sat shocked in front of the television, looking at Jennifer's house in Sydney, with the police and the undertakers going in and out, she'd known she was next.

Once the police were involved how long would it be before the words 'sisters' and 'another bomb' turned up in the same sentence? Then the police would be saying things like, 'What about having a bloody good look at them all, including this Helen, to see if there's anything there that'd get someone revved up enough to be sending out the big firecrackers?'

Once that machine began clanking there would be nothing Helen could do to stop it.

There was another problem. The time. It was six-thirty now. The wretched thing had been here since two, while she'd tried to decide what to do, ditching one plan after another, fumbling and fighting her panic as she tried to think her way through it all. She knew the bomb was safe until someone opened it, but would she be able to convince anyone else of that? Hardly. She could imagine the howls. 'It's a bomb, for Christ's sake! We were all at risk! Why didn't you move straight away?'

Helen closed her eyes for a moment, breathed in and out to try to regain some control, and then dialled 111.

'Which service do you require, Police, Fire or Ambulance?'
'Police.'
'Police here. What is the problem?'
'There's a bomb in the Freyberg Building, in the north-west corner office on the fourteenth floor.'

The voice was crisp and urgent. 'Get out of there now. Walk – do not run. Get out into Queen Street, turn left, walk a hundred yards and wait.' The operator mentioned a small dress shop. Helen knew it. She was told to wait there. What was she wearing so they could find her? They would be evacuating the building. There would be people milling around and they didn't want to miss her.

She hung up and looked at the bomb, and through it to the man who sent it. 'You stinking bastard! You absolute bastard!'

She left and walked out through the foyer, turned into Queen Street and found the dress shop. She sat down on a bus stop bench outside it.

God almighty.

Helen kept herself sitting up straight. She couldn't afford to collapse into panic; she needed to stay alert. This was not the end: it was just the beginning. She'd be going to the police station and she had to stop herself saying or doing anything stupid. Do you want to go to prison? she admonished herself. Do you? Is there something in you, something Catholic, that wants you to confess your sin – yours and Jennifer's – so you be freed of its weight? Is there?

She'd already had one upheaval today. It had been Archie Fallon's farewell that lunchtime. He was one of the partners but he'd got the nod and was off to the Supreme Court Bench. There were whispers that he'd got out just in time after some cock-ups on big cases. Naturally these remained whispers. Judges could steer things in any direction they liked, and lawyers caught spreading rumours could find their cases going sour, their careers and client bases withering on the vine.

Helen was in the pack rolling into the Northern Club for the farewell. Some had gone to shake hands and make contacts. Others trooped in with a weary sense of 'If I'm seen going to other people's send-offs hopefully there'll be a turnout for mine.' Most had another reason for going: they wanted to be sure the evil, smirking little bastard was really leaving.

Helen had once whispered, in strictest confidence, to another woman lawyer, that she thought Fallon was a gruesome sleaze. She discovered that female bonding against the legal profession's predators was a weak adhesive when Fallon slipped the word 'gruesome' into his farewell speech. Everything was noticed; nothing was forgotten. Jolted, she had nearly missed the significance of what happened next. Two men were quietly easing her from the herd. One was a partner at her firm; the other was from the Ministry of Justice, a man both jovial and watchful. The system was up to its waistcoats in royal commissions, they told her, and they were short of experienced lawyers. They'd also like some women in the mix. Helen finally realised what was happening. They were sounding her out for a royal commission and wanted to know her answer before they formally asked her.

As soon as she got back to her office she made full notes: who'd made the approach and what they, and more importantly she, had said. She was certain – well, almost – that she had said yes.

Then the bloody bomb had arrived.

She'd been almost hypnotised by it, as if it were a snake calmly eyeing her before it struck. Its being in her office was its own violation. That office was the reward for her hard years of struggle through real estate conveyancing, divorces and fence disputes. She'd come to this firm, only to be cast adrift two floors down in what the partners called the 'talent pool' but which everyone else called 'The Tomb of the Doomed', marooned to the work of making certain the finer points of a fried-chicken restaurant chain's franchise agreements were properly and neatly spiced.

Now she was sitting on a wooden bench in Queen Street, waiting for the police after she'd risked blowing up the whole place.

chapter five

Wellington, 1947

Feeney forced himself to look up and away from Marie's body. There must be something, anything, lying around that would tell him something about what had happened here. There wasn't. He knew there wouldn't be. She'd been here nearly four months. Weather and time had cleaned away any footprints, blood or anything else that might have been here. They'd still give the area a thorough search, though.

If there was anything good about Marie's death, it was that it had been quick. He could see no signs of her being beaten, tortured, or of a terrible fight to live. That string around her neck would have been dropped over her head and pulled tight. In just a few seconds it would have been over. Marie's killer wanted her dead and him away as fast as possible.

Feeney was about to cross himself as a small thanks to the Furies for the speed of her death. His hand began to move. Then he stopped. No! It'd be straight around the police's Freemasons that he'd been performing Catholic rituals over the body. Things were bad enough between the Masons and the Catholics without him throwing that bit of coal on the fire.

Marie's turning up dead hadn't been too much of a surprise. Right from the day she was reported missing he'd assumed she'd been killed. She was too close to people living with the sort of secrets that could send a man to the gallows. She'd disappeared about the time Wilkins was murdered. Had she seen or heard something? Marie had had a fiery temper: had she yelled a threat frightening enough to force someone to kill her?

Feeney wasn't the only one making the connection between Marie and the bookmakers. He had a drawer full of *Truth* clippings hammering on about it. The reporters' information was too good: they were surely getting help from inside the police. Probably from the Protestants and certainly from the Freemasons – and mostly likely both.

The Freemasons had become a refuge for anyone nervous of the Catholics' growing power and influence. There weren't too many choices. Catholics were close to the heart of both the Labour government and the powerful union movement. The National Party had been either in Opposition or a powerless wartime coalition partner for the last fourteen years. It might be odds on to win the 1949 election, but that was still two years away. So the angry and the frightened flocked to the Masonic lodges.

The tension between the Catholics and almost everyone else had been getting worse since a few years back. New Zealand's army was full of Catholics fighting and dying in the North African desert. The survivors came home on leave and didn't like what they found. The mad, the old, the sick and the rich were exempt. Why, they howled, were the rich being kept safe, especially when the rich tended to be Anglican? The fury was instant. Either the rich found themselves in khaki and fighting, or the 'Furlough Men', as they called themselves, weren't going back to fight.

The 'England right or wrong' ethos of the coalition government twitched. Orders went out from Parliament: Get the bastards back on the ships and off to die for King and Country by whatever means. But how? Turning the military police loose on their own troops was risky – many wouldn't have the stomach for that fight. Besides, the Furlough Men might win a street battle. The government cracked. The privileged felt the breath of military service on their necks and didn't like it. The lodges welcomed them.

The war over, a now roaring and assertive Catholic community looked for more. The rectors of St Patrick's (town) and St Patrick's (Silverstream) steered the best and brightest to the Mosgiel seminary and Victoria University's law school. Cases once settled over a port between gentlemen at the Wellington Club were dragged into the courtroom's bright light. There were bad losses and financial damage. Again the Freemasons let it be known they could help.

Control of the police was the glittering prize in the battle. If Feeney didn't already know that – and he did – there was always the Bishop with his constant reminders: 'Stay where you are, Pat. Protect the faithful because the Masons are coming.' That left Feeney up here in Wellington's mist and cold, looking at the body of a teenage girl, certain that something in that stew of fear, hate, ambition, money and crime got her murdered.

The photographer and the searchers were busy with their cameras and tape measures. The undertakers would be here soon. There would be detectives arriving at Wellington Central and waiting for orders. Feeney couldn't stick around here much longer.

He moved a few steps back to make way for the solid-looking tent over the murder scene. They'd have to get moving – the storm was almost here. Feeney took a long last look at Marie. He would need this picture in his mind for when he became tired and fed up with the case, and the chances were he would eventually be both. He'd need to remember what she looked like so he could avenge her death.

The body was only partly dressed, her panties around her ankles, a thin rope around her neck. He'd know soon enough whether she'd been raped, but he doubted it. There were other motives. Her eyes were closed. That was interesting. Her murderer had reached down and closed them. Why? A rapist wouldn't have cared, but this guy had. Was it a moment of repentance, a plea for forgiveness, or a shivering at the cold, accusing stare of the dead? Was there an emotional connection of some sort? Did Marie and her killer know each other?

Feeney could feel McCarthy just over his shoulder, straining to get a look at the body. Feeney would not move aside for him, but he had to get back to the police gathering at Central, ready for the hunt. He turned abruptly, making sure McCarthy had to grab at a tree to save him from falling down the hill.

'Let's go. I want to talk to the witness,' Feeney said.

'I oughta stay here.'

Feeney didn't care who was watching. Let the junior officers see dissent if they had to.

'No. You're coming with me, now,' he snarled.

McCarthy's eyes opened wide. He was being dismissed from a murder scene? No way. *He* did the dismissing. McCarthy looked around, catching a junior officer's eye.

'You!'

'Yes, sir?' the policeman answered.

'Mind yer own fucking business!'

McCarthy's mouth twisted but he said nothing directly to Feeney. He turned and began a slipping and sliding journey back down to the road. He was only gone a few seconds before Feeney winced at his yelled, 'Get out of my fucking way!' McCarthy had met the undertakers coming up the track. Feeney nodded a welcome as they carried the stretcher and body bag towards him.

Jimmy Byrne was behind them. Feeney smiled. At last, a Catholic detective Feeney could trust. Feeney beckoned him close and whispered, even though the wind would stop anyone hearing.

'I need you to stick close to Murray. He's grief-stricken. He might do something silly. I need to know where he goes, for his own protection. I especially need to know if he goes anywhere near the Wests' place.'

Byrne gave Feeney a shrewd look. McCarthy? Grief-stricken? Bullshit. This was a straight-out tailing job.

'Make sure no one sees you. You report direct to me and no one else. All right?'

The stone-faced Byrne nodded. His eyes shrieked questions but he said nothing as he began picking his way down the hill.

McCarthy stopped when he reached the road. This was bad. That bloody Marie showing up murdered was going to pull up stones all over the place. Stuff best left in the dark. That might be good for the investigators but it wasn't necessarily good for anyone else. Now Feeney had sent that tenacious little prick Byrne after him. As he'd grabbed at a branch on the way down he'd seen him whispering with Feeney and then setting off after him.

That made him, Murray McCarthy, an exposed, jittery antelope sniffing the wind, heart racing, hoping nothing big and dangerous was watching and waiting. With an antelope it was all over in a few brutal seconds. When the claws went into him there'd be nothing slow about it. It'd be detectives and auditors picking over everything, all his cases, looking for every pound note he'd ever spent. There'd be no stopping them. He'd be the bleeding animal in the hot desert, gasping and praying for death. But this wasn't going to end anywhere hot. Unless he was very careful this was going to finish in a cold, damp prison cell.

He'd have to keep the hell away from the West house. Going anywhere near there'd be suicide. The antelope had sniffed the lion's hot, stinking breath, and the antelope had better do everything right or it was dead.

chapter six

Auckland, 1972

Helen had been sitting there for only a few moments but she was already beginning to feel slow and numb as if her whole body were closing down against the attempt to kill her. She'd read about this: how people went into denial so they could protect themselves against whatever horror lay in wait.

But she couldn't afford to do that. The police were coming for her. She couldn't rest; couldn't relax. This was the most dangerous time.

Police were blocking off Queen Street. People were pouring out of the building and being sent off behind the police cars. A uniformed officer was striding down the street towards her. It would only be a few more seconds. For God's sake, she had to get a story together. Something about a client yelling threats. Let them spend the next year trawling through the files.

Police were unloading trestle-type barriers from a van and setting them up around the building. Fire engines and ambulances were pulling up behind them.

She looked up and suddenly realised she was at the exact spot on Queen Street where her career changed. It was just last year, in a noisy getting-ready-for-violence Women's Liberation march. Helen was among them but wasn't yelling. The Law Society was going through an especially conservative phase. Its masters were prone to public fretting and private threats about how the profession was seen by the public. Lawyers getting into fights in the middle of rowdy Queen Street demonstrations were unlikely to be considered helpful to the image of the profession. Helen had found herself among a group of angry women ripping bras out from under shirts and jerseys and hurling them away. One sailed into a building site. A labourer caught it and rubbed it back and forward between his legs. Helen was angry, both at his sexual aggression and at herself for finding it somehow strangely sexy.

His 'Show us yer tits!' blended in with the 'Give us a look at yer growler!' coming from the footpath, to roars of laughter.

Helen's bra, cause or no cause, was staying where it was. But here was trouble. A little thicket of elegantly dressed middle-aged men were just behind the 'Show us yer knockers' chorus. The firm's senior partners were making a point of noticing Helen, and they looked none too pleased. Oh well, if she was finished she was finished. Now she was free to chant and yell for freedom and liberty, and did so until she was hoarse.

That was then. Now there was a bomb in her office and a young policeman was standing beside her.

'Are you okay, Ma'am?' he asked.

She nodded.

'We have to get you out of here. We've got a car, just over there.'

He might have looked young and pleasant but he also looked determined. He had his orders: get the woman and take her back to the station. A Holden police car had slipped up to the kerb and the driver was reaching back and opening a rear door. Helen got in. A policewoman sat in front with the driver. As soon as Helen closed the passenger's door the car was moving, easing down Queen Street and left into Wyndham Street, to circle back up to Albert Street and to Auckland Central Police Station. Helen sat as still as she could. No one said anything.

After the Women's Liberation march she'd arrived back to find a note on her desk. She was wanted, two floors up, now. Hers was the slow, weary walk of someone about to be forced out along the plank to fall to the sharks. It would be back to the suburbs, disputes over boundary fences and overstressed land agents, she knew it.

Instead, the coffee and the bonhomie flowed freely. The

partners had decided there might be something in this Women's Liberation business. Women might be shaken out beyond nursing, teaching and typing. If they were going into complicated jobs and getting bigger money they'd need lawyers, and they'd probably want female ones. The only one in the firm was in the 'Tombs', chained to the wall, in rags and fighting the rats for scraps of food.

Oh no, they couldn't have that.

One of the partners patted her on the back.

'It's time for you to be moving up and on.'

Her picture was booked for a new brochure, replacing the expensive one that had arrived from the printer just last week. The firm went out and found a Maori man doing a law degree in Wellington and hired him. He was insurance in case this Treaty of Waitangi fuss turned sour. Helen was going into the office next to his, both clearly visible from the reception area. First impressions count! The partners had heard about a Samoan finishing a law degree in Hawaii. His parents were in Auckland and he wanted to join them. As soon as they'd seen his CV they'd hired him too. If that fat pinko Norman Kirk got to be prime minister the country would open up to swarms of Polynesians. They'd need lawyers – brown ones who could speak the lingo and explain why they couldn't have thatched huts in New Zealand. They had to have houses. Houses meant conveyancing and sorting out title deeds. Lawyers could take care of all that for them and, why, here we are, with one just like you.

The police car turned into the station. Helen was pleased to be out of it – away from its smell of vomit, disinfectant and sweat. Its radio had chattered urgently about cordons and disposal teams and where was Heather Murphy or whatever her name was. The bomb was apparently covered with lead blankets, above and below. If it did explode, the blast would be contained. They could leave it now for the Bomb Squad, who were on their way.

They got out of the lift on the ninth floor. Would Helen please wait in this room? Sorry it's not more attractive but it's the best we've got. Would she like some tea? Helen smiled and nodded. Of course, she would be only too happy to wait here in this cold, bare, little room. The door closed and she was on her own.

Her promotion at work had seen backslapping congratulations bulleting around the partners' floor. Naturally, these were not for her. No one cared what she thought. The congratulations were for the partners, grabbing the chance to set up a defence against talk that they weren't doing enough for women, and for tapping a potentially lucrative seam of vagino-centric legal work. The accountants would keep an eye on Helen's productivity, and then they could turn back to harvesting the best young men from King's College and Auckland Grammar as they emerged from Auckland University, feeding them into the hoppers that dropped them on the short conveyer ride from 'entry level' to 'highly paid partner'.

Once she was made a team leader Helen discovered that the lawyers assigned to her weren't exactly the diamonds being polished for display. All the other team leaders had quietly grabbed the chance to offload their no-hopers onto her. What was she supposed to do with them? How did she manage them? Did she crash down on them, supervising every moment of their day? Or did she let them run, keeping a guiding hand gently moving them in the right direction?

Archie Fallon had watched all this from the heights of senior partner status. Something had finally stirred in him and he decided to help. He cornered Helen at the Christmas party, away from the small rented stereo belting out America's droningly unhappy tale about riding through the desert on a horse with no name. The younger lawyers were twitching in a gawky series of jerks and jumps that might have had something to do with dance.

Archie's veined and arthritic hand dropped on Helen's knee, moving quickly up her leg. Waves of gin and stale peanuts blasted up into her nostrils. His purple-tinged faced twisted into what he hoped was a soothing smile.

His searing, foul breath was barely an inch from her ear. 'You've finally got yourself a team,' he whispered. 'They're all little bastards. You've got to get them before they get you. Be totally merciless with them – barrel them every chance you get.' She could hear his dentures clicking. She tried to wriggle free but he was too quick, holding her tightly against the wall. This was the Christmas party. What could she do – start screaming?

'They've got their daddies and their little dickies and their connections to help them. I've been fighting that shit all my life,' he snarled, the ghastly smile still pasted across his flushed face. 'I'm from Avondale!' The rawness of Fallon's hate was shocking. Helen knew Avondale wasn't the wealthiest part of Auckland but she didn't think it was that bad. She felt like screaming up to the sky, 'What sort of a fucking God are you? I plead for guidance and you send me a drunken molester!' His tongue was closing on her earlobe as his hand tucked into her panties. Men were in prison for less than this! Helen stiffened, recalling that she'd once heard Fallon referring to the act of physical love between a man and a woman in elegantly nuanced tones as 'whacking the sausage sword into the fleshy scabbard'.

At her reaction Fallon paused for just a second, long enough for Helen to wrench herself free. Her embarrassment was gone, replaced by a red anger. The partners, she realised, were watching and snickering. Oh yes, it was always good fun watching Archie getting up to his tricks.

That had only been a few hundred yards – and a universe – away from this room here at Auckland Central. The door opened. The policewoman was back. 'Bombs are very serious cases. We'll need to talk to you, but unfortunately we'll need to leave you here for a few more moments,' she said. Helen managed a smile and a nod. The policewoman smiled back, but her eyes were careful and assessing. As soon as she was gone Helen did something she hadn't done for nearly twenty years: she began muttering a prayer. There were no paths back now. Her life had changed forever. Whatever her existence had become – a war, a race, a chess game or a duel – there was only one certainty. She was weak and she was facing the strong.

chapter seven

Wellington, 1947

Pat Feeney was being careful about the way he steered the police car into its parking space at Wellington Central's congested yard – far more careful than he'd have been with his own car. Damage a police car and you were in for two hours of filling in forms, and he didn't have the time for that nonsense. He locked the car and was careful to take the key with him, though he was supposed to leave the key in it in case there was an emergency. Huh! Leave the key and the first lazy bugger to come along wanting a car would swoop on it.

Let them get the tram!

Up on Mt Victoria the tent guys had won the race with the storm. Policemen were under it doing a hands-and-knees search. He might be lucky. They might find a tiny droplet of a rare blood group on a blade of grass and some suspect would have the same blood group. It wouldn't be much but it'd be a hell of a good start. Perhaps the murderer had dropped his wallet there, with his name in it and a note: 'Buy soap powder, pay rates, murder Marie.' There had been cases solved that easily, but Feeney had never had one. He'd never expected it so he'd never been disappointed.

McCarthy was the wild card. He was capable of anything, including leading Jimmy Byrne to something or someone they didn't know about, which would break the case open. Feeney allowed himself a little smile. He wouldn't count on it. Still, McCarthy was clearly frazzled and panicky. People like that made mistakes.

The detectives would be in the muster room by now, waiting

to be revved up and sent out to probe and shine lights into every corner of Marie's life. All her family, friends and workmates would receive a visit to say hello. Somewhere in the tears and shock a name might come up. That name would get a visit. Everything was followed up, and more than once. That was how murder investigations went. There was none of that Sherlock Holmes brilliant deduction crap. It was all careful and relentless persistence. By now Marie's post-mortem was under way. With any luck it'd be Filthy Phil doing it. Feeney liked the pathologist, always ready with a cheery remark as he sawed at a dead person's head or flopped their innards into his overhead scale.

A sergeant puffed up to him.

'Pat, mate, they want you on the tenth floor. Compton.'

Feeney had been expecting it. It would've been good to get the detectives going first, but Chief Superintendent Eric Compton didn't like to be kept waiting, especially these days, when the whole place seemed to revolve around him.

'Okay. Tell the guys in the muster room I'll be there in a minute,' Feeney said.

'Yes, sir.'

Feeney walked through Wellington Central's archway and across the road to National Headquarters. As he got out of the lift on the tenth floor the secretary lifted a telephone receiver. By the time Feeney reached her desk the conversation was over.

'Go through. The Chief Superintendent is expecting you,' she told him.

Feeney knew the way – everyone with a big case did. Mostly it was straightforward. Pass on whatever you knew, outline a rough strategy for the investigation's first hours and you were on your way. Reporters would be ringing Compton. As long as he could sound as if he knew what he was talking about he was happy. If he wasn't happy there was trouble. When he'd worked at the wharf police station Mr Compton not being pleased meant someone was belted from one end of the place to the other until the boss got what he wanted. Feeney shook his head. No wonder Compton and McCarthy got along so well. Feeney could think of only one word for them: thugs. If there was a difference between them it was that Compton was slightly smoother about covering the damage afterwards.

Compton looked up when Feeney entered. He was a handsome man with high cheekbones in a strangely immobile face – death with a pulse. He didn't waste any time on niceties. He sat down, leaving Feeney to take the chair in front of his desk.

'What is it – murder? Suicide?'

'Looks like murder.'

'Jesus. That's all we bloody need. Have you seen *Truth*?'

Feeney had, but shook his head. Let Compton have his moment.

'Bloody paper's going on about the police needing changes at the top.'

'Raving on and frigging on about how her going missing is something to do with the bookies. Another way of saying we're sitting back and letting them root us ragged.'

'It's probably a sex attack, too.'

Compton smiled.

'That's better. A lone fiend preying on an innocent young girl and nothing to do with bookies or any of that shit. We can push that. It'll help scare the crap out of the public. Lock up your daughters and all the rest of it. The police stand between them and the terrible nightmare. Yeah, that's good. It'll keep them distracted. But it'll backfire if we don't get someone in the bag quick smart. Then it'll be all police doing nothing while a predator roams loose.'

Compton didn't wait for Feeney to respond. He flicked a copy of *Truth* up from his desk and dropped it again.

'Fucking rag. The sexo angle will make them look like dicks.'

Compton was almost certain to take over as commissioner. Feeney had wondered how he'd would manage the job's ceremonial and diplomatic side. The cosh he kept in his suit jacket was not going to be much help.

'Isn't her father mixed up with the bookies?' Compton's cold blue eyes cut into Feeney.

'There've been rumours. We'll go after that.'

'I'd bloody well think so! Look, you're Catholic, right? You're also a good copper. You've sent tykes away, just like the rest of us. But if this does end up getting tied to the bookies and they happen to be Catholics and there's coppers involved, then we'll need a bloody good clean-out.'

Compton's eyes narrowed. This was how he intimidated people. Let him. Feeney had seen it before. It was never comfortable but he was used to it.

'We're being watched. People are keeping a bloody close eye on this,' Compton said.

Feeney managed to keep a straight face. He'd heard that line in a movie last week at the Majestic.

'I'm bringing in extra troops,' Compton continued. 'I've just finished talking to Bill Thompson in Christchurch and Jim Smythe up in Auckland. They're sending us extra hands. The Auckland guys will be here tomorrow; the Christchurch ones'll be here the day after.'

'Thank you, sir.' Feeney said it, but he didn't mean it. He didn't like the sound of this.

'Jack Smalley and Ted McBride from Auckland. Jock Pollock and Bryce Montgomery from Christchurch. They're all experienced blokes. Use them. Get them at the centre of things. I want a quick result.' He paused to make sure Feeney was listening. Then, 'So do you.'

It was a threat, accompanied by a glare so intense it was near insane.

Feeney took his time. That was the best defence against Compton. If you let him rush you, he'd push you into a mistake and he would have control. Once he got that, he'd never let go.

'As long as we get a good run, without any interference, we've got a pretty good show,' Feeney replied evenly.

That slowed Compton down, and Feeney had meant it to. That was the Frank Wilkins investigation, stuck in the mud with its wheels spinning. Wellington's police had been feeding on rumours that someone had tipped off the owner of the workshop at 100 Adelaide Road, the murder scene, about the forthcoming raid. By the time the raid hit, the workshop had been hosed down and thoroughly cleaned up.

He might have stopped Compton for a moment, but it was only a tiny battle and Compton was winning the war. Those

Auckland and Christchurch names were bad news. Feeney knew three of them, including the two from Christchurch. They were Freemasons with reputations for being ruthless in nailing Catholics.

Compton stood up. It was Feeney's signal to go.

A minute later Compton was putting his phone down. The receptionist had told him Mr Feeney was in the lift and on his way to the ground floor. Of course she would tell him if Mr Feeney reappeared. Mr Compton was going to be meeting someone and did not want to be disturbed.

chapter eight

Auckland, 1972

Helen remembered to sit upright. She could not afford to relax, not for a second. Whoever sent her the bomb would be listening to the radio and watching the television waiting to hear what had happened. If he didn't hear anything the chances were he'd start on another, better bomb. Or he'd find some other way to get her.

But she couldn't worry about that now. She had to focus on getting out of the police station.

She remembered the words of Beverley Martinelli, a doctor friend of hers who looked after people with terminal cancer: 'There are worse things than dying, a hell of a lot worse things.' Beverley was talking about sickness and suffering. Helen was thinking about having to get into a prison van to begin the first of many long years in a cell.

Keep still! she told herself. They might have a camera on you. Someone might be sitting watching you, assessing your body language.

Could anyone work out what she was thinking from how she moved? Did her fidgeting tell them she had something to hide? Were they in front of a screen somewhere watching her every move? Was she giving them clues?

Christ.

Helen clenched her fist.

She mustn't let the police frighten her. Those looks of dripping suspicion were just tools of the trade. They made people think they knew more than they did, hoping to spin people into a confession. Try to convince people that they'd feel lighter, unburdened, freed of their terrible secret if they told all.

Three floors down, someone else was also thinking about Helen. Detective Sergeant Fred Lashing had been given the job of interviewing her. He was not pleased. He had better things to do, hard-working burglars to be catching. But he'd happened to be walking past when the senior sergeant had just been asked to find someone. He was called in. Never mind the burglars, he was told. Just go and bloody do it. Get a statement. Get her to sign it. Get a police car to drop her off home. It's not brain surgery. Off. Go. Do it.

Lashing had waited in the corner of the garage to get a look at her when she arrived at Central. She'd got out of the car and walked over to the lift. Yeah, she looked like a lawyer: middle class, plenty of money in the clothes, and covered in that thin gold jewellery that costs a hell of a lot more than the stuff with the really heavy gold in it. She'd be in the National Party for sure. She might be a bit young for the Navy League and the other patriotic societies. They were a touchy subject with him. He'd heard they were full of women in their fifties, all elegant dressers and educated accents, who lined up fresh young naval officers to rip and tear at them like rabid dogs. He'd heard they nailed them, too. It wasn't the sex that upset him. Well, it was, but it was more the jealousy that was the problem. Straight-out jealousy. There were no horny middle-class women with little gold chains lining up on his doorstep. None at all. All he had was too many hamburgers and the start of a weight problem.

Up in heaven his old dad would love the idea of Fred getting a hard-on for the women in the Navy League. Right from when Fred was a toddler his dad had drilled it into to him that he should 'always fuck the middle class'. He'd died happy at living long enough to see his boy in the police and arresting a company director for drunk driving. Fred's dad was near the end of a working life when the 1951 Waterfront Lockout hurled the country into rage and then revenge. He'd been blacklisted after the lockout, and his life had slid away in hard drinking and never-ending hurt. Fred was sure the idea of him fornicating his way across the Northern Slopes would mesh neatly with his father's Marxism.

Still, he could have done without his dad telling him that if

Fred happened to find himself having sex with anyone middle class he should get out of bed as soon as it was over and wipe his cock on the most expensive drapes before leaving. Fred assumed this was an act of class defiance, to keep him from being enslaved by the enemy, and on a practical note, it might get him an extra day before he had to put on fresh underpants.

Now here he was going upstairs to front this Helen Murphy, who looked like she could whistle up all the sex she liked, as often as she wanted. Sure, he'd take her statement, but he'd also be making damn sure she was actually as innocent as she made out.

'Christ, Fred, be careful,' he muttered to himself. 'That's a frigging lawyer. She knows how to rain shit down all over you.'

Still, a bomb was interesting. Making a bomb took time, care and patience. Someone had to sustain a hate through a long time, and there had to be a hell of a good reason for that. The thing was sent specifically to her, not to the firm, so this was personal. The bomber knew her. So, did she know the bomber? He'd bet she did. He'd have to be careful but the more he thought about it the more interesting it got. Pity she was a lawyer. They were hard to bluff. He'd be better grafting a pig's head on a horse, riding it in the Auckland Cup and calling it a pig of a thing.

He'd got the policewoman to put Helen in a room on a high floor without a view. Seal her off from any reference points. Get her a cup of tea that was half hot water and half sugar: push her glucose levels through the ceiling. Get her sparked up and talking and see where it took them. Give it a few minutes for the sugar to hit and then he'd start.

Upstairs, Helen was looking at the cup of tea they'd just brought her. Didn't the police know how to make tea? Half filling a cup with sugar and tipping hot water over it wasn't the way her mother taught her. Lord help us. They also weren't being too subtle loading her up with sugar, hoping she'd go half manic and lose control over what she was saying. Did they do that with all suspects? That wasn't good. Police thought in straight lines. If they were treating her like a suspect, she'd become one. When did she shift from being the frightened victim of a murder attempt to being a suspect? Had they already connected this with the bomb that killed Jennifer?

Helen looked down at her hand. It was shaking. Christ! Why was she a suspect? Did they have a surprise they were going to throw at her? Questions, questions, never-ending questions! She had to calm down!

The door opened and a man in his mid-forties stood there. The policewoman was just behind him. 'Fred Lashing,' he said, stepping into the room.

He managed to force a smile. He hadn't said anything else – no rank, no greeting, just his name. Helen watched the policewoman standing aside for him. He was senior to her. Up close Lashing didn't look as frightening. He could do with a woman's touch, she noted. His tie was not properly knotted and his suit needed a press. He probably had odd socks. Her guess was that he had been a tough guy, but that had ended a while back, about the time his stomach broke the line between his chin and shoes. It was his eyes that interested her. They were strangely quiet and dull. This man had known failure. Unless she was wrong, his career was already dead, whether he knew it or not. Still, he didn't look stupid. She suspected that people who weren't careful around him could find themselves in serious trouble.

'Mrs?'

'Miss,' Helen corrected him.

'Not Ms,' he said.

'No.'

Lashing filled the silence fiddling with a couple of pieces of paper. Both he and Helen watched each other closely. They realised it at the same time and tried not to share a smile at knowing they were thinking the same thing.

Then, 'When did the bomb arrive?'

'About five o clock,' she said.

Lashing's finger's twitched at his papers.

He knows! He knows I'm lying, and he's caught me out. For God's sake, they've found Margaret! He won't believe another word I say! Christ Almighty!

'Why did you wait until . . .' Lashing looked at the papers, 'six forty-one before you called us? That's over an hour.'

What the hell did she do now? Did she try hiding behind tears? That might work for a few minutes, an hour or even a day. In the end they wouldn't be enough to sail merrily past this. Lashing was more intense now, leaning closer, edging into her space. He'd been eating something with onions and tomato sauce.

'Who sent you the bomb? You know who it was, don't you?'

She fought back the scream that was looking for a way to sweep the panic in her out and away to the sky.

'No.'

'Really?'

He didn't believe her and wasn't bothering to hide it. Should she refuse to talk? No. That'd put the hunt in the open. Then he'd see her as being as much of a criminal as the man who sent the thing. They'd go after everything about her, in Auckland and in Wellington, piece by piece, moment by moment, endlessly pushing until they had everything.

An old lawyer had told her all about the police.

'They're not educated. They don't have every little nuance of the law. They also don't need them. What they do need is what they've got: the ability to be dogged and keep coming at a case for years, decades even. Some of them are smart, very quick. Others plod along, but they all know where they are going. Assume you are brighter, faster and sharper than them and you might face guilty verdicts for your clients and the prison door for yourself.'

Lashing had said hardly anything but Helen already felt as if she were locked in some sort of brutal and exhausting duel.

'You knew it was a bomb the second it hit your desk. And you sat there looking at it for . . . how long?' he asked, very quietly this time.

She'd said five o'clock. Had she said that? Had she said something else? Oh God, was it better just to blurt out everything, all the way back to that winter morning in Miramar? Jennifer was safe, but Helen was not. This had only just started and she was already thinking about prison. What had happened to all her knowledge, her skill, her training? The first real trouble and it had melted away.

Glances flicked between Lashing and the policewoman. They were telling each other there was something deeper, darker and wider here. And Helen was helping them. You stupid, stupid woman! You've thrown the blood in the water – your own. They know it's there. They've smelt it and they are twitching. It's feeding time.

chapter nine

Wellington, 1947

Compton waited. He wanted to give Feeney plenty of time to get out of the building. The last thing he needed was to have him charging back with some extra bit of information.

But judging by the barely hidden anger on Feeney's face when he'd heard about the Auckland and Christchurch troops, Compton reckoned he had other things on his mind. He crossed to the door of his office, opened it and turned back to his desk without saying anything. Murray McCarthy glumly followed him into the office. Compton pointed to a seat. He didn't trust himself to say anything, in case 'Sit' came out, as if he were snarling at the family dog.

'I suppose you brought the tail right here,' Compton snapped. 'Yes, in case you didn't know, you've got one. I got the whisper from one of the guys at the crime scene. He got one of the undertakers to ring me from the morgue. You see, Murray, unlike you, I know what I am bloody well doing.'

McCarthy was silent for a moment. Then he muttered, 'I came into the building through the back way. I could have been going anywhere. Christ, Eric, I went up three flights of stairs before I got in a lift!'

'Don't call me Eric!'

McCarthy knew his mouth had fallen open and didn't care. What the hell was that? He'd been a team with Compton for over twenty years! What about all those nights when they'd beaten confessions out of suspects? Now it was 'Don't call me Eric'. McCarthy swallowed. Feeney putting a tail on him was bad. Jesus, Mother of God. This was worse. It was like having one of those atom bombs dropped on your head.

Compton looked as if he could not care less.

'Okay, Murray. We're going to have this one chat and that's the end of it. You need to understand this one simple thing. From now on, from this precise actual moment, nothing is the same. It doesn't matter about the past. It's gone and it won't be coming back. Frank Wilkins, and now this little bitch West turning up, have changed everything. Surely you can see that?'

McCarthy nodded.

Compton did not give him a chance to say anything. 'We have to recognise it, and respond to it. That means everyone – you, me, the lot – and starting right now.'

McCarthy managed a 'Yes' without being sure what he was actually saying.

'See, Murray, the question is not whether we can change. We don't have a choice. It's *how* we change that'll decide the future . . . our futures.'

McCarthy opened his mouth. Compton waved him silent.

'Me, I'm staying in the police. I'm okay right here. Three or four years from now I'll be commissioner. Once I'm up there I can deal with anything. The real question is you. What about you?'

McCarthy had seen Compton doing this in interview rooms: asking questions that didn't have a right answer. Give the wrong answer and you got socked from wall to wall and back again. Get it right and – what the hell – you got a belting anyway. Christ, surely Compton wasn't going to try that now . . .

'See, the big question is . . . you,' Compton said.

'I was going to stick around,' McCarthy stuttered. 'Christ, I've got to. What the hell else is there?'

Compton shook his head in a sort of mock sorrow. He waited a second for McCarthy to get the message, letting his quiet, cool look chill him.

'Murray, Murray! You're not listening. We've gotta get things shipshape. We can't have any weak spots because we don't know what's ahead, except for one thing. The tykes are all over the place and they won't take it any more. There's Masons after them and they're after the Masons. It's a hell of a mess. It's big trouble and I don't think we can keep it under control.'

McCarthy swallowed. Now he could see what was going on. Compton was slowing the ship down and was getting ready to maroon him, the bastard.

Compton was still talking, quietly and evenly, as if McCarthy were a slow and stupid recruit.

'Look at it another way. Think of it like the weather turning bad. We can't stop it. We can only try to protect ourselves. Look what happens to boats sailing too close to the Antarctic in the winter. It's dark down there. They don't get any light on them. They ice up. They flip over. No one survives. Murray, you see what I mean. Boats that have been in the dark and the cold for too long take people down with them.'

McCarthy held the arms of his chair. His guess was right. He was going over the side. First it was Feeney sending a tail after him. Now Compton was sailing off without him. It didn't get much worse than this. Something in a distant corner of his stomach went tight and made his breathing go weak and shallow.

'Okay, there's another way to see it, Murray. We all went along to the serials at the movies on Saturdays, and the cowboy was mowing down the Indians, to make the west safe for nutcase gunfighters to go around shooting people.'

Compton smiled. He'd only just thought of this stuff, and he liked it. The smile was a chill blue light, showing McCarthy something bloodthirsty and frightening. It did what it was designed to do: it made McCarthy feel even worse.

'Then the farmers turned up. Just behind them it was the public servants and government departments. The gunfighters were history. Get on side or you got killed. You gotta ask yourself, Murray, are you on side?'

Compton was on a roll. Keep the advantage. Kick him when he's down. *Truth* is sniffing around. Your name's come up. Maybe there are records around somewhere. No one wants them turning up. 'Christ, Murray, there are coppers looking for a chance to go for you. I don't know if I could stop them.'

'Eric, I'm going to need some money.'

That brought Compton to a halt. McCarthy could see by the

expression on his face that it had been a mistake. Christ.

'Murray, stop thinking about money. Go and find it. The important thing is to keep moving, like the gunfighters moved west. Maybe you oughta be thinking like that – thinking about going somewhere, moving, keeping ahead, saving yourself.'

'I got a bit put away, but not enough.'

'If anyone owes you anything, Murray, this is the time to be collecting.'

'I was hoping you'd have some . . . to help out.'

'For Christ's sake, Murray! There's a time when we all need to think about our own future. We put it off and we put it off. Well, we can't put it off any more! Look after yourself, Murray. The pack's gathering. Make sure it doesn't catch you.'

Compton was on his feet. He had McCarthy gently but firmly by the arm and was steering him to the door. As soon as McCarthy was out the door he closed it behind him.

McCarthy stood out in the corridor, feeling very alone. He shuffled down to the lift and waited. The door opened. He was still facing the rear of the lift when its doors closed behind him.

The secretary waited. Once the lift numbers showed that McCarthy was several floors down she picked up the telephone, dialled a number and asked for Inspector Pat Feeney. Mr McCarthy had left Mr Compton's office and would be in the Waring Taylor Street foyer in a couple of minutes.

chapter ten

Auckland, 1972

Helen and Lashing stopped and looked across to the door of the interview room. It had opened about six inches and a long bony finger with a gold ring on it was summoning Lashing out into the corridor. He stood up and made for the door. Helen was fascinated by the finger – at not being able to see anything attached to it. Still, she wasn't complaining. It broke the atmosphere.

The 'chat' had begun to turn very sour. If it kept going much longer like this it was heading for more of an 'interrogation'. Now at least Helen had a chance to take stock. That policewoman was still there, so she wouldn't do anything as stupid as let out a big sigh of relief. It was this woman's job to watch, listen and pick up clues; Helen knew to be careful of her. She might start talking about how horrible it was to have something like this happen, and be all feminine understanding and sympathy. Under it, though, she'd be thinking, just as Lashing was thinking, that something was bad in all this and they needed to know what it was. Anything she said now might end up coming out of someone else's mouth in a courtroom, with 'the defendant' or 'she then said' on either side of it. She hadn't been charged or cautioned but she knew she couldn't rely on that. She had to think like a politician did when they were near a microphone: assume the thing was alive. Anything it heard the world heard.

Lashing was out in the corridor. She couldn't hear every word but the conversation sounded sharp. Her guess was that Lashing wanted her in chains and strapped to a prison ship's mast, but he wasn't getting an opportunity to say much. 'Bloody listen to me! Hey! I said shut up!' someone else was saying.

Lashing bit his tongue.

'She's the victim for Christ's sake,' the other voice, a male, said. 'You want to drag us into another one of your messes? If it turns out she did something stupid or crazy or whatever, then fine. We follow it up. We charge her. But for the moment that is it! End of story! Go! Do what you're told.'

Footsteps walked away and a door slammed. Then Lashing was back, kicking the interview room door closed behind him. He was red in the face and obviously struggling for control. A look flew between him and the policewoman, then he turned to Helen.

'Look, we've got your phone numbers, and I assume you're not going anywhere?' he said.

Helen shook her head. She was going home. As if that was a safe place. If a bomber could find her office he could find her home.

Lashing was pasting what he obviously hoped was a friendly expression on his face but it lost its way somewhere and came out as a sullen smirk. He wasn't even bothering to look at her. Why? Was he so sure she was a criminal? He busied himself, sorting out the pieces of paper littering the desk in front of him. Helen waited.

'We'll get you a ride home.' His glance was an order to the policewoman. Lashing stood. 'As soon as we've got anything we'll let you know,' he muttered.

Helen nodded her thanks. What she wanted was a taxi to get her far away from them. But she couldn't do that. She had to take their ride home, be the frightened victim of an attempted murder.

The trip down in the lift was silent. That wasn't a good sign. She'd seen police with victims, and they did what they could to be kind and understanding. Well, there wasn't any of that: only this fraught, accusing silence. If she wasn't worried before, she was now.

As the lift door opened at the garage Lashing mumbled, 'I've gotta go and see what's happening with the rest of it.' He gave

Helen's hand a quick shake, turned and walked away.

The policewoman drove out from Auckland Central, into Vincent Street and up towards Pitt Street. Her mouth, but not her eyes, smiled at Helen.

'There was a bombing case last week over in Sydney. Two people got killed.'

Helen tried to look interested without giving anything away. Was that the policewoman's idea of conversation or was it more questioning? If it was a question she wouldn't exactly call it subtle. Had the police made the connection?

Either way, she was going to have to get moving and track the bomber down. And she was going to have to keep the police away from him until she got to him first.

Oh God.

Helen thanked the operator and put the phone down. Yes, there was a family by the name of Bresnahan still up in Miramar's Nevay Road. The old guy must be long dead. She didn't recognise the initials, but there was someone there by that name. God! It was almost frightening to think it could be that easy. Except that she'd known where to look. It would take the police a lot longer to find the same place. Oh, for heaven's sake, she told herself, stop it. If you keep thinking like that you'll talk yourself to a standstill. You'll be putting yourself on a plate with an apple in your mouth and delivering yourself to their meal room for lunch.

So now what?

Rushing down to Wellington would be dangerous. After the way it went at the police station she had to assume the police would be keeping an eye on her. Wherever she went, they'd go too.

At least she had the time. The firm's partners had left a message telling her to have a few days off. 'You've had a ghastly fright. Take as long as you need.' How kind. Helen had been suitably grateful, not mentioning that she knew they wanted her out of the office so they could run a quiet little investigation of their own. If they'd decided this was the time to make a point about who was and who wasn't in control, Helen would be the perfect target. She was female and had risen quickly. She had a profile and there were partners feeling edgy about it. Had she moved too fast? Was she making others look sluggish? Was she a threat? They might have decided they needed women – but not as high as she'd climbed. This might be their chance to make a stand: we want women, but not in control of anything, thank you very much. If that was going on she'd definitely climbed up on the plate and put an apple in her mouth.

She stood at the liquor cupboard looking at the bottles.

What she needed was a gin.

She opened the bottle, then closed it again. No, better to wait till this was over. She'd need all her wit and imagination.

Bugger that.

She poured a gin and almost no tonic and downed it in a single gulp.

She shuddered as the alcohol warmed through her. Helen, my girl, you really, really do need all your brain cells, she told herself. You mustn't have another one! Then she poured and drank another one.

It was the time! It was the bloody time – the gap between the bomb arriving and her calling the police. The police had been like dogs in heat over it. They'd soon find Margaret, and she'd tell them anything they wanted to know. The partners would be the same. And there'd be plenty of time to agonise about it. God, if she kept downing the gin she'd eventually convince herself she ought to go back to the station and beg to be arrested.

She crossed to the window and eased the drapes apart. She smiled. Her dressing gown had fallen open and she was wearing nothing underneath it. If anyone was looking up at her window she wasn't going to have too many secrets. So? Let them look! She was forty-one. She was still okay. The policewoman, if she was down there, was the same as her, only younger and tighter. Helen pulled the gown back around her. If Lashing was out there he was old enough and looked married enough, or divorced enough, not to be shocked. She stopped. What on earth was she thinking! God Almighty! What sort of blind raving was this?

She turned the light off and looked out the window again. She could see out to the Remuera shops. Something was moving in the florist's doorway. It wasn't a cat or a dog and it wasn't moving quickly – not like the couple who'd stopped there a week ago for a flurry of standing-up sex, jumped back into the Jaguar and sped off as soon as it was over. Was it the coppers? Probably. Well, they couldn't see her now. But that wasn't stopping her hands shaking.

Beverley Martinelli swept through the door to the hospital ward, letting it crash shut behind her. Helen smiled. All these years and Beverley had never done anything without crashing or bashing or breaking something. It didn't matter if it was homework, sport, finding and losing men, studying or not studying; Beverley crashed. You loved her or you hated her, but if you wanted to be around her you had to grab hold of something solid and hang on in case Hurricane Beverley sent you flying.

Beverley stopped in front of Helen.

'Christ, you look bloody appalling.'

'Thank you.'

'I mean it. Come on!'

She waved Helen to follow her and marched off. Wherever Beverley was going was the centre of the world, at least for a while. That suited Helen. Her own world wasn't much fun. Beverley turned left. Good. If she'd turned right they'd be going into the ward where she was resident specialist. Helen didn't feel up to being marched past rows of ashen-faced people waiting for death. She followed Beverley into her little office. Beverley hoisted some files off a chair and dumped them on another chair. She found a small electric jug and plugged it in.

'Coffee all right?'

Helen nodded. You had coffee, or you had water. Beverley had read that the big tea companies were oppressing their growers in India and Ceylon and refused to have tea anywhere near her.

'What's the matter?'

'Nothing, really.'

'Absolute fucking bullshit!' Beverley's mouth was smiling. Her eyes looked straight at and through Helen. It wasn't a comfortable gaze.

'Helen, my love, I happen to be in the denial business. I know it when I see it and most of what I do is getting people past and through it. Meaning: stop it, or I'll have to inject you full of something and get it out of you that way!'

'Inject me full of what?

'I'll think of something. What's going on?'

'Is there any milk?'

'I forgot to get it. I'll get syphilis and die for it. Now, what's the matter? Something is – look at you. You're a hell of a mess. There are people out there in the ward who look better than you. What's going on?'

She wanted to let it go, all of it. Well, almost all of it. To tell Beverley about the bomb, about Jennifer, about the cops, and that maybe they were following her. She'd leave out the Wellington part. She could confess and repent for this later – she'd leave the impression it was something to do with Jennifer. Say whatever she needed to divert Beverley's chillingly focused gaze somewhere – anywhere – else.

After she'd poured it all out, her friend sat back in her chair.

'Shit. I've heard of women having obsessed men following them around . . . but someone you don't know trying to *murder* you? Wow!'

Helen winced. This just didn't end. Now she was lying to people who really wanted to help her. Beverley sat still. Christ, it really was that bad? Anything that could keep Ms Hyperactivity sitting there in silence was up there with the Great Fire and the Black Death.

'The police think something's wrong with what you've told them?'

Helen nodded.

'Sooo. You really are on your own. But you're not. You've got me. Except that I am not sure this is exactly my area.'

Don't say anything.

Beverley fished around in a drawer, reaching right to the back of it. 'You remember Davy, don't you?'

Davy was Beverley's brother. He'd been in a pub fight and the other guy had died of the complications. Davy was found not guilty of attempted murder and guilty of common assault. There'd been talk that Davy or someone near him had got to a witness or a jury member or both. Some friends of the victim wanted to talk to Davy about this. As soon as he heard that, he decided he'd be so much better off somewhere else. Thailand turned out to be sufficiently distant and anonymous.

'There was someone who was able to help him . . . when he had that bit of trouble.' Beverley found a card and gave it to Helen. 'He charges a lot but he might be worth talking to. I'd say you don't have much choice. I'm good for tea, or rather coffee, and sympathy, but I think you might just need a bit more.'

Beverley was what Beverley always was: a realist. And she was right.

chapter eleven

Wellington, 1947

Murray McCarthy's was a heavy tread as he climbed the stairs to John Augustine O'Malley's office. He knew the way to the bookmaker's office. He'd been picking up whispers around the corridors at work that he might have been there a bit too often, that if he spent less time there, the chances of O'Malley doing time might be higher. He knew damn well that some of them hoped he'd be here when they raided the place. He had no doubt they'd throw him in the cells and make him negotiate his way out. So he'd done something about it – taken to meeting O'Malley in cars or pub kitchens. Anywhere but his office.

But there wasn't time to set up anything like that this time. And he was tired. It was late afternoon and he'd been on the go since five in the morning. Most of it had been spent trying to shake off Jimmy Byrne. He'd lost him about ten minutes ago and sprinted around here.

He pushed at the door.

He wondered if this would be any different from fronting frigging Compton. He'd got the bloody runaround there.

Lately there hadn't been many meetings. Everybody knew McCarthy was losing ground in the police. Feeney and a few others were making sure he didn't hear about raids and crackdowns. That was embarrassing. It also made it harder to justify taking O'Malley's money. So far it had been all right. O'Malley kept smiling that thin, bloodless smile of his and whispering, 'Now, Murray, these things happen. It's all swings and roundabouts. You're up and you're down. You'll be back up, so just do your best to be looking out for us all.' More important, he'd kept paying.

McCarthy took a breath as he entered the room. Good. O'Malley was there. The bookmaker looked up, saw McCarthy and nodded to someone standing out of sight. McCarthy stopped. That nod could have been anything from 'Make this a quick, clean kill' to 'Let my friend Mr McCarthy in'.

The 'kill' order was possible. Frank Wilkins had found himself on the end of one of O'Malley's volcanic rages. That night he had disappeared. O'Malley told – not asked – McCarthy to 'do the right thing': 'Turn the investigation into a dog's breakfast or a mad woman's crap or anything else you want, as long as it gives us a chance to get things in order.'

McCarthy had managed it, too. The reward was money. The price was open suspicion. O'Malley hadn't helped by jumping out all over Wellington, spouting pious and giving money to every church charity he could find. McCarthy had complained.

'I only need one juror who feels grateful – not a whole frigging city of them.'

That was the genteel version of the rule John Augustine O'Malley lived by. It had been taught to him by his father not long before he came across two Black and Tans about to rape a North Dublin barmaid.

He'd told John, 'Be ahead of things. Act before they do and never ever turn your back on the bastards, any bastards. If it's you or them, be sure it's them.' The Black and Tans had half-stripped the woman. O'Malley's father killed one of them before the other managed to shoot him. He died next day. His son learned an important lesson. As well as doing it to them before they did it to you, you had to make sure you could kill all of them. If you couldn't, you should keep the hell out of it.

McCarthy could see that O'Malley was looking pale and weary. Not that he ever looked much better. Even healthy and happy he was the most pallid man McCarthy had ever seen. He knew the paler he got, the more likely it was that someone was getting hurt. O'Malley's lips stretched back over those perfect teeth of his. It was hard to tell what that expression was. It might be a welcome. It might be pleasure at the murder to come. McCarthy didn't know. It was frightening.

It was too dark in here for McCarthy to read his watch. At a guess he'd say it was about eight o clock at night. That made it four freaking hours since he'd left O'Malley's office and this was turning into a stone-cold disaster. It wasn't helping that he was hungry, tired and angry. Food, unless he fancied a mouthful of coal dust, wasn't even close to a possibility. All he could do was keep crawling around the floor of this filthy little shed at the back of the Miramar Gas Works, trying to steal the money O'Malley was supposed to have hidden here.

O'Malley had listened carefully to McCarthy. As soon as the policeman had mentioned money he'd cut him off cold. Times had changed, he told him. It had happened that morning. There was no money. That was it: case closed. He, Murray McCarthy, was being turned away with nothing. It was a bloody insult. The worst was there wasn't a bloody thing he could do about it, except choke it back, just as he'd had to do in Compton's office.

He'd got the message. If he wasn't on his own before, he sure as hell was now. Then he'd had more freaking hours of trying to make sure that leech of a detective was off his tail again. He was pretty sure he'd lost him before he'd risked O'Malley, but you never really knew, not for sure.

Christ. He'd just bashed his left ankle against something, and that had to be blood he could feel running down into his thick woollen sock.

'Bastards, bloody bastards!'

He choked the pain back before it got past his mouth and into the open. He bit on his jacket lapel while he waited for the pain to roll from his ankle to wherever pain dies.

Thirty years in the police and he was down to this.

He had run the meeting with Father Horan and Sister Margaret Agnes over and over. In among all the dribble about Spreading the Word and Propagating the Catholic Faith there'd been that throwaway remark about O'Malley keeping money in a shed at the Gas Works. It didn't sound right, but it was just odd enough to be true. O'Malley handled big money and needed cash handy for paying out winning bets. He couldn't keep it at his office in case he got raided. If he put it in a bank the government might find it and sniff around for its share. So, he had to keep it somewhere. McCarthy wondered how an old priest knew about something like that. Maybe he'd heard it in confession or something. Who cared?

Most of McCarthy's money went out more or less at the same speed it came in. There'd been school fees, donations to charity, and on and on. Sure, he had some stashed in his locker at Wellington Central, and some more hidden away at Ruby's brothel. That was for the wife and kids. It was O'Malley's money he was after. He was owed. The bookie couldn't have made it without him. It was a legitimate tax.

Christ but it was dark in here, and he'd just ripped his trousers on a nail. Shit! Keep going. If you end up in prison you won't have to worry about ripped pants – you won't be wearing any. You'll be stretched out on the floor being buggered by anyone who doesn't like cops. And that's everyone. He remembered how he'd twitched when the doctor probed him for constipation. That was bad enough. The idea of a mob of vengeful bastards going at him one after another was flat-out terrifying. He'd never actually been sure if they did screw one another in prison but the prospect had been useful for scaring confessions out of people.

His hands were running out across the floor, through the mouse droppings. Find the bloody money! Never mind prison. Getting caught in here by a crew of O'Malley's oafs carrying baseball bats would be a lot worse.

What was worse than that was that the frigging money wasn't here.

Up in the Gas Works foreman's office Gus Tait looked down at the little shed and scratched his backside. What the hell was he going to do? He had watched McCarthy park his car and bumble his way down the fenceline, past the stockpiles, to that little shed. Why? There wasn't anything in there and hadn't been for years. Hell, he didn't know why the shed was still standing.

But he had his orders. If he saw anyone going into it, and

especially at night, he was to contact Johnny O'Malley. O'Malley hadn't said why and Gus wasn't asking. His other hand had been on the phone for nearly a minute now. It didn't take a genius to see that there was trouble in this. As if there hadn't been enough already. Frank Wilkins's body had turned up just around the corner from the Gas Works and there'd been the bashings at the sly grogs and bookie operations.

Gus'd have a quid O'Malley was in the middle of the lot of it. What was slowing him down now was that Gus's wife worked at the hospital in the Accident and Emergency Department, patching up the wreckage. Turn McCarthy over to O'Malley and there'd be guys in a flash here kicking the lights out of him. Mind you, if he didn't ring, and O'Malley found out, it'd be him his wife would be sewing up.

Murray McCarthy solved Gus Tait's problem by getting himself out of there. Now he was back in his car having a look at his face in the rear-vision mirror. He was a hell of a mess, and there was coal dust all over him. He looked like one of those freaking golliwog dolls.

But what the hell was he going to do about it? Go into a police station and clean up there? Oh sure! Turn up there and the pack would be all over him. Besides, by now the police might have found something he didn't want found, and that'd be him into an interview room for a good going over. He wasn't going to be doing that, thank you very much.

He could also forget going home, at least not until the morning after his wife had carted the kids off to school. He could probably frighten her into shutting up for a while, but it wouldn't last long. Eventually she'd be off wailing to her friends who'd be happily sitting there soaking it up. Besides, she was always having cups of tea with O'Malley's missus – they took turns whining about their husbands. Guess how long it'd take O'Malley to hear about Murray McCarthy coming home covered in coal dust? Once that got back to O'Malley, and it would, he might just stop short of a crucifixion.

Well, he couldn't go around looking like this.

He drove out the Mt Victoria tunnel, down past the Basin

Reserve and St Patrick's College and along to Courtenay Place. A few minutes later he'd abandoned his next plan. What the hell was wrong with all the publicans? The one night he needed at least one of them to be doing some illegal after-hours trading they were all being good boys and had their places locked up tight. He'd only needed a sliver of light under a door and he'd have been in, up to a room with soap and a towel. Half an hour later he'd be fresh as a frigging daisy. But there'd been nothing.

The only place left now was the Taj Mahal, the public toilets in Courtenay Place.

Better not be any bloody poofs there.

He walked in and got to scrubbing at his face and hands. A man of about forty-five walked in, saw McCarthy and stopped, cold with fear.

'Sorry, Mr McCarthy. I'm sorry. Please, McCarthy! I wasn't here for a pull or a bum. I'm not. I'm here for a shit, honest!'

'Fuck off.'

'There's nowhere else!'

'Fuck off.'

The man turned and ran. McCarthy smiled as he splashed cold water over his face. That was interesting. Word can't have got too far around that he was the hunted, not the hunter. So far as they were concerned it was business as usual. Murray McCarthy was still in charge. Good.

He dipped his head in the steel washbasin, running the water through his hair. Getting a bit cleaner and knowing someone was still frightened of him made him feel a bit better. It wasn't much, but it was better than nothing – a little bit of cheer to carry him through what was beginning to look like a long night.

chapter twelve

Auckland, 1972

The partners were all here now, sitting around the table. Helen looked around at them. No one caught her eye. They were in their suits: no shirtsleeves and all the ties pulled up tightly in place. The formal look belied the 'quick word' they'd asked her to 'pop in' for. Helen, if she'd been asked to describe the scene, would have said they looked like witnesses to an execution. So who was going to pull the lever?

Thompson, from Litigation, led the way. 'Helen, quickly run us through the timeline, from when the bomb arrived until the police arrived.' He hit the word 'until' very hard. They already knew when the bomb arrived, they knew when the police had been called, and they didn't like the gap in between. It hadn't helped when she'd used the word 'bomb' to the police, rather than 'suspicious parcel' or something like that. That told them she knew what it was. Add that to the delay and there was the problem.

Thompson looked at her in the way a crab looks over a crippled seagull. We will torment you for the sport. When that turns boring you become lunch.

All that was left was to try to pre-empt the axe already being swung at her head. 'I can only apologise. I did the wrong thing. I appreciate that from time to time we have all done the wrong thing. I do, I must, apologise.'

Thompson's eyes flicked. That had been for his benefit, and he knew it. Go too far and Helen would accept that invitation for tea and biscuits with his wife. The Fiji conference would come up. So would the 'misunderstanding' with the two secretaries Helen had been able to smooth away.

If Thompson had been the only one there she might just have pulled it off. But he was only one of the faces in the crowd. The partners wanted this bomb business dealt with and they wanted a body. Juniors had to be discouraged from being too confident about their futures. That way they were easier to manage.

Gilfedder chipped in. Ah, Gilfedder, the conciliator and peacemaker. 'I think we can accept that all of us have made mistakes. Naturally, we should allow Helen a chance to give some thought to things, and to the way ahead, without feeling any pressure from us.'

This drew nods and approving glances. There it was. The 'guilty' verdict, properly sugared and palatable but clear. No one would be saying it aloud but from this second on Helen was expected to choose the moment when she climbed the steps, pulled the rope tight around her neck and jumped. She could see what was coming. Big cases would be steered away from her. The ambitious and the talented in her team would smell danger and run. The pick of what was left would be seconded away. Deeply regretted cutbacks would sweep the rest into the streets. Helen would be isolated. Finally there would be a decent lunch, suitable remorse at her decision to leave and a cheque slipped into her hand as she walked out the door for the last time.

There were nods all around the table. Good old Gilfedder – he'd hit the perfect blend of sadness and firmness. They didn't need to do anything more. Helen managed to keep a neutral face as Gilfedder sat bathing in the warmth of the reaction. Helen looked across at him. You puffed up little turd!

'Good, good. Take your time, Helen. Take your time. There is no rush. We are behind you one hundred per cent,' he purred.

That jolted her. One hundred per cent? She hadn't realised it was that bad. She'd be lucky to get two weeks before the razors were slashing at her back and the restaurant was being booked for her lunch.

Felicity Castles-O'Brien finished her glass of wine at the same moment as her tale of another man who discovered that his wife actually did understand him and was taking him home with her.

'C'est la vie. Bon voyage. May erectile difficulties always be at your side, travelling with you and forever your friend and companion.' Felicity stopped. 'Ouch. Bitchy. I don't think I should have said that because I don't actually mean it.' She smiled, raised her empty wine glass and muttered, 'To the Gods of Failed Love.'

Helen always found Felicity completely reliable in any or all of the following: being a friend; being intelligent and funny; not worrying about what anyone might think, now or ever; and doing what she liked, when she liked. She was also a sharply effective lawyer and Helen was wondering what she was most going to need Felicity for: her friendship or her legal skills.

She'd told Felicity about the bomb.

'Helen, my sweet, is there another way to be looking at this? Is it possible you might end up thanking God? It'll blast you, pardon the appalling pun, out of that coffin they've been calling an office. God, you're bloody near embalmed.' She looked around. 'Speaking of embalming fluid, where's the wine waiter?'

The waiter was standing behind her.

'We'll have the fish,' Felicity announced. Helen would have liked something with meat in it but it was too late. Felicity had waved him away.

'We have to be very firm with these waiters. New Zealand's only just getting restaurants and we don't want them behaving the way they do in London, as if they're in charge. Get them under control now, right from the start.'

Felicity worked for a firm specialising in anything to do with unions, the Labour Party and the left generally. At Federation of Labour conferences delegates had given her the nickname 'Margarine Thighs' for the speed and ease with which she spread them. She didn't mind. It was a title she'd earned over many conferences.

'Have you been thinking about what could happen if Women's Lib really takes off?' Felicity said.

No, Helen hadn't. She'd been preoccupied with other things.

'Women who have been tarred and feathered and humiliated, degraded and debased and forced to grovel in a pitiful low way might turn out to work rather well.'

Felicity was smiling. Helen had seen that look before.

'Look, it's about guilt. Men's, not ours! I know, I know. They don't think they are guilty of anything. Well, they bloody well are. What we need to do is establish that we, you, are the victims. Look at you: a traumatised mess from having that bomb turn up and look how they've behaved! All they could do was think of ways to boot your arse out into the street. We could do terrible things to them in court. There's a hell of a lot of money there. There's a good line-up of vaguely lefty judges on the Bench now. They love the middle class oppressing the less fortunate, and they like doing something about it even more. It's a chance to be generous.'

'Who are the less fortunate?'

'You!' Felicity answered.

'I'm not,' said Helen. 'But anyway, what's that got to do with anything?'

'Helen, girl, you're a lawyer, for Christ's sake. We're in the guilt and anger business. There is also a bigger picture. It's actually bloody easy. All we need to do is start talking to any journalist who'll listen – which is all of them – about centuries of oppression. We make it fashionable as hell to be female. It's already happening in England and the States. Whole forests full of cute furry little animals have to find new homes because the trees are going to make newsprint to cater for it. We go on about injustice and all the rest of it bloody endlessly. We become the experts. We'll end up on every board in the country. We get to change everything. Now, here is the best hit. We get wheelbarrow loads of money to do it.'

Helen knew her mouth was falling open with surprise and she didn't care.

'Look,' Felicity was in full flow now, 'there are Maori people doing research into the Treaty of Waitangi. Apparently it's all a bloody fraud, and they think there'll be strife over it. Great! We hook up with as many of them as we can find.'

Helen couldn't help it. She was being swept along by Felicity's enthusiasm. She always was. 'What will we, you, need?'

'A law degree! We've already got that. This stuff is so new we don't even have to be very good. We make it up as we go along. If anyone criticises us they're male chauvinist pigs. The other thing you need is breasts. We're all right there too. At least you are. You've got those bloody big tits of yours. Wear uplift bras so they stick out so far they can't be ignored, but don't show any cleavage because that's selling out and pandering to male fantasies, which is a very bad thing, unless you're trying to get laid.'

Helen was paying attention and Felicity could see it.

'It needs balls – not boys' swinging ones, though. I'm talking about the . . . the sheer hide to just get out there and do it, before anyone does it to you. This is like Eve looking at the very first cock. No one knows how big it gets once it starts moving. We can get rich on the back of middle-class pain, guilt and anxiety. Tell me there is something that isn't wonderful about that!'

Felicity leaned forward. 'Now, if we can change the world, we can find a way to deal with this little bomber prick. Have faith!'

Helen couldn't help smiling. Being around Felicity was always good: her cynical optimism was wonderful. Life was looking a bit better. Felicity was busy signalling the waiter, talking to Helen out of the side of her mouth.

'That's a very cute side of beef. Look at that marvellous little arse.' The waiter arrived. 'We're liberals and need to be sustained through the long hard hours of fighting for truth and justice. Have you got any really good burgundy?'

So this is what happens when a career dies. The phone stays silent. The river of invitations has been diverted into other waterways. It was less than a week and Helen was shocked at how quickly it had happened. Most of her cases had been whisked away. The clients were hearing, 'Did you meet Ashleigh? No? Oh God, sorry. Look, we want to swing him and James and Sophie onto your case. Helen's given them a full briefing so you won't notice anything slowing down. Everything will be steaming right along. Oh, Helen? She needed some time to herself: recharge the batteries, as it were. She has been working very hard, and particularly on your matters. We'll be keeping a razor eye on things. It'll be fine.'

And so it was going to go, one case after another until there was no reason for her to be here at all.

She'd been spending a lot of time down at the library, stripping it for anything on bombs, and especially letter-bombs. Eventually a librarian had raised an eyebrow. Helen had to give a reason or the librarian was going to quietly slip out the back and give the police a call.

'I am writing a novel.'

The eyebrow dropped down again. That was fine. Helen was just another dreaming loser heading for part-time school teaching or working here at the library.

Helen had also done long hours sitting in the Copper Kettle, the tearoom on the first floor of Smith and Caughey's department store, making a cup of bad coffee and a good solid scone last for two long hours. She couldn't go on like this. There was this dark little heart out there, probably making another bomb and hoping to slaughter her as he'd done with Jennifer, and she was doing nothing to stop it.

Well, what was she going to do? Just sit and wait for the next bomb? She might as well drive to the Harbour Bridge and jump: save him the time and expense. She fished through her purse and found the business card Beverley Martinelli had given her. She'd ring the man. Today, now.

chapter thirteen

Wellington, 1947

It was midday. Pat Feeney stopped, leaned back and closed his eyes to block out the accusing 'to do' list staring up at him from his desk. He didn't have be too tough on himself. The list was close to being under control. He had detectives trawling Wellington for the God knows who or what that would lead them to Marie West's killer. Jimmy Byrne was out trying to tail McCarthy. Two men were watching that unctuous little prick John Augustine O'Malley. He'd told them to be conspicuous. Make sure everyone and his uncle, cousin and brother knew they were there, and especially O'Malley's customers. That'd interfere with business. O'Malley wouldn't tolerate that for too long. He'd be worried people might get the idea they were exempt from loan repayments. Once the money haemorrhage got bad, O'Malley would make a move. But what could he do? Having coppers outside was going to stop him sending out the guys with the baseball bats. If he came out of that office of his he'd be stopped for a few words.

Build the pressure. Keep building it. Something would give. One thing that was annoying Feeney, though, was a whisper that McCarthy had been in and out of O'Malley's without being seen. He'd want to know how that had happened, and the answer had better be good. Two more detectives were outside Marie's home watching her parents arguing and yelling at each other. That was important. People in a fury could say interesting things. If it turned violent, uniformed coppers would barge in and get it under control. The plainclothes men would be right behind them. If accusations about killing Marie began flying, everyone was to be brought straight down to Wellington Central, in separate cars, and kept well apart while those accusations were thoroughly explored.

Feeney had tonight and perhaps most of tomorrow before Compton's spies arrived from Auckland and Christchurch. From then on, smoke signals would be going straight up to Compton on a regular basis.

The post-mortem must be close to finished now. With any luck it would turn out to be suicide. That'd shift the whole thing into the Coroner's Court and Feeney could wander off to other things. He snorted. Huh! Big black-Irish coppers like him never had that much luck.

This was a murder.

The detectives were due back at four. With luck, one would have a name that was close to Marie, with a motive and no alibi. The investigation would close in on him – or her. Everything would go at it: background, family, friends, all of it, until something fell open.

Then a message came through asking him to phone this number at his earliest convenience. The Bishop would like to meet him and as soon as possible.

Why the hell not? He could get that out of the way and then go and get the post-mortem results. That would take him from the living dead to the truly dead. Feeney smiled. He liked that. There was a joke in there somewhere.

A quarter of an hour later he was turning into Boulcott Street from Willis Street and driving up past St Mary of the Angels church. He parked near the door in the space marked Bishop. Why not? He had always dropped something in the plate at Mass.

He knocked. The door opened immediately. The priest gestured him in and led the way down a long, dark and elegantly panelled corridor. The solid wooden doors at its end could resist anything: a police raid, angry parishioners, nuns wanting to change the Church.

The priest knocked.

'Yes?'

The door opened and the priest whispered something. He

had to jump back as the door flew open and the Bishop was standing there. The hand that once did terrible work in the front row of the Marist scrum and famously ended the All Black hopes of Petone prop Bruce 'The Butcher' Partridge with one cheekbone-shattering punch was planted on Feeney's shoulder and steering him into the office.

'Pat, it's wonderful to be seeing you. Wonderful. We just don't see you enough, and that's a loss for us all. Come on in.'

The Bishop glanced at the priest, his voice changing to a hard-edged growl. 'Thank you, we'll be fine now.' A polite version of 'Go away and don't come back'. The Bishop turned back to Feeney, his eyes watchful above an astonishingly warm smile. 'There's a couple of people come to join us.'

Feeney looked past him. Two men were getting to their feet, both elegantly and expensively dressed. Feeney knew the two lawyers well enough and should have known they would be here. Jamie Johnston and Corbett Wilson stood smiling, hands outstretched. Johnston was a sharp and angry courtroom warrior. Feeney had spent many hours standing in the witness box fending off Johnston's powerful cross-examinations, meeting him in a corner of the court during the lunch break to come to a hurried agreement that a guilty plea to a lesser charge was better than an obviously guilty man going free. Feeney could understand Johnston: he was a man like him, fighting his way in a hard world.

Wilson walked quieter paths. The only times Feeney could remember seeing him out in the fresh air were when he walked between those dingy little rooms of his on The Terrace and the classrooms at Victoria University's Law School, where he quietly promoted eager young Catholic students and laid subtle and vicious traps for the sons of prominent Freemasons. The rest of the time he worked quietly at the intersections where the Labour Party, the Federation of Labour, the Catholic church and, if necessary, the National Party and the employers' organisations crossed and collided. Wilson was always there, whispering in ears and making sure he was long gone when those words resulted in a brawl in Parliament or a poorly constructed case in the Remuneration or Planning Tribunals.

Feeney had no doubt they'd know all about Marie West. They'd probably also know about the police coming from Auckland and Christchurch – that they were all Freemasons, and that McCarthy had seen O'Malley, and they'd probably know what had been said. A lot of information ebbed and flowed from this office, between the Bishop and these two lawyers. They could not be underestimated. Lying to them was a mistake. But then, why would he, when there were far better options?

The priest cleared the teacups and the tray of biscuits. The Bishop rocked slowly back in his leather chair, letting his meaty hand drop down on the expanse of pristine blotting paper. His lips pursed and he took his time. When he did speak, it was louder than necessary.

'You see, Pat, there's a lot for us to be worrying about. There are factions in the police that are resistant to change.'

'Resistant to change' meant opposed to Catholics, good and loyal ones taking their cues from the Bishop. 'Factions' meant Freemasons. The two lawyers nodded, particularly Wilson. Feeney crushed a smile. Of course they nodded. The Bishop signed their cheques.

'We're worried, Pat.' The Bishop was not taking any notice of them. 'We are very worried some will use this poor girl's terrible, terrible tragedy for their own ends.' He stopped for a quick sign of the cross. Feeney kept a straight face. Unless he was mistaken, that was the 'due respect for the dead' part finished. Now they would get to the strategy for using Marie's death to further the church's ends. Why not? Compton was busy doing the same thing.

Instead, the Bishop seemed thoughtful. 'Oh, we know we have enemies. Anyone set on doing right and spreading the word of God automatically has enemies. We're not a threat to them, but they don't realise that. So, if they're given an opening they'll move on us. We could be attacked anywhere we're vulnerable, and this case might leave us vulnerable.'

He stopped and looked at Feeney.

'Do you think we are vulnerable, Pat?'

It hadn't taken much longer than Feeney had expected.

'Not very, not yet.'

'It's possible we could be?'

'Anything is possible, depending on what the investigation turns up.'

The Bishop stopped. This was the place where he knew he had to pull up. Feeney had been here often enough before, long ago tiring of making it clear he would not, and would never, obstruct or skew an investigation to protect the church or the Catholics. It wasn't so much a moral decision. It was just that getting caught gave the anti-Christ more ammunition. It was a realism and a cynicism they could all grasp.

Not that it had ever stopped them finding other ways to apply pressure. The Bishop leaned back slightly so he was out of the light, giving him an enigmatic and dangerous look. Feeney had seen it before and it had ceased to have any effect on him. Still, he did wonder how many priests had sat in front of this desk, to be thoroughly intimidated before hearing their fate. Why did the Bishop bother? He held all the power. The answer was obvious; he did it because he could. He was also a churchman, and Feeney had never met one that wasn't in love with ritual and ceremony.

Feeney waited. He knew what they'd try to do, but he wouldn't let them dominate him. He was powerful and important too. He would not be bluffed into promising anything he shouldn't. It could happen. This was as much a battleground as the dark and the cold where the police slogged a hard living. He was surprised at how much the Bishop's office felt like Compton's. The atmosphere was the same. Influence and darkness seeped out of the walls to bend visitors to the will of the inhabitants.

'You see, Pat,' the Bishop leaned forward, his expression all grave concern, 'we want to offer all the help we can, to help you to make sure right is done, and is seen to be done.'

Huh! He didn't believe that for a second. Unless he was very mistaken they were already working like drovers' dogs to do everything they could to seal Marie West's murder off from the Catholics. They were probably already guilty of obstruction.

Johnston would have talked to O'Malley by now. If O'Malley saw sense, the Wellington hotels would be empty of Catholic bookmakers by tomorrow morning. Naturally, anyone stepping into the vacuum risked ending up in hospital with smashed kneecaps, or being found bleeding among the rubbish tins at the back of the pub.

Wilson would have spent the morning in Parliament Buildings, calling in debts and promising favours for those who had helped. The Bishop would have sent word out to trusted priests. Talk to other priests, to the nuns and the Marist brothers. Listen to everything. All information, no matter how small, would flow back to the Bishop. It would be fed to the lawyers to be used where it would do most good for the church. Feeney tended not to be wired into this circuit unless the offender was a prominent Anglican, Protestant or Freemason.

'What exactly do you want from me, Your Grace?' Feeney asked.

'Pat, we want you to conduct this investigation with the full force of the law, and we want you to know that anything we can do to help will be done.'

Feeney nodded. Well, they'd learned something over the years: to say the right thing to his face, even when they thought and did the opposite.

'Thank you. There's a lot of interest in this case and we want it wrapped up quickly. If you hear or see anything . . .' Feeney replied. The Bishop and the lawyers nodded.

Johnston spoke. 'We heard other policemen are coming in from Auckland and Christchurch, and we were wondering whether they will be sympathetic to . . .' He paused, his hazel eyes lancing at Feeney, '. . . to local conditions and . . . possibly . . . us.'

It'd been less than two hours since Feeney had been told and they already knew. Someone in the Minister of Police's office would have spilled that into Wilson's ear, to earn a credit with the man always able to give something in return.

Feeney said nothing. He let the question float in the air like soft mist.

The Bishop glanced around. No one wanted to say anything.

The Bishop ended the silence by standing up and beginning to shake hands. There was nothing more to be done. Feeney had been told, carefully, of what was required. Investigate by all means, but keep us posted. If a Catholic did the crime, then so be it. There were casualties in war. If he had to go to the gallows then it was regrettable, but they would be able to frighten the rest from straying too far from the guidance of the Bishop and his lawyers.

That was for the future. Now it was time for the other tasks and problems that made work for priests and lawyers. Wilson smiled, his plump, pink hand disappearing into Feeney's. He leaned close. Here it comes, thought Feeney, the message given on the way out the door when there is no chance to protest.

'There's a lot of people watching this one, Pat, watching it very closely. This case is important. I know you'll do well . . . and I hear there is a superintendent job coming up in Auckland in the New Year. It'd make you look good, coming in with the right result in time to get your application in.'

Christ Almighty! That was about as subtle as two goods trains colliding at top speed. If he was helpful the Bishop and Wilson could whisk him out of Wellington, back to Auckland and to high rank. Feeney struggled not to ball his fist and smash it straight into the lawyer's well-fed face.

Pat Feeney did not look back as he drove out into Boulcott Street. He'd had enough of the faith for now. It took only a few minutes before he was pulling into a building next to McKenzies' Cuba Street department store. Being unmarked had not saved Wellington's mortuary from public attention. The owners of the nearby shops had petitioned the council to move it somewhere else, arguing that images of death, slabs, tubes and jars of body parts jarred with the carefree atmosphere of joyous shopping they worked so hard to create. The council turned them down. The other possible site had been near a councillor's own home and any sensible citizen would see that was a wrong thing.

Pat Feeney had always liked the mortuary. The smell of the deceased, the refrigeration chemicals, the formaldehyde, the disinfectant and the methodical searches for evidence and clues were the world of proper policing.

Good. It looked as if Filthy Phil was doing Marie's post-mortem. Better him than Cathcart, a morose little bugger who was always agonising over the finer points of liver function. He was a bore. Why did he worry so much? The only livers he saw had ceased functioning. Still, everyone had their obsessions and perhaps thinking about healthy livers here in the place of death might be something good.

Filthy Phil was never morose. Indeed, Feeney often thought a splash of it might do him good. His search for the Joy of Life had been close to his downfall not just once but many, many times. His full name was Dr Phillip St John Mortimer Price. One day Feeney knew he'd be arresting the impeccably educated Englishman for what Pat Feeney's old mum used to whisper were 'Hunnish practices'. Rumours flew about Wellington that for Filthy Phil, men and women (and anyone in between) made suitable sexual partners, provided they met two criteria: they were over the age of consent and they consented.

Phil had told Feeney: 'There was a bit of a misunderstanding with some debutantes and a couple of officer cadets back in Mother England. Had to relocate, but brought myself along with me, as it were.' He would let a sly grin run across his face as he handed on his mock advice. 'Save yourself, Patrick. Save yourself. Never allow yourself to be yoked to the burden of fornication. It's a terrible, terrible weight to carry through life.'

Filthy Phil's love of fornication had seen him cross swords with Murray McCarthy a few months earlier. This had not been fun and no one was smiling. The doctor was caught up in one of McCarthy's 'poof hunts'. He'd been dragged down to Wellington Central and when he'd refused to tell McCarthy everything he wanted to know, he'd been kicked in the balls. This was in front of witnesses. Filthy Phil's legal team had arrived at Wellington Central, extracted him and eventually a large, and unpublicised, settlement to assist with what everyone quickly agreed would be Phil's long, grim struggle towards the restoration of his psychological well-being. A couple of nights later two nurses helped with this, in a night of exquisite pleasure crossed with moments each would spend years trying to purge from her mind. By morning Phil was sure he was on the track to complete recovery. A week later he was doing 'whatever a chap could do in the circumstances' to satisfy fresh offers.

That was when Feeney cursed the Freemasons for their screaming and howling for McCarthy's head. If they'd just shut up he'd have cheerfully given it to them. But because they made it a religious issue and made it clear they were going to use the case as a lever against other Catholics, Feeney had been forced to muddy the waters and reluctantly save McCarthy.

Phil looked up from Marie West's alabaster-white body.

'Good morning, Patrick. I'm afraid you've definitely got yourself a murder. Strangulation.' Phil moved on before Feeney could ask. 'It's a straight-up one, as far as I can see. No sex. There's nothing in her vagina, anus or mouth that's not supposed to be there. This took real strength. The way this was done I'd say you are looking for someone with powerful hands and forearms.'

Bill West, Marie's father, was a solidly built cabinetmaker.

'It was quick. I doubt she had much idea what was going on. I understand her clothing was disarranged?'

Feeney nodded.

'I'd say that was done afterwards. This was carried out in a few seconds – a minute at the most. There's nothing under her fingernails or between her teeth, no sign of her putting up a fight. I'll get it typed into official language, which of course will be unreadable to anyone who isn't a doctor, and get it over to you. It'll be there in the morning. Okay?'

Phil dropped the file back on his desk and smiled.

'Enough to start with?'

'Anything else I need to know about? Have you been screwing anything you shouldn't?' Feeney asked, smiling.

The doctor returned the smile.

'Oh Pat, Pat,' he gently rebuked. 'Of course I have, and hopefully you won't be involved.'

Well, that was the end of any hope of suicide and a sexo

turning up later to mess around with her clothing. Add that to his session with the Bishop and those two lawyers back in Boulcott Street, and whatever McCarthy was doing out there, and there was only one way to be seeing this.

The whole thing was turning into a very murky stew.

chapter fourteen

Auckland, 1972

For all anyone in the law firm cared, Helen could be slaving over the last of her cases, sobbing in the broom cupboard or stripping herself naked, daubing her body with earth-coloured paints and dancing up and down Queen Street. A couple of days ago she had been reasonably important and occasionally consulted. Now she was a rock in a frothing mountain stream. The fish and water swept past, leaving her behind: cold, exposed and alone.

It would be good to be like Beverley or Felicity: big, powerful presences, able to say anything they liked, whenever they liked. But, legal training not withstanding, she wasn't and never would be. She was quieter, and her first instinct was to keep her profile low. But then neither Beverley nor Felicity had a background like hers. They hadn't grown up having to be careful about what they said and to whom. A word in the wrong ear could have one of Helen's family arrested. Saying too much meant a sharp, instant and often brutal rebuke. You soon learned to listen and keep your mouth shut, and it was a hard habit to break. Still, that level of caution could be useful. She was facing an appallingly delicate navigation: around the police and the firm, and most important, trying to keep herself alive. There was nowhere in there to relax. Nor could she despair, or go looking for more help from her friends. This was too dangerous.

Inside the firm the panic had begun. McGibbons, the best and the brightest in her team, wanted a 'few moments of her time'. She knew what that was about. Another team leader had beckoned: by Monday he'd have jumped ship. Her guess was that he wanted to tell her personally before he leapt over the side. She'd noticed files had disappeared from her desk. Christ, that was quick. No much left now. She could come in and look at the view, because she wasn't getting anything else to do. Oh, her name was still on the internal phone list, and still on the door. French from Insurance and Maritime had dropped by to say hello and spent most of the visit looking around the office. Helen's guess was that it was promised to him. She picked up the phone and began dialling.

Once out of the building she felt better, but that wouldn't last. She hadn't heard anything from the police for a day or two. What were they doing? Were they watching her? How would she know? Would she spot someone following her? Suddenly being six feet tall and having a bold, swinging stride might not be such a good thing. It was wonderful when you wanted to sweep into a room to be noticed and envied. Helen seldom did, but she liked what happened when she did. Men paid attention. Other women's eyes narrowed. That didn't matter now.

Helen walked round and round the Royal Oak shops until she was certain no one was following her. Was it too risky coming out to see this Des Laughlan guy? The police would no doubt want to know why she was hiring a private detective.

She hadn't been here for a long time. The only new thing seemed to be the Kentucky Fried Chicken place, the first of what was supposed to be many. She'd done the legal work and she could confidentially say their chicken, with its eleven herbs and spices, was being served on the basis of the neatest and cleanest legal work possible. A queue of people stretched out the door, waiting patiently for their first Colonel experience. Beverley had laughed about this, telling her Des Laughlan over the road hated the chicken outlet. 'It's putting the place on the map, making it popular. That's bloody horrible for him because if there is one thing our Des avoids, it's publicity and popularity.'

Laughlan looked out his window. Yes, that would be Helen

Murphy over there. They always stood there, plucking up the courage to cross the road and come through his door.

He knew a bit about waiting. He'd been an undercover cop until he'd had one too many years in that schizoid life. He took the wrong personality with him when he left the police. It landed him in what he called 'the bins', known by the medical system as Carrington Mental Health Hospital. There, Laughlan had learned quickly. Blend in. Make the baskets no one wants. Make hundreds of the buggers. Plod along to the group therapy and pour your heart out. Got nothing to pour out? Make it up. If you can't think of something to say, then start crying. Don't miss any meals. Get through the nights of yelling, fear and masturbating. If anyone offers sex, take it. It'll give you something to cry about in the group sessions. Don't even think about getting out. You have no release date. This is indefinite. Do it one day and one hour at a time.

Not knowing his future pushed him deeper into a depression, which in turn kept him locked up for longer. Eventually a funding cut had saved him. Management had to pick, as one nurse put it, the 'cream of the crud'. Everyone else was shown the door. Laughlan was making his three hundred and ninth basket when a nurse walked up with his stuff in his three hundred and eighth. He was given a bus ticket, fifteen pounds and the address of a halfway house.

He put the fifteen dollars on a horse called Group One, the closest name he could find with a connection to the mental hospital. It paid ten dollars. He had a hundred and fifty. He didn't bother with the halfway house. Instead, he signed on for the sickness benefit, without mentioning the hundred and fifty. Forty of it went on a bulk discount deal with a prostitute. Both she and Laughlan were confident he was making big steps in his rehabilitation when the school holidays forced her home to look after the kids.

After that, Laughlan took stock of his skill set. He was going to have a few problems marketing himself to the bright fresh business world, what with his needing heavy medication to stop the twitching and flare-ups of his skin disease. So, he set up as a private detective, ignoring corporate work and specialising in clients at the bottom of the heap. As long as he got results no one cared that he looked like a cross between Frankenstein, Dr Hyde and the family cat.

The more Helen had heard about Des Laughlan the more she liked the sound of him. Word was he didn't look that good but he got the job done. The icing on a darkly flavoured cake was that for a slightly higher fee Laughlan would keep your case off the books. If he was raided you were protected. A lot of his clients chose that particular option.

Helen had another careful look around. She didn't see anyone who looked like police. Go in, do it, take the plunge. She remembered what Laughlan had said about his stairs and was careful to count them. Stairs eight and eleven were broken and Laughlan wasn't getting them fixed. If he was raided the howls of injury would give him the couple of moments he needed to light the match on the bottle of flammable liquid hidden among the files in the smaller of the two filing cabinets. It would be a nasty explosion but at least he, and a few reputations, would survive.

Laughlan smiled as he waved Helen to a chair. Helen liked him. He looked mad and dangerous: exactly what was needed.

'Tea or coffee?' Laughlan was saying.

Helen shook her head.

His smile was telling her, 'It's all right – sit down, spill your guts and have a total breakdown if you want. You're paying.'

Somehow Helen had always known her genes would land her in a place like this. You could do what you liked – get a degree and climb up in the world. Heaven help it, less than a week ago she was being offered royal commissions. Now look at her. Here she was enlisting the help of someone who definitely didn't walk any bright, clean and sunny paths. He looked like her family. It seemed fitting to wind up back in the world of her youth. Des Laughlan certainly belonged there.

She'd bet he was the sort of Catholic boy who believed women were to be either idolised or exploited and very little in between. If they idolised you, they made the finest of friends and allies. If not, they were a nightmare. Anything in between confused them.

'I take it this isn't coming through the firm,' Laughlan prompted.

Helen shook her head. Laughlan already knew Helen's case was going to be . . . complex. On the phone she'd mentioned Lashing's name. Then about half an hour ago Laughlan had seen him over in the queue at the Kentucky Fried Chicken. He hadn't looked too excited about getting his hands on a bit of fried chicken; he'd been more interested in Des Laughlan's doorway. As soon as Laughlan saw him he'd got Errol Schaumkel in to give his office a quick sweep for listening devices. It was clean, although Errol was careful to point out that he'd only had time for the walls, ceiling, floors and power points, not the phones. Otherwise, as Errol put it, Laughlan was free to lie back and enjoy the conversation.

There was a lot to enjoy. Helen's story, beginning with a death in Wellington and ending with a bomb in an Auckland office was hard to top.

Helen's session with Des Laughlan took three-quarters of an hour. Laughlan would be heading to Wellington. No, Helen was best to stay here in Auckland. Be seen living a normal life. Head south and she might drag the coppers down there after her. They didn't need that. If Laughlan needed to pinprick the Wellington bureaucracy it'd be useful that she was a lawyer but she could just as easily do that from Auckland. He had her home phone number. If he called, he would want a quick answer, so she should go out and buy an answerphone.

Laughlan paused. There was something else.

'You know you're being followed, don't you?' Laughlan said.

Helen wasn't surprised at hearing about Lashing buying his fried chicken and walking to an unmarked Holden that shrieked 'police'. A policewoman had taken the red and white box of chicken from him and dropped it in the rubbish tin. Lashing hadn't looked happy about that – he was famous for being ready, willing and able to eat fish and chips three times a day.

'There's another way to look at it. This might be good. They might be keeping an eye on you, to protect you, so if the bomber tries some other way they'll be able to move,' Laughlan suggested. They exchanged glances that said, 'I don't believe that and neither do you.'

If Helen's mail turned up anything fatter than a standard envelope she was to call the police. They were already involved, although it would be good if Laughlan heard first, in case there was anything he needed to get out of the way before they started poking around.

If they blow up a make-up sample she'd only lost out on a couple of free boxes of nail polish. The world had more nail polish.

Now Helen was in her car outside Laughlan's office. It was time to test the Laughlan technique for finding out if you were being followed. She pulled her car out into Manukau Road. Whoops! She was so intent on the rear-vision mirror she nearly hit the car in front. Its driver gave her the fingers. She smiled an apology and waited for him to drive off. That got a horn tooting from behind her.

Not the greatest start.

She drove up Manukau Road to Greenwoods Corner. A Holden was two cars back. Was that the one? She turned left into Pah Road and back down to Mt Albert Road, bringing her back to Royal Oak and its roundabout. The Holden was still there. Good. Helen smiled. There was a Ford stationwagon behind her, but it had painters' ladders on top. That wouldn't be the police. She drove around the roundabout four times. Anyone following her now was definitely suspect.

Lashing came out of the public toilets, zipped up his pants and watched Helen going round and round. The policewoman in the Ford with the ladders on top drove past into Mt Smart Road. Lashing smiled.

'Well, there you go. She's been to Des's school. Good on him. So he didn't lose it in the looney bin. He's done well. She's very good.'

Lashing got a glimpse of Helen's face. She was smiling. Even better! He nodded to another policeman, who eased a battered Vauxhall out into the traffic behind her, keeping two cars back as a relieved-looking Helen drove back towards the city.

chapter fifteen

Wellington, 1947

Splashing water over himself in the Taj Mahal was never going to get Murray McCarthy properly clean. His face and hands were okay, but his hair was a mess and so was his suit. It felt as if it had about an inch of coal dust on it. Getting that clean was going to take professionals. But he didn't have time to hang around here worrying about it. He could be seen. Feeney or Byrne or whoever was on his case would be straight down here sniffing around. He had other things to do, and he had no intention of dragging nosy bloody coppers around after him.

He took a last look in the cracked mirror. 'Bugger it. That'll have to do.'

He did a quick check at the spots he used when he was staking out the Taj. He couldn't see anyone backed into any of the shadows. Next stop was Miramar, to see Weir. He didn't particularly want to be going out there but he had no choice. These days it was just about impossible to get Weir to leave that house of his.

Weir didn't go to the mountain. The frigging mountain had to go to Weir.

McCarthy spat some coal dust out the car's window. That was better. Not that anything was that much better. So far the whole day had been utter crap. Maybe Weir might be able to find something up his sleeve.

Among a lot of other things, Xavier Simeon Weir was Murray McCarthy's legal adviser. He had no formal legal practice. That path had turned muddy on him a few years back, when a surprise audit caused unpleasantness and harsh words. Weir did a two-year sentence. The judge told him that if he'd made a decent attempt at reparations he might do only six months. As far as Weir was concerned, that was out of the question. He knew he'd need a little something to start him off when he came out and opted for the extra time. He'd tried to cover it with a lot of talk about slow horses and fast bookmakers, to be disappointed at the open disbelief and scoffing.

There'd been dire warnings about being at risk of homosexual temptation. To the disappointment of more than one priest that seemed to be an incentive for Weir to do the longer sentence.

The Law Society ignored his bitter complaint that striking him off was a breach of natural justice, punishing him twice for the same offence. The head of the disciplinary committee leaned over and in a deep, sonorous tone whispered in Weir's ear, 'Do us all a favour, fuck off, find a gun, stick it in your ear, pull the trigger and know you've done something decent for the first time in your shitty little existence.'

Well, it wasn't as if he hadn't expected the chop – in his heart of hearts he'd known it was coming. What he didn't like was the way it was presented. For a moment all he could see was a raging red mist and he did something he'd learned to do in prison: he kneed someone in the balls. Unfortunately it was the head of the disciplinary committee, an eminent King's Counsel. Watching him writhe on the floor had been extremely satisfying. It also landed Weir back in court, having to listen to the magistrate chomping away about how this was a sign of the ruin ahead . . . and a lifetime of perdition . . . and crime was a sword over his head . . . and on and drearily on.

The judge gave Weir 'a final chance' and fined him. Weir sprang the fine and the costs from the missing trust funds and spent a long afternoon in the Carpenter's Arms thinking carefully about his future. That future included Jeremy Sylvester Courtenay Norris, whom he hadn't seen since their third-form days at St Patrick's Silverstream. Norris had had a reversal of his own: he was looking at his options after being struck from the medical register for doing one too many abortions.

Weir and Norris did the sensible thing: they went to confession to cleanse their sins and opened a consultancy for those with particularly sensitive and complex problems who had difficulty taking them to the established authorities. They laboured, for good fees, to keep the sons of the rich and the farmers, who might have been playing the Scot's and King's College First Fifteens two weeks before, so seriously debilitated by medical conditions that they could barely stand upright in front of army medical panels. Weir and Norris had to confess, privately, that World War Two had been very good for them, with Weir earning his share of the river of money by keeping the paperwork sparkling.

There had been a rumour or two about McCarthy spending so much time with Weir, who had decided during his prison years that his future sexual orientation was going to involve strapping young men. Why, people asked, was a dedicated poof hunter like McCarthy strangely failing to target Weir in his relentless drive to sweep sodomy and homosexuality from the face of Wellington?

Money.

Weir, McCarthy, and, until he died, Norris could all see there was a place for disgust at alternative sexual practices. That was when they were practised openly and when there was no money in it for Weir, McCarthy or Norris. There was also a bigger picture. McCarthy, for instance, was able to steer the vice squad away from Cynthia Henderson's house in Khandallah, where worried young women could meet Norris and have their problems quickly – and expensively – solved.

There was the room at De Brett's Hotel set up with cameras and sound-recording equipment that had disappeared from the National Film Unit. Under Weir's careful eye it became a solid earner, turning older men's dalliances with younger men, and women, or occasionally both, into envelopes stuffed with ten-pound notes. Norris's death, which was definitely not accidental, had been a crisis. Weir and McCarthy were each pushed to the edges of their talent and influence to get it on the books as 'misadventure' and keep the insurance people from turning difficult.

McCarthy drove through the Miramar Cutting, past the Gas Works and up to the Miramar Fire Station. Weir's place was just ahead, up on the hill looking down over the Marist Miramar boys' school. It was good that it was night. McCarthy wasn't in the mood to sit there as the chubby lawyer gazed down on the playground and the boys playing soccer and cricket, musing at 'my little holding paddock for a great and glorious future and God Save the Queen'. McCarthy pointed out that England had a king. Weir ignored him. McCarthy was a good solid lad, and very useful too, but there were times when he missed the joke.

Thank bloody God.

McCarthy could hear the footsteps crossing the living-room to Xavier Weir's door. He was home. He might have been out visiting the sick or buggering someone, but it was going to be all right. The door opened. Xavier Weir's smile barely creased his cheeks and jowls before it was gone and McCarthy was briskly waved inside. As McCarthy stepped past him Weir poked his head out and looked up and down the street. He couldn't see anyone moving, or anyone watching. Good. Get the door closed quickly.

McCarthy stood awkwardly in the middle of the living-room as Weir marched past him to the drinks cabinet and raised an eyebrow as an offer of a drink. McCarthy nodded. Weir knew what McCarthy liked: neat whiskey and a lot of it.

Weir gave McCarthy his drink, taking the chance to look the policeman up and down. Well, well. His friend Murray had dropped himself in the merde and it looked as if he could not get out on his own. Having him close to panic was an excellent thing. Terrified clients were desperate for help and didn't make too much fuss when they found out what that help was going to cost, and that they'd be paying in cash. They wouldn't be getting any invoices or receipts either. They could turn up in the wrong hands, such as the ones at Inland Revenue. They had far bigger targets than Weir, and he had a policy of not distracting them from the good work they so often did.

Weir waved McCarthy to a seat. Get him sitting down: he'd be easier to control.

'I hear the girl's turned up and the coppers are getting a little bit excited.'

McCarthy nodded. 'Getting a bit excited' referred to his being followed and they both knew it. How Weir knew didn't matter. What mattered was finding a way out of the mess.

'Coal dust, Murray?' Weir asked.

'Yeah,' McCarthy snapped.

'It's all right. Our friend O'Malley has money all over the city. He won't miss some, especially for a good cause.'

McCarthy twitched. Jesus! Mother of Christ, was there anything Weir didn't bloody know about?

'I think I might have to get out. Like you say, things are hotting up and it doesn't look as if this one is going away.'

As soon as Weir had heard about Marie West and that Pat Feeney had the case, he'd decided this might get out of control. He'd spent two hours with his brother Jerry, who worked at the Bank of New Zealand. Between them they had nearly a hundred thousand pounds wired through to the Bank of America branch in San Francisco's Market Street, and without too much paperwork lying around at the New Zealand end. They'd used Peter Fraser's name for the transactions. He was the prime minister. At the first hint of anyone talking about corruption in Parliament the Weir brothers would know the hunters were creeping up on them. They could be gone in two days.

Weir snapped back to the present. McCarthy was talking about getting out of town. Sensible. He was dog tucker in the police. 'It'd be just me for a start, and I'd send for them later,' McCarthy muttered. Weir's was an understanding nod. He didn't believe it for a half second. McCarthy had long since lost interest in his wife and kids. If he was taking it on the run, they weren't going to be a part of it.

'Murray, I think it might be a good idea if you gave me a bit of an idea of what's gone on,' Weir purred.

Out it came: being followed, O'Malley refusing to help, the Gas Works, the Taj. Weir listened carefully. McCarthy would have preferred it if Weir wasn't always glancing at the fly of his pants, but this wasn't the time to be making a fuss.

'Definitely sounds like your police years might be winding down,' Weir said.

McCarthy was struggling to keep control. Weir frowned. He'd better give this guy a bit of hope or he'd go right off the deep end.

'Murray, legging it is just one of the options. There's other work a man with your skills could be doing, and picking up good money. Don't go closing your mind to anything. All right?'

McCarthy didn't try to hide his relief. Christ, he'd take anything that'd get him out of this mess. He wouldn't just take it – he'd bloody grab at it.

Weir sat back in his chair. This was going rather well now. He swallowed back a little flick of pain – another of those blips from his chest. Keep still. It'd pass. It always did.

'There is something I want to show you,' Weir said. 'I think it might be a good time for you to have a little bo-peep at something that might be your future. I tell you what, Murray, it's a good one, too.'

McCarthy stood up. If Weir was offering anything he was interested. Sure, there was this little voice inside telling him to be careful, and that a price tag was always hanging from anything Weir offered. Well, that voice could shut up. He was in trouble. Whatever Weir had in mind might be a way out. He was hot to see it.

chapter sixteen

Wellington, 1972

Des Laughlan had always liked the sound of this job. What could be better than a mix of bombs, lawyers, Catholics and sex? He'd got everything else wrapped up or on hold. Now here he was in Wellington roaming among the cardigan-wearing civil servants. It had gone well. He was nearly finished. The family had been easy to trace, and as far as he could see they were a bunch of brutal fruitcakes. The ones who weren't assault artists were armed robbers and Christ knows what else. The only thing he had to be a bit careful about was not letting any of the throwbacks find out what he was up to. The last thing he wanted was any of the mad buggers turning up on his doorstep, thank you very much.

He'd got a lot from Births, Deaths and Marriages. Sam, who'd been in the same recruit wing with him and who was working in the police records section, had slipped him the rest. They were a bunch of duds who weren't much good at anything, including crime, because they were always getting caught. They could rut, though. He'd counted thirteen of them in the current generation, and half of them under different names. It had taken a while but he had them all sorted out now. He was on the home stretch and going hard out for the finish line.

Helen had been right. One of them had changed his name, picking up the moniker of someone living along the road. Des focused on him. Was he working at a proper job? Did he have a family, and if so, how many were in it? Was he handy with the sort of tools that'd turn a man into a working bomb-maker?

Helen wanted photos of this Bresnahan guy and his house.

Laughlan got a photo of him on the bus that morning. It was easy with the small Leica, which made no noise when you shot. You held it in a handkerchief, you pretended to sneeze and you had your snap. If you were any good – and Des Laughlan was good – that was your up-to-the-minute colour glossy, or black and white, take your pick.

Now he was out here in Miramar, up at the corner of Nevay and Fortification Roads, and he couldn't bloody believe it. There was the house, just as she'd described it from all those years ago – and the garage too! Neither of them looked as if it had seen any paint since.

Now that was a stroke of luck: the garage door was unlocked. Getting a picture of the inside was definitely bonus territory. Carefully Des, very quietly and carefully . . . don't stuff around, in case someone's already called the coppers.

He pushed open the door. It was oddly dark in there. Someone had covered up the windows, and the door at the other end was closed. Get the picture and get the hell out of it. He could feel his pulse begin to race. His mouth was dry. He stepped inside, lifted the little camera to his eye and snapped half a dozen shots. That'd do it. Now, out, out, and on his way.

'No, mate.'

It was a deep voice. Its owner wasn't tall but was strong-looking. Des knew him. He'd taken his picture that morning. He felt powerful hands around his neck. They were tight and getting tighter. He fought as hard as he could but it was hopeless. In a quarter-second of sharp, clear insight, as his knees and legs flopped limp under him, Des Laughlan realised the adventure he'd called his life was ending in a dark, dirty little Miramar garage.

Auckland, 1972

It was just before two o'clock in the afternoon when Helen walked past the offices to the reception area and the lifts. As she passed the lawyers they glanced up and then dropped their heads back to their papers or looked into their telephones.

None of them smiled, or gave a hint they'd recognised her. If lepers were close, you didn't encourage them to come any closer. You could be exposed to the disease.

This couldn't go on much longer; it was too soul-destroying. That was the idea, of course: to make her dispirited and broken and desperate to get out. Well, if this went well she was gone.

The walk down Queen Street to Frank Fitch and Associates took only a few minutes. Felicity was waiting in the foyer. It was suitably left-flavoured, with a picture of the first Labour prime minister, Michael Joseph Savage, smiling shyly down on them. The furniture was chipped and functional with an appropriately musty smell. The odour carried its own message: the poor and downtrodden should always have three things to guide them through an unequal and difficult life – faith, hope and a good lawyer. All three were available here.

An hour later her job interview was over. Frank Fitch, veteran of a thousand battles with the police, the conservative right and the Law Society, a man with a tired, gentle face and the palest blue eyes Helen had ever seen, was shaking her hand, smiling and turning back to his office. Felicity took her to the door.

'Look girl, you did a terrific job. It was a brilliant interview,' Felicity said when Fitch was gone. Helen managed a smile. She wouldn't get the job and they both knew it.

'I don't know, and I am going to fight for you, but I have a feeling he'd like to have a brown face in here. That'd cover everything.'

The only brown faces up at the Law School, or just out of it – and there weren't many of them – were male. Helen was being returned to the elegantly furnished holding pen to rot in the shagpile, the mahogany and the reception area's steel and leather chairs.

Gilfedder, the firm's calm and placid hatchet man, made sure he met her as she came out of the lift. 'Look, we must catch up. I'd like to be in your schedule. Would Monday or Tuesday be all right for you? Do let me know.'

So, there it was. They'd run out of patience. She had until Monday – at the latest Tuesday – to walk out into the snowstorm. After that she was going to be pushed.

At least she had Des Laughlan in Wellington. He seemed to be going well on opening up the pathway to the bomber, the man trying to make any other worries irrelevant. She remembered how, when she'd felt disappointed and under siege, she'd ring Jennifer and they'd talk for an hour.

Days that were gone forever . . .

One day she'd cry a proper goodbye for her sister. Until then, she was going to have to stumble on.

Helen breathed in as deeply as she could. Don't let anyone see you are close to breaking down. Stay strong. Look confident. Go into the office and close the door.

There was a message on her desk. Lashing had rung. God, what did he want? Mind you, if it was really bad – if he'd found out everything – he'd be here with that policewoman and they'd be taking her with them, whether she liked it or not. She musn't panic. It was an investigation. They just wanted more details about something.

She sat at her desk, ignoring the glorious harbour view with the sun bouncing and flashing off the water. Why hadn't Laughlan called? It wasn't like him to leave it this long.

Helen put down the phone. Laughlan was still booked in at the Hollywood Motel in Newtown, and paid up for another two weeks. No, the owner hadn't seen him, but then Mr Laughlan had said he would be meeting a lot of his contacts after working hours and that he'd be doing a lot of coming and going. Oh no, the manager didn't keep an eye on him. The management of the Hollywood respected the privacy of their guests . . . Helen agreed this was good, and yes, if she went to Wellington she would definitely stay at the Hollywood. However, now that Helen had mentioned it, the owner hadn't actually seen Mr Laughlan for a couple of days – not that anyone was looking, you understand. No, there hadn't been any phone calls to or from his room.

Sooooo.

Something was wrong – or was it? Was she panicking? Would she have to go to Wellington herself, and risk being that much closer to the murderer? This was a time when she missed her sister. Having someone to talk to would be wonderful, so she could go over and over it, knowing there was help and support. But there wasn't. She was in her grave and Helen was on her own.

God, she could barely believe it but she found herself thinking about the last person in this place who had been really helpful: Archie Fallon. And he'd been trying to feel her up! Yes, he was a pervert but there were other sides to him. He was a retired judge now and perhaps he'd turned respectable. Oh look, those were pigs flying over the sun and moon. Anyway, did she she actually want respectable? She needed help, and from the filthiest and most cynical mind she knew. That was Fallon.

'Yes, of course.' Fallon had answered the phone himself. 'Love to see you. You know where I am?' She did. He lived at Piha now and she knew the way: out to New Lynn, up Titirangi Road, onto Scenic Drive and just keep going.

chapter seventeen

Wellington, 1947

Thank God. The last of the detectives was finishing droning through his report on how he'd spent the day trying to turn up a name for Marie West's murderer. He needn't have bothered. It was the same as the rest, plugging diligently away and producing nothing. Feeney smiled a 'thanks' at him. The detective smiled back and looked around the room in a vaguely hopeful way. Feeney chilled him with a glance. He wasn't getting any applause for 'everyone I spoke with had eleven independent witnesses who could account for all their movements every hour of the day and night for the past three and a half years'. You got applause when you fronted up with a suspect, a legally obtained and neatly typed confession, good forensic evidence and at least three eyewitnesses. A defence lawyer pointing to his client and yelling, 'He's the filthy scum that did it so hang him now to protect the rest of us', would definitely help. Not only would that get applause, but it would also have Feeney dragging everyone around to the public bar at De Bretts and shouting the first two rounds.

Everything in and around Marie's life had been drilled into. A couple of ex-boyfriends had been frightened into pants-peeing terror but hadn't given anything useful. Friends tried to remember anyone threatening her but came up with nothing. That left the family or some passing nutcase.

Please, please Lord, let it be the family. Passing nutcases were a policeman's nightmare. You relied on chance and their carelessness. The odds were on their side. But the family: no one would call them placid. Clashes were hard and bitter, since

Marie's body had turned up, they had become louder and even more bitter. Feeney kept the detectives on a twenty-four-hour watch. If there was going to be an explosion he wanted people there immediately.

It was nearly six at night. Apart from the detectives rotating through the night outside the West house the rest could go home. They sensed it and were ready to run. These were experienced officers and they lived by a simple rule: once you were out the door, you legged it as fast as you could. If they couldn't see you they couldn't drag you back to do more hours.

Feeney looked up. He bit back an 'Oh shit'.

Compton had arrived at the back of the room. He had four men with him – the Auckland and Christchurch reinforcements. No surprises there. They looked exactly like what they were: solid, 'make no bones about it' Freemasons. They were going to be loyal only to Compton, who left them at the back while he threaded his way through to join Feeney at the front of the room. They exchanged the barest of nods before Compton turned to what had now reluctantly become his audience. He straightened his back, pushed his chin out to a near-impossible angle and swept the policemen with his gaze.

'I won't keep you long,' he said. 'This is a difficult case. But if the trail gets cold it'll turn into the hardest investigation you can have, something that's almost as dead as poor Marie.' He paused, expecting some sort of response. There was nothing. What exactly did he expect? Feeney was thinking. So far he'd told the poor buggers something they actually already knew, that they were getting nowhere.

Compton continued. 'But I have to say, you men are covering the ground well and must, must continue to do so. Remember, always remember: this girl has only us to call her murderer to account. We have to do this. We cannot favour anyone. There must be no shrinking. If anyone obstructs us . . .'

Compton had slipped Feeney a quick little glance at 'favour anyone'. Feeney had stiffened but kept a straight face. The bastard was talking about the Catholics and probably the Bishop. Had he had Feeney followed? Feeney remained impassive. For the audience's benefit he managed a small nod of agreement.

Compton had already turned back to the men. '. . . it is our duty as sworn officers of the law to remove them from the path of the investigation. We must move forward, without fear and favour. Whoever committed this shocking crime must be brought to trial.'

He paused and took a quick breath, winding up for the big finish.

'Nothing else matters. Keep up the good work. I will be providing you with help and support. You can rely on that.'

He stood back, waiting for the applause. Nothing. Compton glared at them until Feeney was forced to start the clapping. The others listlessly joined in. It was a thin effort but enough for Compton, who milked it for as long as he could. Then he snapped the policemen a sharp nod and strode through them to the door, forcing them to make way for him. Feeney watched him go. Arrogant prick.

Still, it was a useful little speech. It told Feeney the Catholics were being watched, and that probably included him. He'd have to be careful.

As soon as Compton was gone, Feeney spoke curtly. 'I want everyone back here at eight in the morning. Apart from those watching the West house, that's it for tonight.' In less than a minute Feeney was alone.

Christ. That was all he needed – having to worry about a tail. What the hell else were they doing? Was there another case being run under this one, hunting Catholics? He really needed to get hold of McCarthy. Where had the big oaf gone? What in God's name was he doing? He hoped Jimmy Byrne was still on his tail, but he'd heard nothing for a while.

Feeney slapped his hand down on the desk, dumping some of his tension and fury. Then his eye caught something. Someone was moving in the shadow of the corridor – a wraith-like figure was slipping away. That would be one of Compton's crew. Great.

Feeney was tired of driving around Wellington's too-familiar streets. He'd been doing it for nearly thirty-five minutes now, and it might take another thirty-five.

He'd keep doing it until he was sure he wasn't being followed.

So far he hadn't seen anyone, or any patterns of cars disappearing and reappearing behind him. Okay, perhaps he could get on with it. Even so, he took the long way around, going through the fruit and vegetable markets to O'Malley's office. Out-of-towners would have to know what they were doing to be able to follow him in and out of there.

He shoved at O'Malley's door. It opened to his touch. Interesting! Every other time he'd been here, and it was mostly on raids, it had been locked and bolted. Still, O'Malley had announced that his bookmaking was on hold so he didn't have to worry too much. By now his money and records would all have been safely moved somewhere else.

Feeney smiled as a tough-looking man walked up to him and stood between Feeney and the little group of people at the other end of the room. Feeney didn't care. He could get a hard-on and play with it all night if he wanted. Then Feeney stopped. The guy wanted to search him before he could talk to O'Malley. Lord, help this simpleton find a hobby. He needed to get out more and stop spending all his time watching American gangster movies.

'Hey, you!' The man snarled at Feeney.

Feeney kept his voice a low, bored monotone. 'I am tired. I have a lot to do before I get home so do me a big favour and fuck off.'

The man bristled. Feeney decided he might wait for a moment after all, but he wasn't going to waste too much time. Let this clown have a few seconds of being a toughie. If he pushed it too far he could see how tough he was when he was in a cell and bleating not to be missed out when the meals came around.

A soft, lightly Irish-accented voice broke across them. 'Why, Freddie, it's all right, that's Mr Feeney come to see us. It'll be fine. It always is when Mr Feeney pays us a little visit.' Freddie, glowering with wounded pride, stepped aside. John Augustine O'Malley was on his feet and walking over to Feeney, all warm hospitality, his hand out and grabbing Feeney's. O'Malley led

Feeney to a distant corner of the room. As always, O'Malley dominated the conversation, a habit that annoyed the priest when O'Malley made his weekly confession.

'Pat, we've been thinking about things. Our time is over. You don't have to worry about us any more. The government's bringing in a totalisator, a legal one. The papers have turned on us, whipping up the public. That's the one thing that we can't hold out against – the public being whipped up against us. I've been telling everyone they are on their own. It's finished.'

Feeney nodded. He'd already have to worry, now probably more than ever. If O'Malley was telling the truth – and that was never a certainty – there'd be thirty-odd bookmakers around Wellington and the Hutt Valley scrambling for control. That'd mean chaos, blood and probably a few more bodies turning up before it all calmed down.

'It's time for me to take the few shillings I've put by for retirement,' O'Malley went on.

Feeney couldn't help a smile. The few shillings! If O'Malley wasn't a millionaire several times over then no one was. Still, if O'Malley was in a mood to talk, then let him.

'There's Frank Wilkins dying a terrible death,' O'Malley said. 'Pulled out of the harbour with bullets in him. There's poor Marie turning up all alone on Mt Victoria. It's too much, and it'll be encouraging those who want to be moving on us.'

His expression got the message across that 'us' included all Catholics, which meant both him and Feeney.

Feeney didn't like that – he didn't count himself with scum like O'Malley. He'd wanted O'Malley in prison for years now, and the bastard was slithering away leaving the bashed, the bankrupted and probably the murdered behind him. A few years back a man had been set on fire. Word had reached Feeney it was O'Malley's doing after he'd been told he could burn in hell before he got his money. O'Malley would have tipped the police off to where Wilkins was killed – at 100 Adelaide Road – and made sure this bit of civic duty came well after the place was safely cleaned up.

'I hear poor Murray McCarthy's been snooping around that little shed at the back of the Gas Works,' O'Malley said.

Feeney knew about that shed. O'Malley had spread the word there was money hidden in it, to flush anyone who'd steal from him out into the open. By now Feeney was deciding there wasn't much point in any of the things he'd come to talk about. If O'Malley knew anything about Marie he wouldn't be telling. Might as well get out of here now.

Feeney stood up. The bookmaker's eyes flashed; he wasn't finished.

'John, I don't give a shit about your problems,' Feeney said, putting his hand on the bookmaker's chest to keep him sitting while he stood over him. 'There's just one thing. If you know anything about that West girl, make sure I hear about it. Otherwise I'll be making sure you get yourself a little farewell present. I'll have honest coppers and tax accountants all over you for the rest of your life. It happened to that fella in Chicago, Capone, and there he was, rotting in a cell for decades. Don't think it couldn't happen to you.'

'If I hear anything I'll tell you.'

Feeney looked at him hard. O'Malley met his gaze. His smirk was gone. Perhaps he meant it. Christ, you just never knew.

O'Malley stood and extended his hand. Feeney ignored it and turned for the door. Freddie stood up and glowered at him. Feeney stopped. He couldn't believe it. The bugger was going to try something. Freddie was walking up to him. Behind them, O'Malley was silent. Well, he can try this, thought Feeney. He shoved Freddie in the chest, sending him back against the wall. Then he swung his knee into Freddie's groin. There was a slow hissing sound from Freddie as he doubled up. His eyes bulged and his face went white as he dropped his hands over his balls. Feeney didn't bother looking back as he closed the door behind him.

Well, that hadn't produced much, although he was inclined to think O'Malley meant it when he said he'd pass anything on. Perhaps there was some good in him. Huh! Some chance. He'd only do that if there was something in it for him.

Feeney walked back through the markets to his car. McCarthy was the next item of business. Feeney would bet the big policeman would be part of O'Malley's 'finishing up the business'. That could mean dead, frightened or seriously hurt. Someone was going to have to pay for O'Malley's world collapsing. He had lost money – he wouldn't like that. Taking it out on a cop would do nicely. So where was the big prick?

Feeney squinted at his alarm clock. Five o'clock in the fricking morning and whoever was belting on his door wasn't going away. At least his wife was sleeping right through it. Being married to him for twenty years, and to the hours he worked, had given her plenty of practice. Feeney eased himself out of bed. Once he was clear of the bedroom and in the hallway it was safe to grumble at the door.

'All right! All right, calm down. I'm coming.'

Jimmy Byrne stood there. Feeney waved him into the house and into the kitchen, the furthest room from the bedroom and his sleeping wife. Byrne didn't wait to be asked why he'd come.

'Johnny O'Malley's dead! He went out his office window and down into the street. Might have been a suicide.'

Neither of them believed that for a second. Feeney felt a chill. He'd been around to O'Malley's. He thought of Freddie, who would love the chance to tell the world Feeney had been there. Great.

'We gotta couple of witnesses,' Byrne was saying. 'One's a chow from up Foxton or Levin. He was with one of those jokers – you know, the ones who've got tits and a cock. What is it?'

'Trans something or other,' Feeney muttered. He didn't know for certain.

'Anyway, this chink, who works at the veggie markets, was having a lunch break about four this morning. He was standing on a box of harchie . . . arts . . . atchi . . .'

'Artichokes.'

If Byrne didn't get on with it, Feeney was going to add the detective to the death toll.

'. . . and he was "serving him" . . . her . . . it . . . whatever the hell it is. Both of them said they saw a couple of guys going into O'Malley's place. So they'd have been facing the same way. I never knew that was how men did it . . .'

'A couple of guys went into O'Malley's?'

'Yeah. Then the next thing there's O'Malley out on the road, dead as a bloody maggot, completely stuffed . . .'

'Where are the chink and the tran?'

'I let the chink go back to Foxton, and the tran . . . whatever it is . . . is in Central. I got him . . . her . . . charged with assault.'

'What?'

'Well, turns out the chinkie didn't blow his load, so he wouldn't pay. When I found them the tran was sitting on his chest, banging his head up and down on the footpath. Must have been a bit confusing for him, cause the tran didn't have any pants on, and his dick was almost in the chink's face, and he had a pile of make-up on – his face I mean.' Byrne shook his head. 'It'd have worried me.'

'Never mind that,' Feeney snapped at him. 'Did either of them give you a description of who went into O'Malley's?'

Yes, they had. It was a perfect word-picture of the two Christchurch detectives.

Feeney felt his knees going soft under him.

'Has this trannie talked to anyone?'

'No. I reckon the cells are the safest place for him. If anyone tries anything the watchhouse keepers will know about it. I don't know what happens if he gets bail.'

'*Don't* let him get bail,' Feeney snapped. 'We want him around. You did the right thing. Good.'

Byrne nodded at the compliment. 'I'm going back down to Central,' he said. 'Um, I'll sort of be around the watchhouse.' Feeney nodded. Good. Byrne could protect the queer. He'd have liked the Chinese in Wellington too, but there wasn't much he could do about that now.

After Byrne left, Feeney put some water in a saucepan and turned on the gas burner under it. There was a time when he'd have had a whiskey, but those days were over now. It'd be a nice cup of tea because he didn't bounce back from the drinking the way he once did. Besides, there was the dawn of a bright new day ahead. It was already piling up its rotting garbage to begin throwing it at him.

chapter eighteen

Auckland, 1972

Helen's journey out to Piha to see Fallon had taken her through New Lynn, and now she was on Titirangi Road. Fred Lashing was beginning to get worried. He'd been following her from the city. That was far too long. Still, she hadn't given any sign of spotting him. That'd change when they got to the top of the hill and past Lopdell House. After that there were hardly any houses and almost no people. Unless he changed the police car into a Volkswagen Kombi van and got himself dressed up to look like one of the hippies wandering around up here, he'd stick out like a dog's nuts.

Fortunately there was a plainclothes unit up ahead and they were happy to pick it up. The two detectives were getting fed up with trying to find witnesses in a case of two barefoot potters half killing each other arguing over glazing mixes. The detectives jumped at the chance to get away from all the mud paths, dripping ferns, overflowing cesspits and angry old hippies telling them Norman Kirk was going to get elected and he'd abolish the police and put the money into communes and marijuana. The detectives would be in their car, out of sight behind Lopdell House.

Lashing stayed with Helen into the Titirangi village and along Scenic Drive. Helen took the right fork where the roads took her out to Piha or around the Manukau Harbour coastline to Huia.

'She's going out to Piha or Karekare.'
'Roger, we've got her now.'
Lashing was happy to leave them to it. From there it was

nothing but bush, streams and fresh air. He wasn't interested in that. By the time he was in back New Lynn the police radio was telling him Helen was past the Anawhata and Karekare turnoffs and definitely going to Piha. The coppers were backing off. They'd pick her up closer to the beach. As soon as Helen was wherever she was going they'd wander down to the beach and flip over the surfers to see if any of them had any hooch in their cars. That'd be more fun than being told 'Piss off, pig' by half-stoned hippies. The worry with them was you'd punch one out and find out he was a lawyer who'd dig out a suit, march you into court and soak you down in fresh crap.

Helen had to concentrate on her driving. The gravel road made the car slide around. It was slow going and making her late. At this rate she'd have to drive home in the dark over the same road. She wasn't looking forward to that.

Would Fallon know about the bomb? Of course he'd know. The legal profession's tomtoms would have got the news out to him. Would he agree to be her lawyer? How much would he want? Was he still a grubby sex-harassing fiend who wouldn't focus on anything above her neck? She looked in the rear-vision mirror and was pleased to see that the car that had been behind her since the Huia turnoff was gone. She hadn't been sure what to do about it anyway. There were no roundabouts in these parts.

Wellington, 1972

It was just after eight in the morning when Jack Gravity spotted the watch on his eight-year-old son James's wrist. Jack sighed. It was more evidence that he'd brought an idiot into the world. Idiots didn't suddenly wear a watch when everyone knew they didn't own one. There were only two ways he could have got it. One was finding it, which might get an owner causing Jack grief by demanding it back. Or he'd stolen it. That'd get the teachers sniffing around, and possibly the Miramar copper as well. Jack had about fifty reasons for not wanting that, and each one of them was a dinner set under the tarpaulin in the garage. He sighed. He was going to have to sort this kid out. James was at the door, kissing his mother and ready to leg it for school.

'Come here, James.'

James looked around.

Christ, he didn't even have the brains to look innocent and pretend he didn't know what his father wanted. Not only was Jack's son a loser, he was a bloody moron.

'Where did you get the watch?'

Jack had a closer look at it. Christ Almighty, he'd stolen an adult's watch. Would this be evidence in court, when he was charged with castrating the boy to stop him breeding and filling the nation with more like him? Jack worked with a lot of idiots and they seemed to be good at only one thing: they bred like rabbits. They ought to be de-balled early.

His son looked back, crestfallen. Jack managed a sympathetic look. He thought about fetching the boy one around the ears, but Davinia was watching and she loved this useless object. It'd only cause more strife if he clipped him. If it went the way it usually did, he'd have to belt her too, and she'd be off to her sister in Naenae and that was him cooking his own dinner for a couple of weeks. Bugger that.

'You didn't get it given to you,' Jack said, as calmly as he could manage. 'You didn't buy it. If you stole it you are going to give it back, or it's down to the police station with you.'

'Please don't get angry with me,' the boy whimpered.

Little clown. Couldn't he see he was already angry with him?

Jack glared with what he hoped was his firm-but-loving-father look down on the brat. He'd better ease back a bit, in case the boy got terrified and filled his pants again.

'I just want to know where you got the watch.'

'I found it.'

This was going to be a long and slow grind.

'Where did you find it?'

James swallowed.

'Are you sure you won't get angry with me?'

Jack swallowed. The little bastard was begging for a slap, but no, Jack would be patient. He would keep trying. It would be unnecessarily character-building but he would do it because that's what good parents did.

'I am not going to get angry.'

'It was from the dead man. He didn't need it.'

That slowed Jack down. The kid had a point. A dead guy wouldn't need a watch. But, Jesus, if there was a corpse in this somewhere it could get very complicated very quickly.

'You're going to be a bit late for school, but that will be all right, because I think it might be a good idea if you showed me this dead man.'

His son nodded.

God help us, if Jack had found a dead man he sure as hell wouldn't be telling anyone about it. Still, he had to make allowances, because that's what happened when the fruit of your loins turned out to be really freaking stupid.

chapter nineteen

Wellington, 1947

If Xavier Weir was offering any sort of future, Murray McCarthy wanted to see it, and right now. But Weir was taking his sweet time, relaxing over another drink and letting that shrewd gaze of his run up and down his guest. Well, Weir could eye him up. He'd done it before and McCarthy couldn't care less, as long as there was a chance of picking up some proper money. He'd have to watch it, though. This was his third whiskey and he hadn't eaten anything for about eight hours. He was starting to feel a bit rocky on it. He'd better slow down or he was going to pass out.

'Now, this might cause a little bit of conflict, with you being a policeman and having taken an oath and all,' Weir said.

'I couldn't bloody care less!'

Weir smiled. That was exactly what he wanted to hear, and he liked that slur in McCarthy's voice. It was time to move things along. He lifted his podgy body out of his chair and nodded for McCarthy to follow him. Weir opened a door on the other side of the kitchen.

'Now remember one thing, Murray. A lot of money's gone into this, and there'll be people who won't be pleased if anything goes wrong. Just so you know. That's not a threat or anything.'

It was a threat and McCarthy knew it. He had an idea of some of the other people who floated around Weir. If they were the ones he thought, then it wasn't just a threat. It was a promise he'd be killed. He shrugged his shoulders. Weir seemed happy with that. He pushed the door open and stepped through it. McCarthy stopped. What the hell was all the drama about? He was looking at a greenhouse, full of green plants and bugger all flowers. So freaking what?

'Murray, forget bookmaking. It's over, finished. There'll be a tote soon and anyone can put a legal bet on. That'll be the end of it. This is the future.'

McCarthy looked at the plants. There was something vaguely familiar about them.

'Yes, Murray, you're getting there. It's *Cannabis sativa*, marijuana, reefer.'

McCarthy got close to one of the plants. It smelt like any other; he'd read the research from the States. A few puffs of some of this stuff and the healthiest, strongest man was only weeks or days away from being broke, skinny, pimply and a dependent drug fiend, crawling in the gutter, selling himself in the desperation to get the next 'fix'. Was Weir's place where the whole of New Zealand started on the slide into drugs? Was he going to be a part of it? This looked like a pretty big operation. There'd definitely be money in it. What was his wife going to say? Who cared? Most of the time she didn't know what was going on, and as long as the money kept coming in she didn't seem to care. Weir had a hand on his shoulder and his voice was soft and reassuring.

'There are hundreds of pounds for the right people. Hundreds! You're the right people, Murray. You deserve it, too. Look at you – a life of bloody hard work and what have you got for it? Do you ever get a word of thanks?'

McCarthy nodded but he wasn't really listening. The words 'hundreds of pounds' had hypnotised him. Weir was purring close to his ear. 'Forget all that nonsense about turning into an addict. It just doesn't happen. That's just the governments trying to keep the world safe for tobacco companies. I've been smoking it for a year and there's never been any problem.'

McCarthy was still stuck at the words 'hundreds of pounds' as they spun and danced around him.

Weir could barely keep the smile off his face. Look at him. McCarthy was a done deal. His police career had gone and he was motherless desperate. The poor sod could barely keep his tongue from falling out. Weir took another quick swig on his whiskey. This might not be as difficult as he'd thought. Still, it didn't matter if it got complicated. He was likely heading for the States. He had good people to keep an eye on things. If McCarthy caused problems he'd be properly taken care of. There was nothing bad anywhere in it.

Weir took a ready-rolled cigarette out from behind a brick, lit it, took a deep puff and handed it to McCarthy.

'This is the express version. These are the samples – the point of sale, the teaser, if you like. Top-grade plants with a little bit more oomph. Get the punters going on them and then wean them back to the ordinary stuff. That's the plan.'

McCarthy took a deep pull on it. He was surprised. The mix of exhaustion, tension, whiskey and marijuana made the stuff work instantly. McCarthy could see why the drug menace was so popular. It was great. His brain told him he wanted more of it. It was all pleasure, and a lot less work than sex. You didn't have to tell it you loved it. You didn't have to remember its name either. Selling this stuff was going to be a hell of a lot easier than catching women doing abortions and giving them a choice: get locked up or service him in any way he wanted. Except for the old ones – they went straight to the cells.

There was no doubt about it. This was the future, and Murray McCarthy was ready and willing.

Weir was surprised at McCarthy's expression. He had a strange twisted leer on his face, his eyes hard and bright. 'Tell me, what's it like, the stuff you guys actually *do* with each other?'

Weir hadn't expected that. He'd wondered about McCarthy always beating up homosexuals and whether there wasn't a bit of denial in it. But this? Christ! Was the fish fighting its way into the net? Well, well. Interesting. He'd take his time. Let the Buddha work right into his mind. It had better. McCarthy was smoking some of the best crop, the stuff he was using to build a reputation for quality.

'What do you mean *you guys* and *actually do*?' Weir asked, quietly. He wouldn't risk anything too soon. He'd make sure – McCarthy might be talking about something else. The cop's leer was beginning to annoy Weir, who was trying to tell himself to ignore it.

'I mean, I've seen it, but you never know if there's something I'm missing,' McCarthy said.

'You want to know – actually really want to know?'

'Yeah.' McCarthy could barely choke the word out.

'You mean all of it?'

Weir's mouth was dry and swallowing wasn't helping. Lord help us! So, the dear sweet lamb was offering itself up without a word of encouragement. Weir felt the pounding in his chest. Be still, be still my beating heart! This wasn't just a 'little adventure'. This was Murray McCarthy, the erratic, violent policeman. He might be hanging onto his job by his fingernails but he could still land Weir in the pokey.

'What's it like, what you do . . . you know?' McCarthy's voice was a choked gasp.

'Murray, it's very exciting. It's very, very exciting. Would you like to find out?'

McCarthy took another deep drag on the cigarette and handed it back to Weir, who took a very shallow puff.

'Yes.' McCarthy barely forced the word out.

Weir tried to control himself. Did anything get wilder, more thrilling and riskier than this? No, it bloody did not. This was Murray McCarthy, the most terrifying cop in Wellington, begging to be screwed.

'Are you really sure?' Weir whispered.

McCarthy's head moved in what looked like a strangled nod. What was Weir to do, run outside and stand in the middle of the road, jump up and down and yell, 'No, no'?

Murray McCarthy was having trouble seeing things properly. Were those plants in front of him or were they miles away? He couldn't tell. His eyes kept fooling him. All he knew was that he felt hazy and slightly giddy.

He said nothing as he sat down on the little bench beside the plants. Weir leaned over beside him, resting a hand on the front of McCarthy's shirt. McCarthy breathed in, then dropped his hand on top of Weir's, who unbuttoned the shirt and let his hand go up and down McCarthy's chest. McCarthy turned to

Weir. Weir stopped. Was this a trap? Was McCarthy going to attack him? Was he going to arrest him? No. McCarthy's eyes fogged with a flowing lust. The big policeman was enjoying himself. Weir let his hand drop to McCarthy's beltline. The policeman eased himself back, to let Weir run down the fly, opening the buttons and dropping his hand into McCarthy's underpants. The policeman was tense now, strong and ready for anything, a low murmur of pleasure rolling from him. There were no words, just this sound from somewhere deep in his throat. Weir eased McCarthy around and down to the floor, so he was on his hands and knees, facing away from him and towards the marijuana plants. He kept one hand caressing the policeman's scalp and ran the other gently up and down him.

'Oh God,' McCarthy moaned. Behind him Weir was shaking his head, still not quite believing this was possible.

Weir felt his breathing and heart rate getting faster and faster as he fought to grasp what was actually happening. He was going to take Murray McCarthy, the man all Weir's friends feared. With his other hand he pulled McCarthy's trousers away and then pulled the underpants down. McCarthy's powerful thighs were there in front of him and parting on their own. Weir was undoing his own trousers. Could he believe this? Could anyone believe this? Was this happening?

Weir stroked McCarthy's hair, running his hand softly down his chest and on down until he had McCarthy's cock in his hand. He began moving it up and down the shaft. He could feel it pulsing in his hand, almost on the verge of exploding. Weir was going to take his time now.

His heart smashed against his chest. Knowing Murray McCarthy in a biblical way! There had never been, would never be, anything that was even close to this. Weir held himself and eased himself close for the final launch. His mouth was dry and he could feel the sweat streaming down his face. He wasn't sure he could cope with the excitement and utter dark, thrilling wickedness of this. But he had to go on. He owed it to Wellington – to all his friends who had been beaten and humiliated. He had to fuck McCarthy. God and all the angels were howling down from heaven for him to go that last few inches. Onwards and upwards! McCarthy's legs were apart and he was sighing as Weir continued to massage his cock. Weir's other hand was on his own cock.

'Right. Now!' Weir gasped.

Something was wrong inside his chest – badly wrong. He tried to grab McCarthy but couldn't. Where the hell is he? That was Xavier Weir's last thought before his heart raced into a thready series of useless little beats. He was falling on the dirt floor beside McCarthy, dying of a heart attack.

Murray McCarthy pushed the soft, inert body away from him. He looked around and then down at the dead man. The sight of Weir shocked him back to whatever he called normal life.

'God Almighty! I was going to let a poof barrel me!'

Weir's face was still, with his eyes gazing softly and silently up at the policeman.

'Jesus!'

He didn't want to look at Weir's eyes, in case he saw triumph at the little fat lawyer having climbed his own personal Himalayan peak, closed on his Great White Whale, come close to planting his flag in the South Pole: the mounting of Murray McCarthy. He reached over and closed Weir's eyelids. That was a bit better. He lay on the floor trying to understand what had just happened.

God Almighty. He'd been on the edge of spreading his legs for a poof. That was disgusting. He dragged himself across the dirt floor. Never mind about his suit. It was already covered in sweat and coal dust. He didn't know why, but he was remembering what the priests had told him. It didn't matter whether you committed the sin. In God's eyes wanting to do it was just the same as carrying out the act.

Oh God, Jesus, bloody hell.

McCarthy flopped forward and lay still. The mark was on him now, and there forever. He crawled across to a rusty old bucket, put his head in it and let his stomach contents roar up and into it. Finally, gasping with the effort of it, he fell back.

He felt a cold draught from the greenhouse door. Christ! His pants and his underpants were still around his knees. Didn't he have any pride? He rolled over on his back and pulled them back up. As he buttoned up his pants he looked over at Weir. What was he going to do with him? Okay, the guy had died of a heart attack – the post-mortem would confirm that – and he hadn't spilled his wad, so there wouldn't be any questions about that. He didn't need to ditch the body anywhere.

But hang on! If he left Weir's pants around his knees the coppers would start asking around. If some neighbour had taken his car number he was in a deep tub of shit. If he cleaned the place up there'd be no reason for an investigation. Yes, he visited Weir. No, there weren't any problems. The neighbour, if there was one, didn't see him leave. So what?

Clean up the bucket he vomited into. No, first things first. He took a deep breath and began wrestling Weir's underpants up into place. It wasn't easy because he was desperate to avoid touching the lawyer's cock. When McCarthy saw it he winced. That was a hell of a thing to be shoving into anyone. It was huge. It looked like a baby's arm holding a tennis ball. Ouch!

He flushed the vomit from the bucket into the toilet and wiped some soil into the bucket to make it look as if it hadn't been cleaned. He looked around. Nothing had dropped from his pockets. Good. He walked through the house, getting closer to a run as he reached the front door.

A last look around. The ashtray and the booze – clean that up. He went back, emptied the ashtray and washed the whiskey glasses. Now it looked better. This wasn't the first time he'd cleaned up a crime scene before the police arrived, but it was the first time he'd had to do it through a marijuana fog.

Now, get out of the frigging place.

He got to the front door, opened it and stopped cold. Someone was standing there with a hand lifted ready to start knocking.

chapter twenty

Auckland, 1972

Archie Fallon offered Helen another cup of tea. She shook her head. Thank you, no. He put the teapot back down.

'Well?' Fallon said.

His change of tone and his question coming out as a sudden, frightening demand shook her. Helen had to be quick to keep her teacup from upending itself over her knees.

'Why me? There's an army of eager lawyers lurking behind almost every blade of grass in Albert, Myers and Eden parks.'

'I don't want them. I want someone completely independent of all the lawyers in Auckland. I have a couple of friends who are lawyers but I don't want them involved. I'll be very frank.'

'Good,' Fallon said.

'They might be traceable to me and that might be risky for them.'

Fallon smiled. 'I am expendable?'

'No, you are distant. I want experience and I don't want anyone close to me. Also, and believe me about this, I don't want anyone who might have any link with the partners at the firm. I've got enough trouble there now, thank you very much.'

Fallon nodded.

'Yes, you do. Word does percolate through the parish. Although not, apparently, to the media. I understand the firm did some of its best work keeping it quiet. That must have cost them every favour they've piled up over the last twenty years.' Fallon grinned. 'Mind you, there wouldn't be many. The mercenary bastards throw an invoice at everything that moves.' He leaned back. 'How long have you got before you get the old heave-ho?'

'Not long. If I haven't gone by Wednesday night they'll do it for me.'

He nodded.

'They must like you. I've seen people gone the same day and for a bloody sight less. Not that it makes much difference in the end. Gone, as they say, is still gone!'

'So, I need help. A lawyer.'

Fallon shook his head in a rueful way.

Helen felt her spirits fall. Had she driven all the way out here to be turned away?

There was a long silence. Fallon got up and began fishing around in a once-elegant writing desk that was battered with use. It took him nearly two minutes to find what he wanted. Helen looked at the single piece of paper. It was a short but comprehensive contract appointing Archibald Fallon as her legal representative.

'It's an old-fashioned formality, but if there are bombs then there'll be bobbies. In fact, I've seen a couple driving past. One is a very competent young detective sergeant. He did a very good job in an arson case I had in front of me a couple of years back.'

They'd followed her all the way out here! Helen had to stop her hand shaking as she signed the contract. Fallon put it in a manila folder and dropped it back on the writing desk. His face was grim and intent.

'This might be the moment to tell me all about it. Everything, thank you.'

Helen closed her eyes for a second. Be calm. Take it slowly. Fallon sat quietly. Then out it came, every terrible detail, all the way back to dressing for school that morning.

At the end Fallon leaned back.

'You have been carrying a rather heavy burden, haven't you?' he said. 'All the way back to 1947 and killing someone. It can't have been easy.'

Helen nodded.

'Right,' he said. 'First things first. You have to get back to town quick smart.' He stood up and fished around again in the writing desk. He found a file, opened it and took out a piece of paper, which he handed to her. 'This is a useful list of files. You will need to find them.'

It was a list of old clients. 'You'll know what I mean, and what to do with them, when you see them. Oh yes, there's something else. There's a chap named Laughlan, Des Laughlan, who is a very good man to have on your side. Very quick, very discreet, knows what he's doing.'

'He's already in Wellington, working for me. I haven't heard from him for a couple of days, though.'

'Good,' Fallon answered.

As she walked to her car she was careful to look around. She seemed to be on her own. That was good. But then that's what she'd thought on the way here.

Wellington, 1972

Jack Gravity's son was still wearing the watch.

'But not for much longer,' Jack murmured to himself. Except that taking it off the little retard might put Jack under pressure to buy him another one. There was also always a chance one of the bigger kids would steal it from him. That might not be too bad. The evidence would be gone and Jack might pick up a few quid from the insurance claim.

James led his father into the bushes behind Holy Cross School at the top of Miramar Avenue. Sure enough, the body was there. Jack felt a moment of paternalism, pushing his son out of the way behind him. No child should have to see this. But then, the kid had already seen it. Hell, he'd already looted it, and if he had any sense he'd have the money from the wallet salted away somewhere. No, his son wouldn't have done that – he wasn't bright enough. The body was a man in his forties. His face was white and his mouth was open. Jack turned away from his open staring eyes. They were too cold, too intense and penetrating. For a second it felt as if he were looking straight into Jack's mind, to his sins and his deepest, most hidden thoughts. People had tricks to divert the living from that. There were none to keep them from the dead: they were out of reach.

Jack choked back his fear. He grabbed James's wrist and

undid the watch. He took the man's cold, white arm and strapped the watch back on it.

'Now, come on!'

He marched James back to the car, glaring at him ferociously. 'Just don't say anything. Not one word, all right?'

Jack was looking for a phone box. He was not going all the way home to call them, in case there was some way of tracing the call. Ah, there was one right there, just over by the dentist's surgery, where the ticket counter of the old Capitol picture theatre used to be. He dialled 111.

'Police, Fire or Ambulance? Which service do you require?'

'Police.'

A male voice came on the line.

'This is the police.'

'There's a body just behind the Holy Cross School, at the end of Miramar Avenue. It's sort of round behind the shithouses, and up in the bush.'

'The toilets aren't in the bush?'

'No, the body's there.'

'Is it a male or a female?'

'It's a male.'

Jack paused for a moment, then added, 'It's got its watch on, all right. No one took its watch, okay? Have you got that written down? The watch is still there.'

The voice had a slightly puzzled note.

'The watch is still there? What's the . . . er . . . significance of the watch . . . sir?'

Jack didn't like that. Every time a copper had started calling him 'sir' he was about to be marched off to the police station, where no one would believe a word he said, and they'd soon stop calling him 'sir'. Go through that system a few times and you learn to notice the details.

'Dunno,' Jack blurted out. 'I dunno.'

He put the receiver back. He walked over to his car, got in and drove back up Miramar Avenue, heading for home. He flicked a cold glance across at James. 'Just shut the fuck up. I'll talk to you when we get home.' James shrunk back. He'd heard that before and it never ended happily.

chapter twenty-one

Auckland, 1972

Fred Lashing read the file again. So Des Laughlan's ticket had just been cancelled. He'd turned up dead behind the bogs of a Catholic primary school. Lashing was not sure about whether the 'dead', 'bogs' and 'Catholic primary school' were connected or not. What was certain was that Laughlan was history.

Hearing about Laughlan jarred him straight back to the Helen Murphy case. She'd had to go on the back burner while he sorted out this armed robbery. The bloody thing happened right in front of him. He'd been minding his own business, enjoying the sun and a stroll down Vulcan Lane to have a look at a new takeaway bar in Queen Street when this little shit of a robber ran into a shop right beside him, waving a gun and yelling.

'This is a robbery so hand over all your money and no one will get hurt,' or something like that.

The robber had quietened down when he realised he was in the wrong shop. Instead of being in the highly profitable women's clothes shop he was in a martial arts place with about twenty black-belt holders enjoying a preview of the new season's karate outfits. About now he'd begun having a bit of trouble with the gun. The black paper he'd wrapped around the ballpoint pen to make it look like a pistol began unravelling. The karate types took it in turns to make citizen's arrests, beginning with the black-belt holders and working down to the lowly white belts. By the time Lashing got there the robber was on the floor pleading for someone to call the police.

'I am the police, but I might need these guys to help me get you up to Central.'

The robber took the hint and began blurting a confession. There was a lot to confess. He was looking at six other robberies, eighty-three burglaries, a couple of hundred car conversions and hundreds of petty thefts. The case turned into an all-consuming monster. All the follow-ups and running around meant Lashing didn't have time for meals and he'd started losing a worrying amount of weight. If it kept going like this he'd have to splash out on a new suit.

In between, he'd checked in on the bombing case. He'd perked up when one of the Sydney victims turned out to be Jennifer Conlon, who used to be Jennifer Murphy. That was Helen Murphy's sister. So that's how Helen knew it was a bomb and not a big toaster arriving in the mail with its wires hanging out. She'd known it was coming. It was also why she'd spent half a day trying to decide what to do. Then she'd whipped out to see Des Laughlan. He'd legged it down to Wellington, where she and her sister came from, and he'd lobbed up freshly deceased in Miramar.

Well, well, well.

With the Auckland police stretched by a run of murders, Lashing hadn't had too much trouble sidling back into the Murphy case. As a case it was a loser: a hell of a lot of work and only one offender and one crime, unlike burglary, where nabbing one offender could mean wrapping up dozens of crimes. Still, it involved Helen Murphy and that got him going. Something about her just yelled 'experience' and 'middle-class leg-over'. Those were definite bell-ringers for Lashing. She could have all the degrees, fancy clothes and flash offices in the world but he just knew, don't ask him why, that having those long, middle-class legs wrapped around him would be an experience that'd linger with him all the way to the grave. Naturally, it wouldn't just be for him. There was his dad and the class war. He couldn't forget that.

Lashing didn't like to admit it, not even to himself, but he'd caught himself thinking about what might happen to her in the long nights in the women's prison. Did he want to be there to protect her? Or was he hoping for the worst? Did he want to watch? It was definitely bothering him. Why? What was it about her that was hooking him? He felt like a big salmon flopping around on the end of a spear. Did he want to control her? What did he want to do? Was this some sort of homage to his old dad up there in heaven?

He tried to focus on the case. Helen Murphy and her sister had done something – something bad enough to get one of them killed and a bloody good attempt at the other one. What was it? What had Laughlan found out? The questions just didn't end. Was there another question, one he'd been dodging? Was he in love with her? He didn't want to think about that, not while he was working on ways to get her into jail. God, what a mess.

She hadn't left town. That meant she hadn't killed Des. But she was somehow connected. This might be a three-for-one deal. Find the bomber. That's who killed Laughlan and sent her the bomb in the first place. The last time Lashing hit something like that it was in a lucky draw down at the hardware shop. He'd ended up with these steak knives that weren't any good. They kept breaking. Eventually he'd given up and gone out to buy a proper chisel for getting the mortar off the old bricks.

He'd left a message for Helen to call him. He didn't have anything he particularly wanted to say but it wouldn't do any harm to remind her that he was here. Boom! Ten minutes later she was in the car and off out to Piha to see that evil old scum Archie Fallon.

Well, well, well.

Was that a little sign of nerves? It sure looked as if she might be pulling up the drawbridge. Give her another tweak or two and she might do something stupid. It wouldn't be the first case broken by having a bit of pressure applied.

The Wellington coppers had sent up everything they had on Des Laughlan's killing. It wasn't much. It looked as if it had happened somewhere else and the body was dumped there afterwards.

Had Helen gone to that school? Was the murderer sending a signal? There was some stuff on the Murphy family that was interesting reading. They were a pretty tatty line-up, though it had been a while since any of them had been arrested for anything. The Wellington coppers were trawling them but they didn't seem to be getting far. The few family members still living in the country weren't being obstructive – they simply didn't know anything about it. Plus, they'd more or less lost contact with Helen.

There was one odd thing. Des Laughlan's watch was around the wrong way on his wrist. Whoever rang the police about the body had made a song and dance about the watch. Something needed sorting out there. The Wellington cops had been looking up books on the occult, to make sure wearing a watch around the wrong way wasn't some sort of witchcraft symbol, and this wasn't the work of a mass murderer or Satanist group. It seemed to have been a good excuse to do the rounds of Wellington's witches and warlocks. There'd been plenty of volunteers for this. As far as Lashing could see from the file, meeting the actual witches seemed to have been a let-down. The police had expected lesbian rituals, slinky women wearing bugger all and lots of really weird stuff. What they got was middle-aged women in dressing gowns, smoking cigarettes, and a lot of Weetbix and tea, lamb chops for dinner and jobs in accounts at government departments. Disappointed officers eventually gave up and trooped back to the main investigation.

Lashing wracked his brain. Something had happened, and Helen Murphy and her sister were in the middle of it. What was it? Who did they do it to? And why?

chapter twenty-two

Wellington, 1947

It was three hours since Jimmy Byrne had knocked on his door to tell him John Augustine O'Malley had departed this life. Feeney was alone in his office. The detectives were out for another day of knocking on doors and prowling for names with any connection to Marie West. If they hadn't hit something by tonight the case was officially going cold. Some would begin being clipped off for other investigations. That would gather pace until eventually Feeney would be the only one, and he'd be expected to pick up other cases. Marie would become a watching brief. If something came up he'd look into it; otherwise it was down to luck, a tip or a confession, which could be years away.

Feeney sighed. At least he was being spared Compton barging in to take over. Compton didn't have to. His guys were keeping an eye on things and they'd be reporting back to him. Speaking of which, the two Christchurch detectives hadn't turned up for the morning briefing. No messages of apology or explanation from either of them. Now there was a surprise. If Feeney had committed a murder in the middle of a homicide investigation he wouldn't be sending in absent notes, and he wouldn't be sticking around either.

Feeney had taken two of his toughest detectives aside. You've got the green light. Get tough, really tough, with the bookies. If they're not helpful, make them helpful. Helpful means telling the police what we want to know. If that means tuning them up with a cosh then so be it. Don't get caught, don't do anything in front of witnesses and don't break any bones. But do leave fear, anxiety and ill will all across town. Make it clear it keeps going until Marie West's murderer gets dropped off at Wellington Central.

It was immoral, it was definitely illegal, but there might be a greater good. There'd better be.

McCarthy was another problem. No one knew where he was. The Miramar cops had been doing passes of his house and hadn't seen him. Still, McCarthy would turn up. He was too big, too clumsy and too violent not to. His wife had rung in. He hadn't been home. Did the police know where he was? Feeney had to mutter something about a 'tricky undercover investigation'. She'd believed him, which would buy them time. Feeney had shaken his head and dropped his face in his hands after that. Now he was lying to policemen's families. Where did this shit end?

Some clown had given the transvestite bail and he'd bolted. No one knew where he was. There was a whisper he was on his way to Auckland. Feeney had the Auckland coppers keeping an eye out, but so far, nothing. Then the Levin police rang to say they couldn't find the chink. He was gone too.

He was going nowhere on all fronts. So just what was so exciting and glamorous about murder investigations? Nothing. Bloody nothing.

Only. If Byrne was right, and he probably was, he had two murders: Marie West and John Augustine O'Malley. The first was too bloody public. The second was too secret. If O'Malley's killing got public, Feeney knew what would happen next. Compton would swoop on it. Another team would be assembled, with 'Catholics need not apply' stamped all over it, and Feeney would bet his house, car and pension it'd stay unsolved.

He forced himself out of his chair. If he kept thinking like that he'd never move again. It was time for another talk with Filthy Phil. If anyone asked what he was doing, and no one would, he was following up Marie West. If those two creeps from Christchurch were still following him it'd be another chance to get them out in the open. Catholics weren't the only ones who could have accidents, and Wellington was Pat Feeney's home ground.

He walked down to the yard and as he was getting into his car a young policeman ran over waving a piece of paper. Feeney wound the window down.

'Excuse me, sir, we got this message about five minutes ago. The person would not say who it was, but they'd like you to call.'

It was the Bishop's private number. Now there was a surprise. He'd have heard about O'Malley and would want to know how Feeney was going to help defend against the pagans smashing at the church's very doors.

'Thanks, I'll deal with it.' Then he thought of something. Compton. There was something odd. O'Malley had died violently, but Feeney hadn't been marched up to Compton's office for a briefing. What did that tell him? That Compton already knew everything he needed to know about John O'Malley's farewell from this earth?

Feeney drove out of Wellington Central, into Waring Taylor Street. Well, if he wasn't nervous before, he was now. Were they going to have a go at him? Was he next? Was he making this up? Was he going mad? At least he was going up to the mortuary. He could rely on something. There was a certainty about the dead. They didn't sit in rooms hatching evil little religious-based plots.

Filthy Phil was solemn-faced. No cheerily mordant tales from some distant sexual frontier, just a dull, careful slouch. Feeney hadn't seen this before and didn't like it. Phil looked slow and broken, as if something had reached in and drawn the spirit up his throat and out of him.

John Augustine O'Malley?

Phil's was a dull and precise monologue. 'The injuries are consistent with a fall from a third-floor window. A series of skull fractures, some spinal injuries, which probably would have killed him on their own, and a fractured pelvis. One of the bone fragments that got loose in his left leg severed the femoral artery. Without getting to surgery immediately he would have been dead in ten minutes from that alone.'

Phil closed the file and waited. Feeney said nothing. He sat still and watched the doctor getting more and more nervous.

'What?' Phil snapped.

'That's what I'm wondering. What? When were they here?'

Phil ran a hand across his face, as if he were trying to wipe away an unpleasant memory. It didn't work. When he looked back at Feeney his eyes were shining with fear and pain.

'I dunno what you mean, Pat, no idea at all.'

'Bullshit.'

'Is there anything else? Because I am busy.'

'Phil, you know exactly what I bloody mean.' Feeney leaned forward, letting his strength and bulk send its own signal. I am stronger than you, meaner than you, and if you keep lying to me I want you to know I am under strain and that might make me do something I shouldn't. He wouldn't, but years of experience told him the look produced results most of the time. As it did now. Phil closed his eyes for a moment. Then he spoke, his voice weary and resigned.

'Two and a half hours ago.'

'How many?

'There were two of them. Plainclothes. I've never seen them before.'

The Christchurch detectives. They were still here!

'They didn't touch me.'

'Christ, Phil, I know they didn't bloody touch you. They didn't have to. What'd they say?'

Feeney had seen this often enough before: a frightened and overstressed man finding the strength to tell the truth, one not necessarily in his best interests.

'There was a spot of bother at a party in Karori.'

'That place in Ararua Road?' Feeney asked.

'Yeah. There was me . . .' Phil stopped, his hand going across his face again. He took a deep breath and then looked Feeney right in the eye. 'There was me, and a chap who works at Parliament. And there are some snaps. Good quality. Very clear.'

Phil sagged back. Feeney should have known it would be this simple.

'Did they have the photos?'

'Yes.'

Had they asked for anything to be altered or covered up? He

could have a go for attempting to pervert the course of justice, only that'd need Phil to co-operate and he didn't like the chances of that.

'They kept saying they thought he'd fallen or jumped out the window and they said it about ten times. Eventually you get the message.'

Feeney nodded.

There was a silence. Phil took a deep breath.

'Look, bugger it. This is just for you, okay?' Phil said. Feeney nodded. The pathologist lifted a sheet from John O'Malley's body and touched the point of the dead man's jaw.

'That's bruising. Any boxer knows that's the knockout one. It's all about disconnecting the direct pathways to the brain. If it didn't knock him out he'd have been groggy enough for someone to do whatever they liked.'

Feeney had seen the glazed-eyed look on the rugby field and in pub brawls.

'The injuries from the fall are on this side of the head, the opposite side to the bruising. When his head hit the footpath it was at this angle. There are no other fractures or bruising to this side of the face.'

'So someone hit him.'

'These bruises are not consistent with injuries from the fall.'

'I might have to get you up in the witness box saying that.'

'You can get me in the witness box if you like.'

Feeney knew what that meant: 'Forget it.' By tomorrow Phil would have done his report and O'Malley would be cremated. There'd be nothing to check. Besides, he had other things to worry about. Was O'Malley the only one, or were those two starting a little 'clean up Wellington' campaign? He'd also need to find the photos or he could never rely on Phil again. Compton's safe was a good bet. His secretary was an ally, but that might be pushing it a little too far.

Then he smiled. Hang on. He wasn't thinking straight. He wasn't thinking at all. There was a way.

To go after O'Malley's death would be a juicy inviting tangent, but he wasn't going to do it, at least not yet. Feeney's job was to keep the focus on Marie. Besides, it was obvious that solving her murder would take him straight to the reason for O'Malley going out the window: policemen taking money, the killing of Frank Wilkins. He'd stick with her. She was the innocent one – that made her the most important. Oh yes, all humans are created equal and are entitled to the same respect. So endeth the Gospel according to Feeney.

O'Malley could wait. There was no news from Central. The detectives were still battling away, but no winners. It was narrowing down to Marie's parents, and dragging her father back for yet another interrogation. As if he didn't know where that was going to go.

He could see big stolid Bill West sitting there, denying everything, answering 'Yes' or 'No' to all questions. No, he didn't know anything about the murder. Yes, he knew some bookmakers and he helped them out from time to time. He would go that far and no further. Eventually West would go home to another round of painful and vocal arguments with his wife. She'd get the police. They'd arrest him. She'd turn up a few hours later to drop the charges and they'd let him go again. She'd accuse her husband of killing Marie but be unable to back it up with anything close to evidence. She'd told them over and over again that Marie and her father had fought the night Frank Wilkins had gone missing. Marie had wanted to meet her boyfriend. She didn't know what had happened after Marie sneaked out through the back bedroom window. Did Bill stay in the house? She didn't know. He called her a traitor. She screamed at him that he was a murderer. Feeney shuddered at the isolation, the hatred and the pain of these two people welded together in a marriage of horror. It seemed to tunnel endlessly deeper into each other's most sensitive and agonising nerves. Every time they found one they'd stab at it hard, triggering a vicious response. And so it went, on and horribly on.

The police had searched their house twice. There was no twine in the house to match the string around Marie's neck, nor anything else to link them to the killing.

Feeney let out a long breath. The mother was obviously the weaker of the two – or was she the stronger? Was there a strange strength in her weakness? Was she the opposite of Pat Feeney, who appeared strong but wondered if he was actually weak? Would the accumulated suffering finally break the dam and let the truth flood out?

That might happen now, or it might happen in twenty years' time. He didn't want to wait that long. Wasn't he the angel of vengeance for the dead, the one who would let Marie sleep quietly in her grave knowing the man who did her wrong was to suffer for it?

Then there was O'Malley. Wasn't he entitled to the same tranquillity on his journey into eternity? Who would speak for him? Who would bring peace to his soul?

Feeney rubbed his eyes. He was tired and angry, and didn't have answers to any of the questions endlessly pushing at him. If there was a manhunt for Marie's murderer then surely O'Malley deserved the same. There were witnesses, if only they could find them again. There was medical evidence. It would not be that difficult. One or other of the Christchurch detectives would likely decide on survival over loyalty, turn King's Evidence, and send the other to the gallows. But was there justice in that? O'Malley had murdered Frank Wilkins, or if he didn't do it himself he knew who did. O'Malley paid off policemen who would be dancing for joy knowing he was gone. Why would anyone speak for him, or be at one with him? More bloody questions and no frigging answers. Feeney stood and stretched. He could go on and on and on with this. What sort of man was he and who would he choose?

When he got like this, and it was more and more often, far more than he liked, he could understand Jesus screaming for the burden to be shifted from him. Pat Feeney wasn't nailed to any cross – yet. It wasn't much consolation but McCarthy was probably nailed to one of his own making. He'd been seen late last night driving out towards the Mt Victoria tunnel. The coppers said he looked wild, panicked and desperate.

Then they'd lost him.

chapter twenty-three

Auckland, 1972

Helen breathed a prayer to any gods that might be interested when Colleen Jones said she'd help. Colleen was a senior secretary. She knew everything at the firm and, more important, where to find it. It had been a hell of a risk, asking her to find and copy sensitive files. If Colleen had run to the partners Helen would have been out the door within minutes. But, after a terrible pause, Colleen had said yes. Helen had been right in guessing that the secretary hated the partners, individually and collectively, with a passion so deep and so strong that Helen began to wonder if she wouldn't turn up one day with a knife and kill them slowly one by one.

Their constant demands that Colleen make them coffee, do their shopping and run errands without losing any productivity were the least of it. Worse was the frequent unscheduled overtime. She was a solo mother and desperate for the salary, with little choice except to cave in and they knew it. If they felt like working late, Colleen was forced into desperate and expensive negotiations to organise meals and find babysitters. She had tried assertiveness classes. She had tried reasoning. She'd even begged. She'd tried flat-out refusal. Nothing seemed to work. The partners' power was complete. What they wanted they got. Helen's request for help was an opportunity for a seething Colleen to do something – anything – to fight back and to shake their smug little world.

It was Saturday morning. Colleen and Helen were in the office. Colleen's two little boys were out in reception, playing with the toys she'd brought with her. She'd been unable to find a babysitter, and anyway the three and four year old were an informal alarm system. They had been told that any adult turning up was a friend. Go up to them and say hello. Both Colleen and Helen would be listening for a chirpy little voice. The back-up plan, if someone did arrive and get pointed about what was going on, was that Colleen would get distressed and out of control and plead with the children to tell her what the visitor had done to them. Even the slightest hint of a child molestation charge should be enough to make anyone malleable.

'Reduce them to a quivering jelly. Break the bastards. See the fear. God, I love it.' Colleen had beamed. It was the first time Helen had seen her anywhere near this joyous.

Colleen had looked down Fallon's list of files. 'They went looking for most of these just after you went out the other day,' she said.

That was Helen's trip to Piha to see Fallon.

'Some of them are in Edgar's office.' She could forget those. Edgar, famously suspicious, always made sure everything – door, drawers and safe – was locked whenever he left his office, even to go to the toilet.

It took just over twenty minutes to find enough files to make it worth doing. Helen worked the copy machine. Colleen ran a shuttle between the offices, finding and returning files. It helped that she had the managing partner's master key, which had gone out for lunch with her the day before, been dropped off at a key cutter's where it became a twin, and was put back into his office.

McKenzie's office was the bonanza. Four of the files they wanted were in his second drawer, sitting neatly stacked for the sacrifice. Two were copied now. Helen was halfway through the third when the machine stopped. A red light was blinking. She pressed the buttons. Nothing! They lost ten minutes going through the manual before concluding whatever was wrong would need outside help. Helen was shaking her head, beginning to despair.

Colleen smiled. 'It's all right. No problem at all. Mother is equipped and ready. Look, we just photograph the pages. I'm all set, and I've brought plenty of film, just in case.' This wasn't the moment to ask Colleen how she knew about photographing documents.

They were finishing the fourth file when they heard the footsteps. What about the kids? Helen looked out. The little one was curled up asleep and the older one was engrossed in a puzzle. It was obvious what Helen and Colleen were doing. They'd had it. Colleen would be sacked. Helen would be lucky to avoid being prosecuted.

The fresh-faced young man standing behind Helen didn't seem interested in the copy machine, the papers beside it or in Colleen's camera. He was intent on the way Helen's blouse fell slightly open when she turned around. Let him look. She would have been quite happy to take off her blouse and bra, let her breasts swing free, jump up and down so he could watch them bounce and let him spend the rest of the day playing with them.

It was John Brill, one of the juniors, bright and loyal but probably destined to be an outsider for his time here.

'Um, I was just coming in to drop off a letter,' he mumbled.

'Sure,' Helen answered. 'Is it anything I can help with?'

Brill shuffled from foot to foot.

'Um, it's sort of about you.'

Helen was beginning to enjoy his oddly gawky and rather charming embarrassment.

'As soon as I heard you were going I put out a feeler at another firm and I think I might have found something at Laan, Parker, Priddey, Hodge and Lack. Um, look, I'd better go. Perhaps later?' he muttered.

Helen tried to paste an encouraging and understanding expression on her face. So, the juniors knew she was gone. Great! So much for all the talk of this being a matter of the 'gravest confidentiality'. McGibbons was someone she could understand. He was well connected, with sources running everywhere. Brill was different. This was the most junior of the juniors diving over the side.

Colleen waited until Brill had gone, then she turned a stern look on Helen. 'You look terrible. If you don't sit down for at least five minutes I'm going to ring all the partners and tell them what's going on, what you are doing and why.'

She was right. Colleen was an ally, but she was also taking a big risk. If anything went really wrong she was finished too, and her chances of another job would be nil.

'All right.'

'What about him?'

Colleen smiled. 'Leave him to me.'

Helen looked at Colleen's wide smile and coolly focused eyes. If John Brill had the slightest idea of what was good for him he woundn't utter a word about anything he had seen until everyone working at the firm had been safely dead for years, and even then it'd pay him to be careful.

Helen was still having trouble staying composed. For heaven's sake! If she was going to fall apart at something like this, what was it going to be like when things got really ugly? Once Des Laughlan's report came in she would be up against much worse than this. Did she have the strength for it? She'd better. She didn't have much choice.

Archie Fallon had been right when he'd talked about the meeting with the partners. 'They'll set it up like a convocation of cardinals: plenty of august presence and ceremony, formality ladled over it like custard on a pudding. There'll be plenty of 'putting aside any other agenda items' and 'moving on to the one piece of business in front of us'. Fallon's chuckle, along with the pace of his departure to the Bench, told Helen he knew exactly how these meetings went.

'It's all tedious, pompous crap but they like it. No, they love it, and they'll do it because they think it'll intimidate you.'

Fallon's script was accurate almost to the word. They were even wearing their best funeral suits, a row of softly coloured zebras.

'Look them right in the eye,' Fallon had said. 'Imagine them rising slowly off the toilet, their trousers caught around their knees. It's not the prettiest sight but it does make them manageable. Or, if you really want, think about them locked in the coital embrace. No, on second thoughts, don't do that.

You have a good mind and it shouldn't be scarred.'

McKenzie was leading off, with a polished drone about 'collegiality and confidence in the ability and sensibility of each other . . .'

Helen was tempted to count the 'ilities' but decided against it. It might start her laughing and that definitely wouldn't be helpful. McKenzie finished and looked around the table. Helen was surprised that, by his standards, he'd been so brief. She'd expected him to go on and on, as he usually did, until everything was drowned under at least six feet of words. Someone must have had a word with him: 'There are no clients to impress. You're not being paid by the six-minute time unit, so don't go stuffing around, just get on with it.'

Still, he'd done what he set out to do: build the equivalent of a crucifix right here in the boardroom, ask her to pop on this little hat of thorns, sit still for a good long whipping and hop up on the cross. Don't worry about the feet and hands; we'll take care of all that for you. Helen remembered the last time. Then it had been the gallows. The atmosphere now seemed far more violent, which was appropriate. It was the moment they were finally getting rid of her.

Two or three of the partners had the decency to look away and be embarrassed. The rest met her head on, slavering for the execution. These she tried to imagine surprising on the toilet or straining at sex. Fallon was right. It was too ugly.

Some of them had been outspoken, on the radio and in print, about how everyone had the right to legal representation. They would provide this to anyone who needed it, and who could pay, although the 'who could pay' part was downplayed for public consumption. That came later, in private, when the client had been reduced to incontinent terror at what could happen if he or she didn't have the kind of legal talent available only from this firm.

No one was rushing to defend her.

Fredericks hit the only vaguely reassuring note. 'Helen has been a superb servant of the firm and we have to recognise that.' The others glared at him. He decided not to say much more and quickly wrapped it up. There was a silence. They were looking at her. It was her turn. She reached down to the briefcase and found what she was looking for. It wasn't the greatest card in the world but it was all she had.

Let the games begin.

chapter twenty-four

Wellington, 1947

Murray McCarthy stood on Weir's doorstep, squinting through the whiskey and marijuana haze at the woman standing on the doorstep. She looked about fifty, expensively dressed in a plaid skirt, sensible shoes and the sort of beige cardigan that'd cost nearly a week of his salary. She didn't look too patient, either. But then, as far as McCarthy could see, these women never were. They lived in places like Karori and Seatoun and relentlessly herded children, vicars, husbands, priests, shopkeepers and tradesmen along like sheep. Churches and charities could not survive without them. Which was fine, but it didn't explain why she'd turned up at Xavier Weir's house in the middle of the freaking night demanding drugs. McCarthy was struggling to understand exactly what was going on.

'Look, I am sorry but I don't happen to have a lot of time for shilly-shallying around,' she snapped in a cultivated accent, one piercing enough to command the helpers across a busy 'bring and buy' sale in a large church hall. McCarthy bristled. Who did she think she was talking to? He could arrest her and give her to the moustachioed police matrons, who'd give her a search she'd never forget.

Only he couldn't and he knew it.

'I have an arrangement with Xavier,' she was saying. 'He knows why I am here, for some of his little cigarettes, and I want to get on with it – now, please. I don't have much time. People will be arriving soon and there's a lot to do. Come on. Busy, busy.'

By the time McCarthy had digested this, she'd loosed off an

impatient sigh, swept past him and was in the house. She knew exactly where she was going, across the living-room and straight for the greenhouse door.

'It's the horse trials this weekend. I've got friends coming down from Hawke's Bay and the Wairarapa. There's been quite a lot of fornication. There's going to be more of it and some of Xavier's little cigarettes will help things along no end.'

McCarthy was still standing at the door struggling to take this in. She was so far outside the normal run of crooks and criminals he couldn't quite figure it out. The dope wasn't helping either. That bloody thing had been incredibly strong.

'Oh dear. Look, I know where everything is. I'll do it myself,' she snapped as if she were talking to a doltish child. She stopped at Weir's body.

'Xavier, Xavier, Xavier! I have told you about this sort of thing. Still, it's better than hanging around those ghastly toilets.' She turned a knowing smile on McCarthy, who blinked back his surprise.

She thinks I'm one of *them*!

The woman marched to the back of the greenhouse, lifted a stone pot, found a tin full of joints, scooped them out and dropped them in her handbag. Then she fished through a purse and shoved a handful of five and ten pound notes into McCarthy's hand. She hadn't said a word and didn't need to. She was moving so fast he didn't have a chance to say or do anything to stop her. He'd guess that no one ever had.

'You'll give that to Xavier when he wakes up?'

McCarthy nodded, not sure what to say. The only thing he could think was, Don't tell her Weir isn't going to be waking up.

He looked at the notes crumpled in his hand. Christ! There must have been forty or fifty pounds. His weekly pay was fifteen pounds! Weir was right – this was big money!

'Well now, we know we can trust you, Mr McCarthy, don't we?'

She knew his name! He didn't need that. Now he had only two choices. Kill her, or let her go and hope she wouldn't do him in. If he was going to kill her it'd have to be right now.

She was already back across the living-room and opening the front door.

Then she stopped, looking thoughtfully at him. What was she thinking? She smiled. It wasn't warm. It felt chilly. Her eyes were looking straight at him and it made him feel uncomfortable.

'You can come to our place tonight if you like. You'd be welcome. You might find you rather enjoy yourself. It's at 176 Ararua Road, in Karori.'

There was something cold underneath her smile but he didn't know what it was. His brain wasn't working fast enough. Ararua Road! That was up in money country – another planet from him, even though it was only about a quarter of an hour's drive away. She smiled another of those thin, quick smiles and opened the door.

'Xavier is welcome too. He knows where to go. Lord knows, he's been there often enough.'

He wasn't going to be killing her. She was out the door and already crossing the road. McCarthy watched. Two big men were standing by her car and getting into it with her. Thank God he hadn't attacked her or those two would have come looking. He wouldn't have stood a chance against them.

The large black car slithered away from the kerb. Let it. He had plenty of other things to worry about. What the hell had just happened? Had he just turned into a homo? Christ! He'd done long, dirty years of keeping Wellington safe from queers and there he was, spreading them for Xavier Weir to take him like a woman, and he'd been sighing for it. Christ! How could he walk among decent people with something like that weighing down on him?

He closed the door behind him. His car was not far away. He didn't look back. He pointed it towards the Miramar Cutting, for Kilbirnie and the city. Then he stopped. There was nowhere to get cleaned up and he wasn't finding any company. What was the point? He turned the car around and headed back the way he came.

McCarthy sat in the cold beside the Worser Bay Yacht Club building. He'd been there for a long time now, perhaps an hour.

He was looking in a quiet, dull way out over Wellington Harbour's black water. The tiny waves in front of him gleamed in a sliver of whiteness before they fell on the sand. It was time to make up his mind. He knew what he should be doing. The right thing was to fill his pockets with stones and walk out into the sea until he drowned. Or would he fail himself one more time, just like he failed himself when something slipped and he begged for a buggering? Huh? What was he going to do?

If he killed himself then everything would come out. He'd be the dead guy and everything could be blamed on him. It'd be all wringing hands and sad talk about 'bad apples'. He might be out of their reach but it'd hit his wife and kids. He might be more or less separate from them now but he still felt a bit of an obligation. They'd have the tax people sniffing around for every single ten-shilling note he'd ever salted down. Those barracuda would take the flesh off a baby and not blink. The family wouldn't stand a chance.

What about him?

Looking after Weir's business wasn't exactly an option now. Whoever was keeping an eye on it would make a move. There wouldn't be room for him. His bet was that they'd bury Weir in the greenhouse, report him missing and just carry on.

He could make a run for it. He had a good idea where he'd go. Disappearing would create doubt and the family would have time to put up some defences against whatever would come at them. He'd done enough favours for Corbett Wilson. He'd promised to help the family if it all went wrong.

Bugger it.

He stood up. Murray McCarthy had made his decision.

Bloody bugger it.

He was gaining in confidence. It was going to be all right.

Fucken bloody bugger it.

He buttoned up his shirt, pulled his tie more or less into place, walked to the car and drove up the hill towards Miramar. Never mind being a dunny philosopher. Leave that to the university students. He had other things to do.

He'd managed one good thing. He'd been up to the Devon Street house. He'd knocked. No one had answered. He'd looked in the windows. No one was there so he'd had to break into the place. Once he was in he'd gone straight down to the basement and found the lists he'd help hide there. Then he'd gone straight down to Corbett Wilson's office, walked in, dropped the papers on the lawyer's desk and taken off. There'd been hardly a word said.

Marie West. This whole mess was her fault. Why couldn't the little bitch have done what all other teenage girls did and just quietly buggered off to let the boys pump away at her for a couple of months? That'd have stopped her getting into fights with the family and seeing and hearing things that weren't any of her business. Then she could have declared herself a virgin again and gone home. It'd have been all hugs and tears and forgiveness and off to confession to unload the sin of the shagging she'd been doing. She'd still be running around and not causing everyone all this grief. Stupid little girl!

Feeney was out there somewhere too. McCarthy shuddered at the thought of that big black-browed coalminer of a copper getting him somewhere quiet. Feeney knew everything, if he didn't, he had a pretty good idea. If he decided to close the book on McCarthy it'd be long years in the pokey. Christ, he'd been a bee's cock away from going inside after the Filthy Phil mistake. He could forget another chance. There was only one way to look at this. He, Murray McCarthy, was wading slowly up a narrow valley and watching a flash-flooded Shit Creek coming straight down at him.

In the rear-view mirror he could see back to the hill behind Marist Miramar, where Xavier Weir lay dead in his greenhouse.

Filthy swine! When someone finds you it's off to hell and you can bloody burn.

God help him. In the last couple of hours he'd boiled his way from despair to fear to despair to self-loathing and now into some sort of strange dark hatred. He knew what was going on. He'd shamed himself. Someone was going to have to pay for it. He wasn't going to be the only one feeling bad before this was all over. His grip on the steering wheel was so tight his knuckles were white. The wheel's ridges were imprinted on his palm and he'd started enjoying the pain coming out of it.

To think he was gonna bloody top himself! Jesus! He was gonna kill himself.

His chin jutted out and the corners of his mouth curled an ugly, snorting determination.

They'd bloody love that, the lot of them. They all wanted him gone. And they'd be lining up to do him in.

He drove through Kilbirnie and up towards Newtown. Then he stopped. No. He'd go around the harbour. He'd have its ink-black water on one side and the rough scrubbly bush on the other. That'd be better. It'd feel right. They were dangerous elements. Cold water and unforgiving bush could kill. That was the right atmosphere for a man who'd almost been screwed by another one.

This was the time for Murray McCarthy to have his redemption, just like Jesus had got it on the cross. The only difference was that McCarthy's redemption wasn't going to involve him getting hurt. Oh no. It was going to be a lousy homo feeling it. That would sponge the sin away. One of them had caused it – one of them was going to have to pay. If he didn't balance this, he was finished as any kind of man.

What did God say?

Vengeance is mine.

McCarthy smiled. He liked that. God was telling him he was right.

He drove around into Oriental Bay. The Taj was just ahead of him. He stopped near the Majestic picture theatre. It was just up ahead where they'd found the car that'd been used to cart Frank Wilkins around to Evans Bay.

He got out and waited in a doorway. He could see the toilets from here. It was just a waiting game now. About ten minutes later he smiled as a man, slow, overweight and wearing glasses, looked around to see if anyone was watching. He didn't see McCarthy and quickly disappeared into the Taj.

The fat one would do nicely. Salvation was right there, waddling into real trouble. He'd be the sacrifice through which McCarthy would sweep away the filth Xavier Weir had heaped on him.

Murray McCarthy would be a man again.

chapter twenty-five

Auckland, 1972

The partners were glancing at their watches. The atmosphere was telling Helen they wanted to be on their way. McKenzie had fired all the bullets they'd need. The bad business was done and it was time to move on. There were lunches waiting out there. Helen was on her way to Calvary. The only thing left to sort out now was whether she'd go quietly or they'd have to deal with rage and hysteria. They hoped not. That would affect their digestion. It had already been stressful enough.

She dropped the files on the table in front of her. Glances flicked around the table. What was this all about? She looked at the names on the front of the manila folders, as if to sort them, even though she already had them in the right order. Make them wait. Soak up all the oxygen in the room. Get everything focused on you. Was this how actors felt when they walked out into the light at the Mercury and looked out over the silent and attentive audience?

'I've been able to help some or all of you in managing some very, very difficult matters,' Helen said. She made a show of looking at the files. Prolong the suspense. On the other hand she wouldn't milk it too much or they'd find a way to grab the initiative. She began quietly listing the cases: the ones she had files for, and the others Fallon had told her about. The atmosphere was cooling but not as quickly as she'd hoped. Was something wrong? Well, she had no choice now. It was too late to turn back. She'd chosen her road and she was going to have to travel right to the end of it.

There was the McAnnally business, with its allegations of

kickbacks to the city council officers, supposedly funnelled through the firm. The widow Fitzgerald, losing everything after spectacularly bad legal advice, was saved only after the partners had a whip-around among themselves to stop her suing them. That had disappointed a long line of lawyers itching for a chance to have a go at them. There were the Jamieson and the Fa'afua cases. There was the legal attack on the Waikato Maori that had come badly unstuck. Without some quick help from a couple of MPs that one could have sunk the firm.

The partners were calming down. Most of this was old news. In a couple of the cases the key people were safely dead. In others the payments went out with claw-back clauses: go public and the money comes back. Helen hadn't shown them anything they couldn't manage. Still, there might be some fallout that was best avoided. Helen sensed the concern and blessed Archie Fallon. He had created more than one of these problems in the first place. That was why they wanted him out the door and off to the Bench, where he couldn't do any serious harm. Helen kept reminding herself not to even think about uttering an open threat. She'd present the cases as examples of how she'd helped, or could help. They'd get the message. She knew where the bodies were buried.

Then it was over. Her case for the defence had taken only slightly longer than McKenzie's argument for her execution. The glances around the table gravitated to McKenzie. He cleared his throat and allowed his chin to move forward, almost independently of the rest of his face. Then Gilfedder interrupted.

'I think we might be able to see a clear direction as to the way forward. Thank you, Helen, for making your points so well and so clearly.'

Helen's acknowledgement was silent but, she hoped, gracious. If they felt comfortable it'd be easier for them to be generous. Generosity might be important. Missing out on the job with Felicity's firm meant it might be a while before she could count on an income.

'Perhaps if we could ask you to give us a few minutes . . .' Gilfedder cut across her.

Helen nodded and stood up. This was it: the bit where they

talked about the money. It was: 'Bugger off, Helen, so we can work out what it'll take to get you out without a fight, without tears and without upsetting the slaves down in the Tombs.' She began putting the files in her briefcase.

'It may be,' Gilfedder purred, 'that you choose to leave those behind.'

Fallon had anticipated that. Give them up without a second glance, he'd said. They'll assume you've made copies. They've all made their own for when their own time comes. She stood and nodded. The files were on the table in front of her now-empty chair. For a second she had a vision of a furious scramble while they leapt to check whether she'd been bluffing them with sheets of blank paper.

She sat in her office. This was the hard part: the waiting. Would they buy her silence, or were the files so old that it didn't matter? They might decide to hurl her out with almost nothing and dare her to do anything about it. It would be a signal to the rest.

A secretary knocked and put her head around the door. It had only been a quarter of an hour. Was Helen free to talk to Mr McKenzie? Yes, she was. The secretary looked relieved that Helen was not going to be difficult. She obviously didn't want to go back to McKenzie and tell him Helen was barricaded in with a pistol in each hand and shooting at anyone who came into her office.

McKenzie waved her in. Jackson, the managing partner, was there too. He'd be writing the cheque – or issuing the writs against her.

'Obviously, this is an unfortunate business,' McKenzie began.

Helen nodded. Most unfortunate.

'And of course, we want to recognise your contribution – a strong contribution – to making the firm what it is today. Naturally, we have been looking at recognising this and we have an offer.' McKenzie nodded to Jackson, who handed over an envelope. It was not sealed. She glanced into it. Seven thousand dollars! Fallon's advice thundered in her mind.

'Look, if it's anything over six grand, grab it, shove it in the waistband of your knickers, bugger off down to the bank and get it on a fast clearance. Don't go back to your office. Don't pass Go. Don't pass anything. Just get the – excuse me for this – fuck out of there. They'll clean out your office and send your bits and pieces on. By then you should have made sure you don't have anything too compromising floating about for them to see.'

As soon as the cheque was cleared he'd suggested talking to any other lawyers she knew. She could mention sexual harassment – but without bringing up Fallon's name thank you very much. Imply the place is full of slavering predators. That would be her only defence against the whispers of incompetence the partners would be spreading to justify the departure of a high-profile woman lawyer.

She looked at the cheque, and then at McKenzie and Jackson.

'Thank you.'

There was an indemnity form. By accepting this payment she was forfeiting any right to take action against them. She'd expected that and signed it. The handshakes were silent. Would they send her personal items to her home? Of course they would. She shook hands with her secretary and her team. It was a grim moment. No one quite knew what to say. Her secretary struggled to hold back the tears.

Helen walked down the corridor to the lifts. As she went, faces rose and dropped back to their desks. They couldn't be seen as allies. If Helen was just the first, the Stalinists who ran this place might decide to purge any allies next.

Thank God, the lift was empty. She stood still, holding her head up. Why? She did not have to keep up appearances any more. She didn't have to hide behind the persona of a crisp 'take no nonsense' lawyer. The last of her resistance broke and the tears rolled down her face.

Helen paced her living-room. Where the hell was Des Laughlan? What was he doing? She'd talked to everyone who might have seen him and it sounded as if he'd done everything she'd hired him for, but she'd heard absolutely nothing.

Where on earth was he?

Someone was knocking at the door. She walked across and opened it.

Lashing stood there, his policewoman offsider behind him. As soon as Helen opened the door Lashing moved forward slightly in a practised and professional move. She would not be able to close it without moving him. Try that and she could be arrested for assault.

'I wanted to catch up with you. There are a few things happening.' Could he come in?

Helen didn't have much choice. She stood aside.

'I hear you've moved on from the law firm,' he said.

That hadn't taken long. It was also jarring. Was that the idea? Was he telling her, 'We're watching and we don't miss anything?'

'There are a couple of things,' Lashing said. 'Des Laughlan's one of them.' Helen knew she showed surprise and Lashing's eyes glowed with triumph.

'He's been found dead in Wellington, in the bush behind Holy Cross School in Miramar. It looks as if he was murdered.'

Helen felt her knees go weak. She put a hand on the table, pulled out a chair and let herself drop down onto it.

'As far as we can work out he died a couple of days after he last talked to you.'

Helen nodded. No point denying it. They'd been outside Laughlan's office. Give away the known and try to keep the unknown. But what the hell was the unknown?

'We'd like to know what he was doing for you, so we can follow up. We've been out to his office. He'd finished some work for a couple of criminal lawyers but that was it in Auckland. You were the next client through the door. Suddenly, he's ringing people in Wellington and a day later he's in a motel in Newtown, and now . . .'

Helen nodded. She couldn't afford a mistake here.

'Can you leave it with me, at least for a little while? I'll sit down and write you a list.'

The policewoman's eyebrows flicked. Helen didn't like her expression. 'We'd prefer it if you could sit down with us and we'll work out the list now,' she said.

Little bitch. Helen took a breath. Keep calm, and don't let them push you. Take as long as you need to think this through, and above all, don't bloody panic.

'What's happening about the bomb that was sent to me?' Helen asked.

The policewoman didn't like her changing the subject. Lashing saw the hard glare between the two women and cut across it. 'We're still going on that,' he said. 'There are Wellington detectives going back through everything at that end. There's work going on in Sydney, and the bomb's being taken apart in the lab. We're following up each component, trying to find where it was bought, see if anyone remembers anyone. There's a lot happening.'

He waited for a reaction.

'That sounds very thorough,' Helen said.

She had to get them out of there. She didn't like the sound of Wellington detectives going back through everything. Waiting back there was what had happened to her and Jennifer in July of 1947.

'I am not sure how much I can tell you about what Mr Laughlan was doing for me, but I'll make a list of all the places he might have gone. I'll do it this afternoon.'

This time Lashing's frown matched the policewoman's. Clearly he also thought 'now' would be better. Helen tried to keep the initiative by walking to the front door and opening it. Lashing stood still for a moment, then moved to the door.

'So, there'll be something this afternoon? We'll get someone to pick it up. Four o'clock,' the policewoman said. It was an order.

Once the door closed behind them Helen leaned against it, trying not to start shaking again. Laughlan was dead. Detectives were going through her life. Lashing wanted a list of everything Laughlan was doing. Whatever she came up with now was going to have to be good – believable, but vague enough to keep them away from what she wanted hidden. This was frightening. If the bomb was telling her she'd been found then killing Laughlan was saying the murderer was right behind her.

What was she going to do?

There weren't many choices. She could sit there in Auckland and hope the police solved the problem for her. But she couldn't rely on that. They might find out too much. No, she had to go to Wellington and deal with it herself. She would feel like a cat, dipped in honey and dropped into an anthill, but what the hell else was she supposed to do? Where was she going to go if she ran? She'd never been out of the country. Going anywhere beyond Australia meant getting a passport, and Lashing would hear about that in no time. Even Australia wasn't safe. Jennifer had been there, using her married name, and he'd still found her.

How exactly did you fight against something so still and silent, like a log in a lake, just under the surface and waiting to tear the bottom out of your boat?

chapter twenty-six

Wellington, 1947

If there was one place in this world Pat Feeney knew too well it was this corridor down to the Bishop's office. There'd been times when he'd enjoyed coming here. Then there'd been the times when he'd wished he'd never heard of the place.

He'd told the priest he could find his own way, but no, the priest's job was to escort him to the Bishop's door and that was what he was going to do. Feeney backed down when he saw the flash of terror across the young man's face. He didn't like to think what would happen if the Bishop felt that a guest, an important one, had been slighted.

The Bishop had the two lawyers, Johnston and Wilson, with him.

'Ah, Pat, come on in,' the Bishop purred. He glanced over at the priest. 'A cup of tea or coffee for Mr Feeney?' It was a question for Feeney and an order for the priest.

'No thanks, I'm fine,' Feeney answered.

The Bishop gave the priest a curt nod. That's it. Go away and stay away.

He did not waste time. 'We're very worried about things, Pat. There's the terrible business of the young girl, Marie West. How is that going?'

Feeney kept a straight face. Yeah, sure! These guys were long past worrying about Marie. But, okay, he'd stay non-committal until they got to the real point: John Augustine O'Malley.

'It's turning into a long hard go. If you don't get something quickly it's like quarrying rock. But in the end we'll find him. When? I don't know.'

He'd said the same thing to the reporters from the *Dominion* and the *Evening Post*. They'd all read it and none of them could care less. It was a formality and it was out of the way. Corbett Wilson leaned forward, his eyes drilling at Feeney.

'There's the terrible business of John O'Malley.'

'We're not sure exactly what's gone on,' Feeney said. 'We don't know whether it was suicide or an accident.' He was keeping the word 'murder' out of this.

'Of course it does look that way,' Wilson answered, hitting the words 'does look' very hard. Feeney got the message. Wilson thought it was a murder.

The Bishop was watching them, intent and sharp. 'Johnny came to us, a distressed soul, but not to repent his sins, which was a great tragedy now his soul is on its way to his maker and him facing the accounting with the darkness still on him. He did say that he was a worried, worried man, and that things weren't right, not right at all.'

Wilson snapped a glare at the Bishop. He didn't want him telling Feeney too much. For a moment the Bishop seemed to shrink from the power of Wilson's gaze. Interesting.

Careful, sonny, Feeney thought. Remember, he did play in the front row. He won't always back down. He's got good contacts, he signs the cheques and there are other lawyers.

'Johnny gave us a couple of things that might be a bit of help,' the Bishop said. Feeney could see the cleric's flash of annoyance at Wilson for suggesting he had a loose mouth. 'Corbett here has been looking after them for us.'

Well, well. The 'few things' O'Malley had given them were too hot to keep on church property, obviously.

'What things?' Feeney asked.

That came out harder and faster than Feeney had intended. He must have been more tired than he thought. He'd better keep an eye on that. Tired people made mistakes.

'It's details of his business. I've got the only copy and I'm arranging to get it all photographed,' Corbett answered.

'I'll come over with you now and pick them up.'

Wilson's quick look told Feeney that was not the plan. What was? Was the lawyer frightened of what he'd seen, or of even a whisper of power moving out of his control? Feeney's guess was the latter.

'The post-mortem examination suggests it was an accident or a suicide,' Feeney answered.

The Bishop's mouth went tight as he leaned back. Furtive glances slipped between him and the lawyers.

'I see,' the Bishop said.

'That's how it stands,' Feeney said. 'Of course I've a man having a closer look into it, going over all the details, looking for witnesses and so on, but that's where we are.'

'There is something else that might be useful to you.' The Bishop handed Feeney an envelope and stood up. The meeting was over.

Feeney sat in the Humber and opened the envelope. The photos of Filthy Phil and the Minister of Forestry's private secretary, a male civil servant, dropped into his lap. Christ, if the Bishop had these in his office, what was bad enough to get out of the office and into Wilson's safe? Feeney glanced back up at the house. The Bishop was standing at a window looking down at him. Then he turned and was gone.

Pat Feeney booted the chair across the room. The detectives in the briefing room scrambled to make themselves scarce doing whatever was necessary to get out in a hurry. Climbing over the backs of the slow and the weak. Hurling them from the lifeboats. Anything to escape the boss's wrath.

Once they'd gone Feeney stood quietly. Temper tantrums weren't going to do anyone any good. That had been both childish and stupid. But, Mother of the Lord God, finding a way through all of this – the Bishop, Marie, the bookies, the lawyers and Filthy Phil – without feeling frustrated and angry was going to take the patience of a saint and Pat Feeney could forget ever being one of those. He flopped on a chair and ran a hand through his hair. What a bloody mess.

He felt sorely tempted to smash the whole place, but he wouldn't, and he knew it. The expense voucher for replacement furniture would have to go past Compton and he didn't need to give him any more ammunition. He thought about Filthy Phil doctoring the pathologist's report on O'Malley. He had the photos now and could stop the cremation. But he'd have to persuade Phil they were the only prints. Where were the negatives? He wouldn't blame Phil for not taking the chance. Was it better to let O'Malley slip away? And what was Corbett Wilson up to? What was in his office? Did dead men tell tales?

None of these was the real problem. It was him. Feeney was tired and overwhelmed and wasn't sure even his bull energy was going to get him through this. He felt weak and hollow. Was it depression, exhaustion or self-pity? Had he simply lost his faith – in himself, God, whoever? Whatever it was was dragging him down. He'd seen detectives lose control of big investigations. The troops sensed the panic, got their heads down and kept away from the problem. They were so keen to avoid becoming targets, they went off on tangents. Smaller crimes got solved while the big one was left lying abandoned like a beer bottle on the side of the road.

Piling up behind everything else was his guilt at not having visited his mother.

He had to get out of here. Find some distance and perspective. Sitting in the rest home listening to the shards of memory spinning from his mother's fractured brain was never pleasant but he had no choice. He had a debt. She'd carried him, fed him and loved him, always struggling to do her best for him. Soon she'd be dead and he'd never have another chance.

There was something he needed to do first. He had to have a quick chat with Wilson's assistant about the contents of the lawyer's safe. Feeney didn't expect too many problems. Her sister was a busy abortionist and that'd be the deal – a warning that the police knew and that it was time to get out of the business before she was caught, in exchange for a detailed list. He smiled. He could do the work of both the police and of God. Wasn't that him solving crimes and keeping little babies alive? Who said he never did anything for humanity?

Pat Feeney's mother sat in a big comfortable chair near the hospital's window. Mantovani dripped from the radio. Feeney hated that music. What was wrong with crooners? But this wasn't his home, and the people who lived here liked it. If he wanted crooners he could go home and listen to them there. The word 'home' hurt. This place was so far from his memories of his joyously chaotic boyhood. Sure, the staff did their best to make it friendly, but it was always going to look like a hospital, with its long benchtops, industrial-strength cleaners and rigid schedule. Seeing his mother, the once free spirit who would impulsively run down bush tracks or up into the sand dunes leaving the family trailing behind her, being so regimented and restricted often had him near tears.

The eyes that looked down at him when he was a little boy crying from the grazes and bruises of some adventure and smiled away the pain looked straight past him now. Feeney bit his bottom lip. If he was important to her years ago, he wasn't now. In all the hours of listening to the words falling from her mouth he'd never once heard his name.

He was the only one left. Her husband, his father, was dead. The other three children, Johnny, James and Siobhan, had all died with him when their father rolled the car on the Brynderwyns, on the way to Whangarei. Pat had brought her to Wellington, applied to get her into this hospital and been turned away. He'd mentioned this to the Bishop. Next day there was a call from the nun who ran the place. There had been a clerical mistake and yes, of course there was a bed.

Today was especially hard. If he didn't get out of here soon he'd break down. Finally he stood up, leaned over and kissed her on the cheek. 'I love you, Mum.' He said it every time he visited. Who knew whether some door to her mind might open and let the words through, and she'd register one last time that he was grateful for everything and he did, truly, love her.

He waited a moment. Nothing. There was always nothing. He swallowed back the familiar lump and nodded to the nurse as he left. She was on her way to his mother, carrying what looked like fresh nappies. By the time he reached his car the tears were rolling down his face and dropping onto his shirt.

He sat in the car. God help him! He was old enough to face anything. At least he had a choice. Marie West didn't. Someone had grabbed her from behind. Seconds later she was unconscious. A couple of minutes later she was dead, strangled and left to rot in the bush.

That was what he was supposed to be doing – solving the poor girl's murder. All he wanted was to be with his wife and children, talking about everything and nothing, so long as it was gentle and funny and warm and made him feel wanted, needed and loved.

Come on, Pat, he told himself. For Christ's sake, come on.

Jimmy Byrne was waiting for him at Wellington Central. He was stone-faced.

'Boss,' he said, 'we couldn't find the chink and it looks like the trannie . . . or whatever . . .'

Feeney cut across him. He'd had enough of debased humanity for one day. 'Call him a him, okay?'

'. . . is gone. I talked to some other ones. They'll call me when he turns up. I had to give away a couple of things, but they seem pretty sure he's gone.'

Feeney had a good idea what 'the couple of things' might have been. Jimmy had negotiated someone's charges down or away in exchange for information. Feeney couldn't care less. If it ended up with even a hint of justice for O'Malley, scummy parasitic bastard that he was, then it was worth it.

Damn it. Someone was getting away with killing Marie because he had to divert Catholic coppers into chasing two Freemason policemen who had killed a Catholic bookie. The bloody police were devouring themselves. Oh sure, the murderer might be terrified of the knock on the door and drinking away the sight and sound of Marie choking to dead. They might even have decided it was all too much and gone off and killed themselves. But whatever they were doing it wasn't happening in a cell or the dock of a courtroom.

'Good on you, Jimmy.'

Byrne looked relieved. As he followed Feeney into the station he saw Feeney's jaw jut out. Good. That had always been a sign something was going on, and probably aimed at the Freemasons. Jimmy Byrne would do anything to help that along.

Feeney stopped, turned to Byrne. He'd made a decision.

chapter twenty-seven

Wellington, 1972

Lashing resented having to sit quietly and obediently like a good boy while Inspector Alistair Henderson lazed his way through the report Lashing had spent the morning typing. Henderson could feel Lashing's impatience burning on the other side of the desk and couldn't care less. Lashing had no choice.

Henderson made a point of sneering from time to time as he read, looking over it to Lashing and muttering, 'I'd say we might have to get your typing spruced up a bit. It's pretty bloody bad.'

Lashing flashed him a glare. Henderson was unmoved. Lashing could glare until his eyeballs joined his teeth in a glass of water beside the bed at night. Henderson had to give the go-ahead or Lashing wasn't going to get in the same street to what he wanted. Lashing didn't know he'd done a speed-reading course and digested every syllable in the report at least three times. But he needed time – time to figure out what to do with Lashing and the bomb case. Henderson had been asking around. General opinion was Lashing had the best line on the case and was the most enthusiastic. Besides, it was a chance to get rid of him, so he wouldn't be mooching around the place sharing his takeaways with his burglars.

Finally, Henderson looked up at Lashing, who blurted impatiently, 'Look, sir, her sister's dead from a bombing. They're from Wellington. The bomb that went to Sydney came from Masterton, which is only over the hill from Wellington. So did the one that Helen Murphy got. Then she hires a bloody private detective who goes down there and gets himself killed. I think it's important I head down there.'

'Yes, I know. It's all here in the report,' Henderson snapped.

It came out more aggressively than he'd intended but he had to shut him up. Henderson knew Lashing would get what he wanted, but there was a protocol here. He had to do the decent thing and grovel for it, instead of all this 'reasonable case' nonsense. There was a silence. They both leaned back, which irritated Henderson. Lashing wasn't supposed to be looking at ease; he was supposed to be like a dog begging for a favour from his master.

Lashing had seen that look in Henderson's eye before. It was going to be all right but he would have to work a bit harder for it yet.

'Here's the best bit,' Lashing said. 'She's on her way down to Wellington right now, as we speak. She'll get there in about half an hour. I took a bit of a punt that it'd be okay and asked the Wellington guys to keep an eye on her.' He saw Henderson's look and quickly added, 'Observation only, nothing else. Strictly long-leash and no contact stuff.'

It didn't help Lashing's case and they both knew it. Getting Wellington to do a tail was supposed to go through Henderson's office. Upstarts like Lashing didn't jump the gun – not if they knew what was good for them. Maybe Lashing was getting a bit big for his boots, assuming he was safely over all the jumps and racing for the finish line, the trophy and the big bag of oats. Henderson couldn't have that. No sir. It was a few years back now but he hadn't forgotten the wrap-up of the Dominion Road payroll robbery. Lashing had called him a 'fat, slow bloody dickhead'. Henderson didn't mind dickhead too much, but the fat part had cut. Okay, he might be slightly overweight, perhaps even drifting up towards the lower end of corpulent, but he was definitely not bloody fat.

'I . . . er . . . I would like to go down to Wellington and stay with it,' Lashing was saying. Now he was leaning forward in a properly respectful way, which helped. 'She's trying to find whoever sent the frigging bomb. What I want to know is why she isn't hiding out somewhere and leaving it for us to find the prick. I've never seen anything like this. There can be only one bloody reason.'

He was silently cursing himself. Damn! He'd forgotten to throw in a couple of 'sirs'. Henderson was sticky about rank. Without due deference he could go all surly and then anything was possible – he might even turn Lashing down flat.

Henderson shrugged his shoulders. He'd had as much grovelling as he was getting. He might as well move on.

'Yeah, you can go to Wellington. Stay on it and I'll ask them to back you up.'

Lashing nodded his thanks and stood up.

Henderson smiled. He wasn't getting off that easy. This might just be the moment to remind Lashing about who was running things. 'You can take Jan Peters with you. It'll be good experience for her, and she's already been on the case.'

Jan Peters was the policewoman who'd been at Helen's interview at Auckland Central. Lashing didn't want her, and not because it was her. He didn't want anyone. Losing her was going to take finesse. If he made a conspicuous fuss it might give Henderson an excuse to pull the pin on the trip. The Wellington coppers would take over the case and Lashing would be back to burglary. He found himself thinking again about Helen Murphy, about those long legs and the way that expensive fabric wrapped around her when she was walking quickly.

'Yes, sir. That'll be fine. I'll get things moving.'

Henderson gestured at Lashing's report. His sneer said he didn't want it on his desk or in his office. Lashing picked it up and trudged out to the main CIB office. There was a lot to do – organise plane tickets, find a place to stay, check on how the Wellington police were going, and come up with a way to lose Jan Peters.

Henderson sat back and smiled. He felt like running a sweepstake on how long it'd be before Jan Peters was in here with some reason for not going to Wellington with Lashing.

Helen had always felt relieved when the plane taxied up to Wellington airport's terminal and she could wrap her coat around her for the wind-whipped sprint across the tarmac. Buying a ticket to fly into Wellington always felt like placing a bet. It'd only take one of those big southerly gusts to come in from Cook Strait and you'd be coming up red when your money was on black.

The two detectives standing near the baggage claim watched her collect her bag and walk over to the rental-car counter. After she had gone, one of them sidled up to the counter, showed his badge and got a look at the rental agreement. She had a red Hillman Hunter and she'd given the Hollywood Motel as her address.

Why would anyone stay in a crapper like that? One of the cops had been there with a policewoman for some 'special inquiries' and they'd ended up covered in bites from whatever lived inside the mattress. Hang on. Wasn't the guy who'd come down from Auckland and got killed and dumped out in Miramar staying there too? Perhaps the clowns up in Auckland had stumbled on to something . . .

They were still watching as she came out of the Births, Deaths and Marriages office in Lower Hutt. Helen was pleased with herself. It had taken only a few minutes to find that Des Laughlan had been doing a good job. The woman behind the counter was most helpful. 'Gosh, you're the second one in just a couple of weeks looking for that family. The other person wanted to know if they had changed names or anything. But we can't really give that out, not without their permission.' Helen shivered at the idea of that family knowing who was asking about them. Des Laughlan had got this close and been murdered for his efforts.

'Thank you, but no.'

Next stop was the Land Transfer Office. The woman there raised an eyebrow. A man had been in here a week or so ago looking for the same information. Ignoring the woman's suspicious eye, Helen found what she was looking for: the names of all the neighbours on either side of the house she was interested in. Then it was back to Births, Deaths and Marriages. The woman there was enjoying this. She took Helen's list.

'I don't need to go and check these – I already did it.' She disappeared into an office and came back with a piece of paper. It was upside down but Helen recognised Des Laughlan's handwriting. All except two of the names had been crossed out. Surely it couldn't be this easy? A few minutes later she was in the Hillman Hunter heading back to town. Mack Bresnahan. That was the name howling out from the lists at her.

But was rushing out to Miramar a good idea? Hell, she could drop out of this, give his name and address to the police anonymously, and if they found bomb-making stuff at his house that'd be the end of it. But then it might not . . . He'd know where the police interest had come from. He might have a bit of evidence of some sort hidden away and it would be enough to take Helen down with him.

Don't forget, she told herself, you're a lawyer, and that makes you prime fodder for a detective's trophy case. You'll get nothing from them.

No, no one was getting anything until she was sure she was safe.

From the Hutt motorway she could see over to the Miramar peninsula: brooding, dark, strong and bush-covered, it shoved itself out into the harbour. Right at the top, where there should have been some sort of memorial to faith or hope, like they had at Rio De Janeiro, there was Mt Crawford prison, a monument to hate, malice and lost dreams.

She drove past the Ngauranga Gorge and the inter-island ferry wharf. A blue Ford Falcon had been behind her on the way out to Lower Hutt and there was one behind her now. Was it the same one? Was she being followed? She had to get a grip on herself. If she got too jittery it'd only end with her frozen and too frightened to move while a hunter was about to pull the trigger. She couldn't afford that. She had to keep moving forward, stay on the offensive.

chapter twenty-eight

Wellington, 1947

Murray McCarthy had been in interview rooms and in court looking murderers in the eye and watching their faces when the jury foreman said 'guilty': the moment they knew they were bound for Auckland's Mt Eden Prison, to listen to the carpenters out in the yard build the gallows they'd be hanged from.

There had always been just the one question.

Why?

They were alone and all the resources of the state were aimed straight at them. If the police wanted a forest search, the trucks arrived and the soldiers tumbled out. If a house was to be searched to destruction then that's what happened.

And people still went out and did it.

Why?

Now that McCarthy was about to become a murderer he knew why. They didn't think of anything beyond the act. It consumed them just as it was taking control of him. He stood still in his hiding place not far from the entrance to the Taj. He was going to kill someone he didn't know. If he didn't kill him, he'd be crippled or brain damaged, carrying McCarthy's mark for the rest of his days.

Well, they put their mark on me, McCarthy muttered to himself.

He didn't look in any shop windows. He didn't want to see his face – not after what he'd discovered about himself, and then what he'd thought while he was in the cold at Worser Bay. He couldn't look at himself until he was a man again. There was only way for that to happen: his pain had to be shifted onto someone else.

One of them had been going to bugger him, like a woman! Why?

Why did he need to kill? Only three people had any idea of what had gone on at Weir's house. He was one. Xavier Weir was another, and he was dead. The woman who knocked on the door might have guessed but didn't care. All she wanted was her dope and to be gone. But *he* knew, and that was all that mattered. He was the man with the stain that needed to be cleansed, and only blood would do it. Wasn't that in the Bible? An eye for a tooth or some shit like that; if it was good enough for the good book, it was good enough for him.

So far he'd seen three men going into the Taj. None of them had come out. He'd have to wait – attacking three of them was too dangerous. Only one of them needed to land a king hit and he'd be at their mercy. What if he slipped on the Taj's wet, slippery floor? They would have a chance to run. Hell, they might not. They might finish what Weir had started. He couldn't risk that. He'd have to wait. The last one out would be the one who died.

He was surprised he didn't hear any inner voices telling him to turn around, walk away, find somewhere to sleep. There was only this silent, running certainty that he was going to kill. No clubs or knives or guns, either. It'd be fists and feet, as close to the victim as he could get. Look into his eyes. Belt him hard enough to stun him. Turn him into a helpless animal being moved up to the slaughter. McCarthy peered through the dark. He was a one-man freezing-works crew: fast, efficient and forever.

Christ! When were they going to bloody leave? He stamped his feet and looked at his watch. Get on with it. Have your sex and then come out to die. His fists closed and unclosed almost beyond his control. Ah! One man came out and near-sprinted to a car parked just up the road. He leapt into it and was gone.

'You just saved your life, but there's tomorrow,' snarled McCarthy. 'Someone else'll get a chance at you.'

Another man ambled out, buttoning up his pants. He didn't

see McCarthy standing in the shadows. Why would he? He wasn't expecting anyone to be around, not at one in the morning when Courtenay Place was a desert.

McCarthy crossed the road to stand in the dark just outside the door. His mouth was dry. He could feel his heart trying to bash through his chest. Now he knew the murderer's 'why'. Getting ready to kill was exciting. It was better than sex!

The third man walked out. Now! By the time the man's eyes behind his thick spectacles had opened wide and the awful warning had reached his brain, McCarthy had hit him in the stomach. The man sagged. McCarthy grabbed the lapels of his coat, lifted him up and smashed his forehead onto the man's nose. Blood sprayed across them both as the bones in the victim's nose turned soft and smashed under the force.

He spun the man around and rammed his head into the concrete wall. The excitement, the dark little thrill of anticipation was going now. All he had left was this cold curiosity. What was the quickest way to finish this and how long would it take?

As he kicked and punched at the man McCarthy reminded himself to be careful not to hurt himself, not to break a knuckle or damage a toe. The suit didn't matter. It was already covered with coal dust from O'Malley's shed, dirt from Weir's floor and the sea dampness from the long hour sitting at Worser Bay. A bit of blood wouldn't make any difference.

The man was on the ground. His head was exposed and flopping around. He had lost any hope of protecting it. His arms were dropped down beside him. McCarthy could keep kicking without having to worry. The man was helpless. Whatever was left of his brain had ordered him into a foetal position, in a hopeless attempt to protect his head, chest and abdomen from McCarthy's endlessly pounding kicking.

I'm getting tired. I've had enough. Why don't you just die?

Killing the guy had turned into hard boring effort, like digging over a garden. He had to keep going. He couldn't risk this man talking to Feeney or Byrne or any of the others. Not that he needed to worry. The eyes looking up at him were eerily blank and calmly unseeing. Finally McCarthy stopped to let his breathing drop back to something near normal. Surely the guy was dead. He had to be. McCarthy didn't have much energy left. His rugby days were long gone and there'd been too much beer, too many pies and too many long hours of sitting in police cars and police stations. Christ! He wasn't even fit enough to kill someone quickly.

If the man wasn't dead now he was close enough. Now he had to get rid of the body before some street cleaner came around the corner and caught them. He'd have to die too, and McCarthy had had enough for one night.

He drove his car to beside the body, opened the boot and spread out one of the canvas sheets used for preserving evidence at outdoor crime scenes. It took longer than he expected to get the body into the sheet and heft it into the boot. It was hard, sweaty work, especially as he was exhausted from all the kicking. Finally, the body rolled in and he slammed the boot shut.

Except the boot hadn't shut. The man's hand had dropped on the lip and was sticking out in a creepy way. He couldn't get squeamish, not now, so he opened the boot again and flicked the hand back inside. This time the boot closed and he could go round to the driver's seat.

Oh Jesus, he could have done without that.

Apart from when his forehead smashed down on the nose there hadn't been any actual flesh-to-flesh contact. Until now it had all been safely distant, but now there had been that gentle and almost kind connection with his victim. It made the man seem almost human. There were going to be nightmares, and they would be coming from that hand . . .

Ten minutes later the man was jammed behind some oil drums at the back of the wharf sheds.

McCarthy took a last look. Now a voice was coming up from inside him: that man was a human being. His fists clenched. No he wasn't. He was a poof.

He was scared now. The finality of it was making McCarthy feel odd. That man had been living and now he was dead. Forever. This was the time to go back out to Worser Bay and take that walk out into the water.

No!

That'd be the coward's way out. What he'd do was go home in the morning, grab his clothes and be gone. That'd be better. Except that morning was still hours away, and he was standing here like a dork, waiting to be caught by the first young beat copper who wandered along. Act as if you have half a brain. Get out of here!

He tried to pull himself together.

He walked back to the wharf fence and stopped.

Christ!

A bread truck was driving past. The driver could put him here at the moment Filthy Phil would estimate as the time of death. Jesus! He shook his head. He could feel the panic rising as he ran for the car. Once in the car he managed to stop his hand shaking long enough to get the key in the ignition.

Please bloody start. Just . . . start!

Thank God. He eased out of Courtenay Place and into Tory Street. Behind him a beat policeman looked up from some rubbish someone had tipped out on the footpath. Interesting! That was Murray McCarthy. Inspector Feeney had put out a notice for anyone who saw him to let him know immediately. Huh! That'd be the same high and mighty Feeney who'd stopped him getting a chance to join plainclothes. If Feeney thought he was getting any help from this constable he could whistle Dixie right up his big fat freckle.

chapter twenty-nine

Miramar, 1972

It must have been at least twenty-five years – 1947, and that terrible July – since Helen had stood here on the corner of Nevay and Fortification Roads. It felt strange. She could almost hear the sounds coming back down the years. She'd been one of the kids playing cricket and soccer in the street with the boys, the howls for leg-before and the soccer ball smacking against the garage door, or refusing to play with them because they were too rough, and flouncing off to the fussy world of the little girl, with its bars and barriers to keep the boys out.

Now she saw that childhood world through different eyes. This would be a good place to invest. There were world-class views in every direction and big strong houses. Let what was calling itself the 'smart money' rush to Thorndon's shaded dampness. Then again, perhaps Miramar might not appeal to the hipsters. This had always been a neighbourhood for families, for people with jobs and children, going to church, growing old and watching their children go out to make their way in the world. Trendy had never been a part of it.

Looking at the garages brought her back hard. That garage was still there! She'd hoped it would have gone, and taken its tale of death with it. But it was still here.

She had Des Laughlan's last report in the briefcase on the back seat of her car. Mack Bresnahan would be here soon, getting off the Fortification Road bus and walking over to his house. Laughlan had followed him for three days and it had been the same routine every time.

He wouldn't see her – that was the idea. She'd see him, but

he wouldn't see her. She looked across at the house. A woman stood at the gate, looking back and forth. She looked thin and anxious and her clothes would have cost less than Helen's watch. That would be – what was her name? – Gwen.

'Daniel!'

There was an almost panicked look about her.

A little boy's head popped up from behind the next-door house's fence. He was about seven. He smiled.

'You come here now!' she yelled.

There was shrillness about her, almost desperate, as she waved to the boy to come. He seemed happy to stay where he was, watching the bus wheeze and rumble around the corner.

It stopped outside the little shelter at 144 Nevay Road and people got out. Three men in suits, carrying briefcases and newspapers, strode away. A woman hefted some bags of groceries into her arms and trudged off. A fourth man was in overalls. He was strongly built and unhurried. His face was strong. If it hadn't been for the reddening from too much alcohol he might have been good-looking. Too many years of taking orders had given him a hard, sour look. He saw the boy at the fence.

'Hey, you bloody get home.'

The boy instantly ran towards the woman at the gate, making sure he stayed out of his father's way. The man reached the gate.

'I thought I told you to keep them bloody kids on the property. Eh? Did I?'

Helen felt a stab of cold go through her. She'd seen that look on the woman's face before, on women who had been beaten up by the husbands. She stopped herself. Don't do anything. You are only here to look. You can get her help when this is over.

Bresnahan looked around as he shut the gate behind him, then stopped. He'd seen her. He didn't move, just kept looking at her. The woman and the child had gone inside but he stood looking straight at Helen.

She fumbled with the car keys. Get out of here. Get out now. Now. Now. Now! She sped away down the hill to Darlington Road. When it was safe to stop, she let the shock run through her body. Her fingers clenched and unclenched on the steering wheel. She'd been right. That was him all right. That man standing there looking at her was the one who had tried to murder her. How could he? How could he cold-bloodedly kill her sister, try to kill her, then simply stand there calmly.

It was obscene.

Inspector Alistair Henderson watched Jan Peters as she closed the door on the way out of his office. How the hell had Lashing done it? There had to be something more than her wanting to stay in Auckland to use her technical institute accounting training to work in fraud. Mind you, being stuck with Lashing wasn't exactly his idea of a good time. He shuddered to think what a twenty-three-year-old woman's view of it might be. But he'd done surveillance jobs with Lashing, and while he wasn't exactly a sparkling mint, there were guys with worse body odour problems.

Jan Peters closed the door behind her and almost sprinted away in case Henderson changed his mind and ordered her to go. God! That had been close.

Lashing's suggestion that as budgets were tight they could share a room had been the final straw. Just the possibility of seeing Lashing wandering around in his underpants and washing his socks in the kitchen sink had nearly made her gag. From that second on her entire being was devoted to freeing herself of that horror.

As she reached the fresh air and drew a deep, healing breath she tried not to think one disturbing thought. Had Lashing been trying to hide a smile when he'd told her about his laundry habits?

The pins in the map marked the places Helen had been since she'd arrived in Wellington: the Hollywood Motel, the government departments in Wellington and the Hutt Valley, and then up to Nevay Road.

'What was she doing out there?' Lashing asked.

Maher, a tall and melancholy-looking Wellington policeman, recited from his notebook as he looked carefully at what he had written.

'Dunno. She drives up there, straight from Births, Deaths and Marriages. Then boom. We have to ask ourselves whether she found something to get her Pied Pipering up to sunny Miramar.'

He pointed at the pin.

'We've a chap busy finding out what she discovered in the Hutt. In the meantime she gets up to Nevay Road, parks the car, stands around looking up and down the road. That's good. You don't get run over. You don't stuff up our road accident statistics. We get a chance to see what's going on.'

It was obvious Maher liked doing briefings, and Lashing was a fresh audience so he was getting all the flourishes that had long since bored the locals.

'She seems interested in a house with a Bresnahan family living there. The wife's nothing. He's a lad. There are a few Shit-for-Brains-of-the-Week awards, and he's had a couple of holidays – three years for robbery and then two for smacking a joker who pissed him off and was left with a very untidy, scarred look to him. Friend Bresnahan isn't someone you'd meet at the Wellington Club to while away a few hours over a sherry.'

Maher flicked the pages of his notebook. Lashing raised an eyebrow. Was there anything he wasn't being told?

'Shopping lists for the missus.'

Maher looked back at the notebook. Ah, yes.

'Anyway, she's there about two or three minutes, and it's back to the car and off. She gets down to Darlington Road and sits in the car for about twenty minutes. Just sits there. We aren't sure but we think she might have had a wee cry. Don't know for sure but that's what we think.'

'What about Bresnahan?'

'We don't think he had a little cry. His mum owned the house. Our boy did a few years in Australia – working on quarries, not doing time. Comes home. Gets married. He moves back in with mother, dragging wifey along with him. Then the kiddies arrive. That must have been a thrill for the wife, because until Mummy handed in her knife and fork and went off to look after all the other bad angels, she was – and this is the kindest way of putting it – a truly evil bitch.'

Lashing could feel the other detectives becoming restless.

Maher took no notice. 'He's a bit different to the rest of them. He must have decided on a complete new look. He changed his name to Bresnahan, probably because of his dear departed brother Vincent. Dunno why. A sense of shame at wrongdoing never worried this lot. Anyway, new name and all he just keeps on living with Mother, who kept the old name. I assume it pissed her off, but pissing people off never worried this lot. There's a story his daddy was a copper who topped himself. It's not a subject we're exactly keen on at the moment, not with the crime clearance figures down. The commissioner's bitching that the only crime we have managed to solve was the one no sensible policeman should have anything to do with, which is of course a whore' – Maher pronounced it 'hooer' – 'on her way home from a Cabinet Minister's place with a couple of marijuana cigarettes in her bag. He's having to go to cocktail parties at Parliament and getting the silent treatment from her customers, which turns out to be almost everyone. He isn't happy – meaning, of course, none of us are happy. There's Miramar Rangers failing to win the Chatham Cup, Athletic losing to Marist by 25–0, my horse running last in the Wellington Cup, a Labour government on the way and the price of beer and smokes going up. My missus wants more sex, even though I am having to work extra hours. I haven't spent a lot of time on *his* suicide in case it starts to look inspirational.'

Maher stopped for breath. Lashing couldn't believe it. He was like a bloody actor standing there waiting for a round of applause. Better not give him one, in case he wasn't. Maher was not the kind of man you wanted to be guessing wrong about.

'Yeah, someone did, about a year ago. We don't know who. The detailed records have gone. The person who did the search for our mysterious customer kicked it about six months ago. Electrocuted putting in a new bathroom. Exactly why you'd want electricity in a bathroom is beyond me, but who knows where style and fashion can lead us. There were no cheques we can chase either. They must have paid cash.'

Lashing said nothing. If that was Bresnahan checking on Jennifer and Helen then there was a whopping starting point.

He finds them: the bombs go out. They'd get him in. If he didn't talk they'd get the interview along to where he asks about a doctor because he's worried about all this blood he's pissing. He confesses and he gets his doctor. Confession signed. The doctor will see you now. It'd be case closed, cell door slams and detectives immediately report to beer stations.

It was a nice fantasy but that's all it was. Get Bresnahan in for something that big and he'd be wrapped in cotton wool. Lay a hand on him and it'd be straight into the ranks of the ex-police.

Maher waited until Lashing's attention was back with him.

'Now, cue the drum roll because we are close to the big finish. Laughlan, the guy who was working for her and who got dead, turns out to have been following the same pee trail across the carpet.'

The same what?

'Pee trail. Animals find their way through the bush . . .'

'Yeah, yeah, I know. I had a cat till it buggered off.'

'He was out at Lower Hutt doing the same stuff as her. Same names, same houses, same everything. Next day he gets karked. Now this lawyer's blundering around, and looking to make it a hat trick. Question? If everyone who gets seriously close to the Bresnahan house ends up an ex-person is this something that should interest us?'

'Yes, it is.'

chapter thirty

Wellington, 1947

Pat Feeney looked across the interview room's table into Bill West's broad, open face. He let the silence hang there. People often became uncomfortable and started talking just to fill in the void. It was a good theory and it got results. But it wasn't working now. West sat there, calm and unmoving, with the placid presence of a powerfully built man. Feeney wasn't hearing silence. He was hearing failure. Dragging West in here was its own way of broadcasting from the rooftops that the investigation into Marie's murder had turned up exactly nothing. No one was even close to being charged. Sure, they'd caught half a dozen burglars, a peeping tom and a crew stealing and repainting cars, but no murderer.

If he was honest, all he was doing, dragging West in here, was trying to show he was doing something. But what? Hoping to rekindle the team's fading enthusiasm? Probably. Was that ethical? Barely. Was it cruel to be shoving West's daughter's death in his face again? Definitely. So, did that make him a righteous investigator or some kind of torturer?

Anyone could see that under his silence West was flickering with nerves. Look at the arms, tightly and defiantly folded across his chest. What could Feeney learn from that? Most likely nothing. Being in a police station made anyone nervous. There were only two ways out. One was walking free. The other was being taken downstairs to be charged, fingerprinted and photographed and having the doors close to leave you alone in a bleak concrete cell.

Or was there something else worrying West? Was he

struggling to remember the lies he'd told last time he was here, or because he was innocent and no one believed him?

Finally Feeney spoke, mostly for the benefit of Jimmy Byrne, who was sitting there ready to take notes. 'It's nine-thirty on the morning of 14 July 1947. In the room are Inspector Pat Feeney, Detective James Byrne and Bill West. He is the father of Marie West, murder victim.' There was a pause while Byrne wrote all that down.

West had arrived without a lawyer. 'I haven't done anything. I don't need one.'

Did he know that a statement taken without a lawyer was harder to sell in a courtroom? Should Feeney attack from the start? Or go slowly and try to build a web to let him slowly ensnare himself in it? He'd tried both tactics and neither had worked. Everything ended the same way: West folded those strong forearms across his chest and announced that he was saying nothing. This was not going to be easy.

The police lawyers had been clear about this.

'Unless you've actually got something good on him be bloody careful. Keep drilling at him and it'll be howls of torture and Gestapo tactics. If the judge goes for that, and the chances are he will, you're in for a long hard road home.'

But then Feeney couldn't forget that West was number one on the suspect list by a long, long way, from the very moment Marie's body had turned up. His name had also been in play for the Frank Wilkins case. He was close to O'Malley. It wasn't hard to think Marie might have seen or heard something. Add in her tendency to yell first and think later and it was a lit fuse. Filthy Phil said it had been a strong male who had killed Marie. Look at those ham-hocks of forearms!

Jimmy Byrne glanced at Feeney. Was he going to do anything? This silence stuff wasn't doing any good. Feeney chilled him with a glance. Keep still. Getting restless would undermine the intensity Feeney was trying to build.

There seemed no point in waiting any longer.

'We need a bit of help, Bill. We're working hard. We're all over town. We're turning up all sorts of things and eventually we'll get a proper bite. We'll finally reel him in and that'll be that. I want to know what you think. Who do you think killed her? Who put a piece of string around her neck, and when she was dead played around with her panties to make it look like a sexo job? Who did that, Bill?'

West shook his head.

'Someone came up behind your little girl, Bill, your daughter, and wrapped that string around her neck. She'd have kicked and struggled, gasping and trying to live, but he was going to kill her no matter what she did. It was someone with big strong arms, too.'

Feeney made sure West saw him looking at his powerful forearms. He waited for a reply. Nothing. Bloody nothing. The guy had shut up shop.

'He knew her,' Feeney said. 'You want to know how we know that? Because he closed her eyes so she wasn't looking up at him any more. He'd done something terrible and he knew it. Those eyes were accusing him. Suddenly he was feeling empty and wrong and bad. He knew those eyes would always be there looking at him, following him, tormenting him, and he had to do something to stop it. What would it be like for someone who'd created that life, loved it and guided it into the world? What would it be like for someone like that?'

West bit his bottom lip. Feeney stopped. If he was feeling something, let it build and grow. Would he say something to make it stop? Was he fighting something? West's face was blank. Feeney could only guess at what was going on behind those eyes. Well, he didn't have much choice now but to keep going.

'After she was dead he reached under her dress, your daughter's dress, and pulled her panties down.' Feeney leaned forward. 'He was having a good look at her, Bill. She was out there in the open for him. We don't know what he did, whether he did something to himself. Christ, for all we know he gave himself a pull over her. That's your daughter, Bill. Who could have done that? Can you help us find the sick bastard who did that?'

Had the expression in West's eyes changed? Had the blinds slipped up, to show a room full of pain and suffering, and then slammed closed again? Perhaps yes. Perhaps no. Feeney couldn't be certain.

'He didn't have sex with her. He didn't have the balls for it. That was too much for him. So he just stood there looking at her. He never touched her clothes from the waist up, never looked at her breasts, nothing like that, just looked at the bottom half of . . . your daughter.'

West still didn't react. Feeney heard the warnings coming up from inside him. If he kept going like this West was not going to be the only one with his pride and dignity stripped. Imagine if he was innocent and he was planting this in his mind!

'You must have an idea, Bill. You gotta have some clue about who'd do that.'

Nothing.

Pat Feeney sensed Jimmy Byrne wincing. Hell. If it was getting too strong for him then it was really bad.

It had been half an hour now. West was staying dug deep behind the sandbags of 'I don't know' and 'Dunno'. Feeney could ask anything he liked. He could walk around the room, stand over West, invade his space or create a sense of distance. It all ended in the same place. West gave no hint of cracking.

Feeney slumped back. If they didn't stop now, or get something useful, he was worried he might lose his way, smash his fist down on something – the table or Bill West. Byrne had been careful to be close enough to grab Feeney if he did anything stupid. But Feeney wasn't Murray McCarthy. He didn't go around belting people just because he could. Feeney quietly looked from West to Jimmy Byrne's notes and back again. It was over. They'd got nothing. Feeney waved West to the door. 'Look, thank you for coming in. We may need to talk to you again but you can go now.'

West said nothing. He lifted his heavy body out of his chair and followed Byrne out the door. He lumbered out to the Waring Taylor Street exit, trudging out and up to Lambton Quay without glancing back.

When Byrne got back to the interview room Feeney was sitting with his forearms on the desk, staring at the wall.

'What's next, boss?'

Byrne wanted Feeney to have got something from this. It didn't have to be much – just a crumb to take them past the interview's failure. Feeney didn't look at him. He sat still, looking straight ahead and shaking his head.

'How could anyone sit there, looking at pictures of his dead daughter with her panties around her ankles, and not feel anything, not say anything, not do anything? How the fuck could he? No reaction, no bloody nothing! It's sick!'

Byrne kept quiet, letting Feeney rage. Let the storm pass.

'If he's shut down that much he's blotting it out. Is that some sort of grief reaction? Or did the bastard do it?' Feeney stopped, drawing in and letting out a long breath. 'I think he did it but I can't prove it. We just can't get ourselves over that last bridge. It's too long and too narrow and we're nowhere near it.'

Feeney got up. If all the prowling and trawling through Marie's life was going nowhere there was only one other road: a full-on attack on Wellington's bookmakers. He'd already given the green light to a couple of detectives who'd been heating things up. Now it needed more. More fear, more violence, more everything. Most of the people on the end of it were Catholics, but too bad. Yes, he'd be doing the Freemasons' work for them, but so be it. He could repair the damage later.

'Get Mahoney, Gregan and Farrell and get started, especially on any bookies with anything to do with O'Malley, which is the frigging lot of them, or anything to do with West. I mean get started. I want it full-on. Turnovers, tipping everything out, the lot, starting right now.'

Byrne nodded, moving to the door.

'I've had enough of all this bloody tiptoeing around it,' Feeney said. 'If a Catholic killed that girl then a Catholic swings for it. Go straight at it! Everyone gets the treatment. No excuses. Everyone! No one hides behind a crucifix or the bloody Virgin Mary. What's that thing they say about eggs – cooking them or whatever it is?'

'You can't make an omelette without breaking some eggs,' Byrne obliged.

'Yeah, that's it. Break the bastards. Go!'

Byrne was only too happy to get out of there. Feeney gathered up his papers, lifted himself out of his chair and turned to the door. He stopped. Compton was there.

'I couldn't help overhearing that. Good work. We have to get on top of these bookies once and for all. They've got too much money and they're too well organised.'

Just like you and the bloody Masons, Feeney thought but did not say.

'That's the story, Pat.' Compton was glowing at the prospect. 'Flush them out. Go in hard. All out's what we want. I'm proud of you. You know these types. Get after them!' Compton slapped him on the shoulder. It was all Feeney could do not to slap Compton's hand away.

'I'll approve whatever you need.'

The hard line of Compton's mouth flickered slightly. It might have been a smile or it could have been a predator's leer. Whatever it was, he was taking it with him as he strode away. Feeney looked after him. Approve anything he needed – hearing that from the tight-fisted Compton was something new. Was he desperate? Was there something he wanted buried? Still, if we go at the Catholics we can go at anyone, and we've got Compton funding it. Well, well, well. Perhaps there is a God.

Feeney stood up. His shoulders were straighter now. There was someone who was going to experience a full-on attack, and it wasn't a bookmaker.

chapter thirty-one

Wellington, 1972

It was two hours ago now but Helen was still struggling with the idea that Mack Bresnahan could just stand there looking at her with the casual disinterest he'd show a meter reader. He had to have known who she was. She'd grown up there. He'd tried to kill her. He must know! But he hadn't done anything; there'd just been this bored indifference. It felt frightening. That man had spent weeks and months tracking her and Jennifer down and made the bombs. Hours of slow and careful work had gone into them. Then, nothing!

The television in the Hollywood Motel unit was blaring about Norman Kirk, Jack Marshall and Keith Holyoake and the election later in the year. She had more important things to think about. Why had she gone anywhere near the man's house anyway? Was it straight-out curiosity? Was something in her saying she'd had enough of the fear and the tension and decided to present herself as a neatly wrapped victim just so it could be over? Did she *want* the police to break the case open so it would all come out? She was forty-one. She'd still have good years ahead when she came out of prison.

Stop it!

She wouldn't be telling the police anything. And she'd seen Bresnahan's face, which made him human, more or less. She'd seen what she was dealing with. She thought about Des Laughlan. Had he got too close to Bresnahan, perhaps face to face? Now he was dead.

She knew Bresnahan was her man. It was the right family, name change or no, and he was the right age. She knew where he lived and worked. But that was not enough. She needed more. What did he do on the weekend? What did he do at home? Did he love, or like, or hate his wife and children? She had to find a weakness so she could go through it straight at him. He'd be thinking the same now he'd sniffed the air and smelled danger. And no matter what else she did, she should never forget the police were out there somewhere, and they weren't stupid.

She drew a line down the middle of a piece of paper. On one side she wrote positives, on the other negatives. Halfway down the page she wrote plan. She wrote for about ten minutes, then crunched the paper up and threw it away. The she had second thoughts. What was she thinking? If someone found that it wouldn't be paper. It'd be evidence. She picked it up and smoothed it away to put in her bag. She'd have to find somewhere safe to get rid of it, and the pieces of paper under it, in case it ended up in a police laboratory with someone carefully going over it for pencil impressions. That sounded paranoid, but paranoia might be the only way to steer herself through this mess.

She walked out of the motel and across to her car. She drove down to the Basin Reserve, and up through the Mt Victoria tunnel. It didn't take long to get back out to Miramar. As she drove up Nevay Road and the little rise past Napier Street she realised she was tired. Surely this was a mistake. Stop. Was she thinking clearly? Was she too loaded down with planning, thinking, relentless pushing to go back over and over every possibility? She might not be able to react quickly enough.

She stopped near the corner of Nevay and Fortification roads.

Still, she needed to know the territory exactly. She had to be sure she knew exactly where everything was – each house, the bus stop, the way the roads turned, everything. She had half a plan now, and it would depend utterly on having everything right. She couldn't risk a surprise if things began moving quickly.

Oh God Almighty! She'd just made a terrible mistake. She had been here yesterday at the exact same time, and she'd parked out in the open. Why hadn't she gone around the corner and walked back?

Mack Bresnahan was getting off the bus and was looking straight at her. Their gazes locked until Helen forced herself to look away. But this time he reacted. She could feel his hard anger coming across the road in high-voltage waves. Christ, he was coming over. No, he was not. He was going into his house. He'd stopped at the gate and was looking back at her.

Oh God, she was so stupid! She just couldn't help coming back for another look. Get out of here. Get out of here!

She smashed the car into gear and got it back down the hill. She drove along Darlington Road and finally stopped near the Miramar Fire Station, just up the road from the Gas Works and the Miramar Cutting. She let her head fall forward.

Why? Why had she done it? She could have gone up there anytime – while he was at work. What in the name of everything had possessed her to go anywhere near that wretched man? Did she want him to kill her? Is that what she wanted?

She sat in the car hitting the steering wheel, trying to let the great lump of fright and fear push free of her. She had failed: utterly, totally and miserably.

She had a trained, logical mind. Why wasn't she using it? Des Laughlan knew his way through this world and his body had been dumped in the bushes. What would happen to you?

Where was she going to go – back to the miserable and lonely Hollywood Motel? She had to think this through. All right. She'd just done something stupid. He knew she wasn't going away. He couldn't pick and choose now. He couldn't sit in a shed somewhere slowly and carefully making his bomb. He had to act. Neither of them could run – she'd known that from the moment the package arrived at her office. Her office! There was a life gone forever.

She heard it before she saw anything.

Smash!

The sound was fast, hard, frightening and pieces of glass flew at her. Someone was attacking her car! A man was at the back of it, with something in his hand. He lifted it and smashed it down on the car's roof, then slammed it through a side window.

It was Bresnahan. His face was still. His eyes were lit like fires. Insane.

'Christ! Stop it!'

She had one hand over her head, trying to protect it from the flying glass and from the next blow. She rammed the car into gear and hopped and jerked forward. He was still attacking the car. Move! Get moving! Get out of here!

She shot through the Miramar Cutting and out around Evans Bay. Wasn't that where they had pulled a bookmaker out of the water, full of bullets, not long before her own horror? She kept driving, past Kilbirnie and over the hill to Newtown. Finally, somewhere, she stopped.

She sagged, eyes closed, hands resting lightly at the top of the battered car's steering wheel. The streams of excitement and terror were slowly ceasing the chase through her veins and arteries. Her heart thumped and jumped in her chest, and it felt as if there was a steel rope around her forehead, tightening and squeezing the life out of her. She could feel the back of her blouse heavy with sweat and fear.

She had to attack. It was too late for anything else.

Mack Bresnahan did what he always did when he arrived home from work. He dropped his Gladstone bag inside the front door and used his heel to kick it shut behind him. His wife had asked him not to do that because it gave the children a fright, but he ignored her. This was his house. Who brought in the money that kept them? He did, and if he had to hit her again, to make sure she understood, then that's what he'd do.

He clumped through to the kitchen, and stopped. His wife and the brats looked up at him. Never mind them. It was who was sitting at the other end of the table that stopped him.

Helen met his gaze. From the moment she'd been invited into the house she'd known this was the moment to set the tone. She mustn't even hint at being scared. This guy could smell fear and that'd take him straight through his surprise. Just being here would be enough to throw him off centre. It might even panic him. He wouldn't notice what she was looking for.

Gwen Bresnahan chirped across the silence, at the same time reaching across to gently push one of the children's hands away from the blood-red jelly. 'Mack, this is Helen.'

Helen could see his eyes narrow slightly, his mind flicking across all the questions and choices.

The gaze between Helen and Bresnahan chainsawed straight through Gwen's anxious joviality.

Bresnahan stopped in front of his wife. She swallowed and seemed to shrink away from him. Helen watched. If she wasn't here he'd hit her for letting her through the door.

What had she done? She knew why she was there, but what had she done to her?

'Helen used to live over the road, in the house up behind the bus stop,' Gwen said. 'She's here from Auckland and she's taken the chance to come up here and have a little look around.' Gwen added, as she almost always did, a desperate-sounding 'Isn't that nice?'

Bresnahan cut across her. 'Didn't I tell you about people coming here that I don't know?'

Gwen was close to panic.

'Isn't that nice?' she said again.

'No.'

He looked around the kitchen.

'Are you staying long?'

'Now, Mack, that's not the way to be talking to our guest!'

A hard glance stopped her. Gwen swallowed back whatever she had been about to say and began fussing with the children and the food. Helen could see that Gwen knew trouble and the atmosphere it came in. She was doing what she'd always done, retreating the way she always did. She'd protect the children, make sure she was the one getting hit and give the little ones time to flee or to hide. Her fear sheeted across the room. The tiniest flick of a smile ran across Bresnahan's mouth. Helen held back a shudder. The bastard was the Lord again. But Helen was here. How was he going to beat her with a witness around? Helen watched his indecision. Good.

'Look, I don't want to interrupt your dinner,' Helen said. She'd got what she came for. It was time to get out. Gwen dropped a hand on Helen's forearm, much more firmly than necessary. If a grip could beg, this one was saying, 'Stay, don't leave us.'

'You are welcome to stay with us. It's all right.' Gwen's insistence was close to pleading.

Helen couldn't miss the agony behind it. Gwen looked around at the children. 'You'd like our visitor to stay, wouldn't you?'

The little faces nodded. They couldn't care less. They were intent on the dinner. Helen could see Bresnahan regrouping. Witness or not, he was gaining confidence. He might try something.

Gwen's fluttering anxiety, her dedication to the children and her endless hunting for a way through her brutal existence were close to heartbreaking. What would happen to her if Helen killed their provider? Bresnahan might be a bastard but there must once have been love of some sort to pull them down the aisle and carry them this far.

She had to get out. She heard herself saying, 'It was wonderful being in one of the houses from the old times. I've loved it. Thank you for being so nice to me, but I have to go. I really do.'

She was on her feet and heading for the door. Bresnahan stood his ground as she approached and passed him. His eyes still showed doubt but his mouth was ripped in an ugly sneer. Helen kept telling herself to be strong. Send him a message that he's in a war.

As she passed close to him she felt something different. The mix of danger and Bresnahan's stolid male presence fired a blip of a sexual charge through her. Where had that come from? Bresnahan's eyebrows twitched. Had he felt it too? Slowly he moved to allow her to squeeze past, but made sure he brushed against her. Then she was past him and opening the front door.

She ran to her car, struggled with the key and sped down Nevay Road towards Totara Road. She kept going until she was off the hill. This time she was not stopping, speeding away from Miramar until she was around the harbour and into Oriental Bay. The further away she got from Nevay Road the better she felt. She had what she wanted, and she was ready to move.

chapter thirty-two

Wellington, 1947

It had taken Murray McCarthy a lot longer than he'd expected to find the house in Ararua Road. He didn't know Karori all that well and he'd taken a couple of wrong turns. Who wouldn't? He wasn't exactly in the best state to be looking for houses in flash suburbs. It hadn't helped that he'd seen a beat copper back there and that made him lose time going through the back streets. Then once he'd got up here he had to sit watching the house. It was in darkness and he couldn't risk knocking on the wrong door. The rich and the middle class didn't like people going around knocking on their doors late at night. They'd be on to the police in a second.

It was all right now. He'd just seen people moving around inside the place, including the woman who'd been out at Weir's. She'd answered the door, wearing the same no-nonsense blouse, only now it was open so far he could see almost everything.

'Mr McCarthy,' she smiled. 'I'm Moira. Why don't you come on in?'

Her words might have welcomed him but she wasn't moving. 'Not official, is it?' He shook his head and she stood aside.

That had been about ten minutes ago. Now he was sitting at the back of this large, elegant room working his way through a glass of beer while others around him sipped wine or puffed on reefers. Moira stood in front of everyone.

'Well, well, it's just wonderful you're all here, in Karori, in the middle of the night. All the good church-going people are asleep and it's time for all the wicked devils to come out and play!'

Moira's tongue rolled across her lips when she spoke. McCarthy liked that. It caused a stirring in his pants. She was a good public speaker. He peered through the smoke. Hang on – he'd heard her before. Where was it? He had another mouthful of beer and fought back a burp. Yeah, that's right, the Catholic church, out in Miramar Avenue at an appeal to help the poor little piccaninnies in Africa. She was representing the Anglicans or someone.

Well, there wasn't much church about this, not sitting here watching the woman lying next to him running her hand up and down the pants of the guy beside her. In between she paused to inhale a reefer. Both of them had a vacant, lost look on their faces. McCarthy wouldn't have minded being on the end of that hand. He wasn't as keen on sharing the reefer, not with her having an open sore on her lip. But then, why worry about his health now? They'd be finding the poof's body down by the wharf sheds and it wouldn't take too long to trace it back to him. What difference did it make if he caught something now?

Moira was saying, 'We've got a special, special treat, a wonderful, wicked little show for us all to enjoy.' McCarthy couldn't help thinking she sounded as if she was handing out presents to the Cubs and Brownies. Actually, hadn't she had something to do with Brownies? Or was it the Girl Guides? It was something wholesome and healthy.

'Jane and Wendy have volunteered. Aren't they wonderful?' Moira smiled and pointed at the two women, leading a round of applause for them. They were climbing up out of the people in front of McCarthy. They weren't sisters, at least McCarthy didn't think so, but they looked alike: tall, brunette, slim and both of them looking as if they had years of sports or dance behind them. They picked their way to the front with an easy, relaxed athleticism.

Someone put on some jazz and it eased a slow melancholy saxophone solo out over the room. The main light flicked off and some table lamps went out too, leaving just enough light in the dim, smoky atmosphere. The woman beside him had her hand in the man's pants and was taking it out now. With a dazed, slow movement he was licking himself off her hand. Up at the front Jane and Wendy faced each other and began swaying in time to the music. Moira stood behind Wendy, her hands on the younger woman's hips. Wendy let her hands roll up above her head, letting Moira gently run her hands up to each of her breasts. Then she dropped her own hands on top of Moira's and guided them down to her nipples for Moira to hold between thumb and forefinger, gently turning Wendy around so the audience could see what she was doing. Jane was dancing gracefully to the other side of the room, and without missing a beat she reached up under her dress and whisked out her panties, dropping them near the expensive-looking drapes.

McCarthy wasn't bothered about his beer now. He didn't need a reefer either. The air was so thick with marijuana smoke all he needed do was breathe in and let himself float into this strange, and getting stranger, world.

Jane danced her way back to Wendy and Moira until Wendy was sandwiched between them. Moira stepped back, letting her hands drop from Wendy's breasts and down her stomach to reach around and stroke gently between her legs. Jane leaned forward and kissed Wendy on the mouth, moving her head back so everyone could see their tongues touching and duelling, their heads moving back and forth. Jane began pulling Wendy's blouse out from her skirt, undoing its buttons and pulling it back over her shoulders. Wendy's back arched as she swayed in time to the music. Moira stepped back into the darkness behind them, leaving Jane holding her hands in the air and Wendy running her hands up and down her body.

There was a sudden moment of silence. Moira was backing in to be near Jane and Wendy again. McCarthy could see why the sudden quiet. She was dancing with a black man, not tall but powerful and with thick, strong arms. He had one arm around Moira's waist; the other was holding a reefer up to his mouth. If McCarthy's mouth was half open, before it was wide open now. Where had they found the black guy? McCarthy had never seen one before. The man lifted Moira's dress and his hand was under it, rubbing her. Even from this distance McCarthy could see her eyes softening with pleasure. Her hips rolled back and forth in time with his hand's pushing at and releasing her. No one in the audience moved.

McCarthy reached down and eased his underpants to let his cock stand. Beside him the man and woman had stopped and were watching the show.

Jane and Wendy, both half undressed now, were breaking apart and circling Moira, stripping her clothes with quick nimble flicks. In just a few seconds her blouse was open and her skirt was falling to the floor. As Moira had stroked Wendy's breasts, now Wendy was doing the same thing for Moira. Jane was behind the black man, running her hands down his chest to his belt, loosening it and reaching down to pull his trousers open. She hooked her thumbs into his white underpants and pushed them to the floor, letting him step neatly out of them. Wendy pulled Moira's skirt away from her and rubbed her hands down Moira's back. Now it was Moira's turn to be in the middle, with both the man's and the women's hands exploring her body. Her panties were gone. She was naked now, her dark patch contrasting with the greying hair on her head. Then she dropped to her knees in front of the black man, her mouth going around him, taking him in. Her head pushed back and forth against him. Behind him, Jane was pushing his legs apart. Wendy was kissing him, open and full-lipped, her long legs on either side of Moira, still with her eyes closed, sucking on the man.

Someone turned the music up.

Now Wendy had Moira by the shoulders and was pulling her away from the man's cock, back down on the floor, gently pushing her legs apart. Jane was helping the black man to his knees in front of Moira, rubbing his back and kissing his ears. The strong muscles in his arms moved as he worked himself around until he was on top of Moira. She slipped a hand down between them to help him into her. Her knees rose to form triangles, the soles of her feet on the carpet. His taut buttocks rose and fell as he thrust into her. McCarthy could see her eyes opening and closing with the pleasure of having him.

A man got up from the audience, fumbling with his trousers. He wanted to join in, but Jane pushed him back. Wendy pointed at him – stay there or he'd be thrown out. Everyone else in the room quietly clapped in time to the music and to the black man's heaving.

Moira's face was softly blank. Her hair drooped with perspiration. Her back arched and dropped as the man worked. Her mouth opened and her tongue rolled across her lips as she savoured the pleasure. Jane and Wendy stood beside them, kissing. Now they were stripping each other. When they were down to their panties they stopped and looked out over the audience clapping in time to the black man as he rose and fell into Moira.

McCarthy was hypnotised by Moira's heaving and moaning and the strength of the black man's thrusting. It felt like his eyes were forcing themselves out of his head as he strained to watch. Moira was rising with a surge of pleasure. McCarthy looked up. The two nearly naked women were working their way through the crowd, stepping over everyone, pausing to let male, and a couple of female, hands touch and slide across their bodies. Heads were turning. Where were they going? Who had they chosen? McCarthy wasn't watching them. He was trapped in fascination at Moira and the black man. Moira's legs tensed. He could see the muscles go hard down her lower legs, then soften and relax. Now the man was rolling off her, a trail of white seed running down his blackness.

What the hell was this? Jane and Wendy were coming straight at McCarthy.

Murray McCarthy could not decide if he was excited or terrified. The two women, their breasts close to his face, reached down. Each of them took one of his hands.

Christ Almighty, what the hell was next?

Yes, he had a hard-on, but he wasn't going to say it out loud. After tonight, with his scrambling around the Gas Works, being out at Weir's place, trying to decide if he was going to swim out into Wellington Harbour, and then killing the queer, he'd had enough. They wanted to screw the black bloke and give each other a seeing too, then fine. Getting him up out of the crowd for Christ knows what was a hell of a lot different. But he could feel hands behind him shoving him to his feet. Some of them were on his arse. He tensed. They'd better be careful about that. If any of these wispy-bearded creeps thought they were going to give him a touching up they had a few things coming – like a boot in the balls.

His legs felt strange and almost rubbery under him. Jane turned his chin around to face hers. She kissed him, letting his tongue fall deep into her mouth. Wendy ran her hand up and down the front of his pants. This warmth was coming up from his sex. Any idea of running away was gone. He let himself be led up to the front.

Moira and the black man were standing at the side of the room with sheets around themselves. McCarthy could easily see the outlines of her breasts and his cock under them. He'd heard about black guys, about how they lugged around things that banged against the insides of their knees.

Jane's hands were inside his shirt and running up and down his chest. He could feel his breathing getting faster and the blood surging through him. Wendy was behind him, easing his shirt back over his shoulders. Jane reached up and kissed him again, letting his tongue do whatever it liked.

Christ, he liked this!

The audience was slipping out of sight somewhere into the foggy mist. He felt alone with these two women rubbing themselves up against him, and God, he liked it. Wendy slipped his singlet back over his head. Jane knelt in front of him, pulling his belt buckle open, and he could feel her fingers against his straining cock as she undid his trouser buttons. She lifted his feet, one after the other, so he could step free of his pants. She had her hands in the waistband of his jocks, and was slipping them off too. He could feel himself, hard as hell, spring free as his underpants followed his pants down over his shoes and off to the side somewhere.

A tiny voice inside him made him glance over to make sure he knew where his clothes had ended up. Now Jane had him in her mouth and was licking and sucking at him. He let the waves of soft pleasure run up through him, holding her hair in his hands, guiding her up and down on him.

Behind him, Wendy had her breasts against his back and was

sliding her hands through his chest hair and up across his face. If this kept going he was going to faint, right here in front of the lot of them. It felt odd, being buck bloody naked. He'd have to be careful, too – the way this Jane was going down there, he'd be spraying his load all over the place. Not that it mattered, with the pleasure making his head swim.

Then the two women stepped back from him. Suddenly he was alone and naked in front of them all. In the distance he could see someone gathering up his clothes and taking them to the door. That was bad. Suddenly, McCarthy was frightened.

He looked around at Moira. She was smiling at him. The bloody bitch. They'd set this up. He should have guessed by her expression back at Weir's when she'd invited him here.

A soft male voice was behind him. 'Remember us, Mr McCarthy?' There were three men there. Poofs. Eyeing him up and down. He looked at them. 'You were very rough with us. Perhaps we should be rough with you?'

McCarthy gulped. One of them was holding a heavy belt. He lifted it and cracked it across McCarthy's shoulder, who took off. As he sprinted for the door he felt hands grabbing at him. Almost everyone was smacking at his backside. Behind him the man with the belt was whooping, 'Let's see your little red bottom!' and thrashing at McCarthy with it. It hurt.

Run. Get out of here. Please, God, let me escape.

chapter thirty-three

Wellington, 1947

All throughout his career Feeney had been careful to teach, and occasionally preach, that violence was the refuge of the unimaginative, debased and animalistic. Police should never use it. Besides, if the court found out, and most of the time it did, anything you'd got through violent means might as well hop into the grave and lie down because it was already dead.

Well, times had changed. He was the man who had just turned the police loose on the bookmakers. Give us anything we need to know – or else. That was bad enough. And right now he was using Corbett Wilson's tie to squash the lawyer's face down on his desk. This was wrong. He knew it and he should be ashamed. The problem was, it was also dark and guilty fun.

He knew Wilson wouldn't be going anywhere near a court, and wouldn't even think about an official complaint. He'd endure it until Feeney either stopped or he got what he wanted. He'd have his revenge later.

Feeney had expected better from Wilson than these funny little chicken squeals. Where was the resistance, the threats, the fight, the offer of a bribe? Dear, oh dear, oh dear. It was poor. And this from a lawyer who promoted himself as the toughest of the tough.

Feeney's mouth was close to Wilson's ear. 'Now, we are all agreed that I am common as shit and that I have no education or breeding or understanding of the ways power works in Parliament. But what I do have is you by the head. If I want, I can have you by the balls. Would you like a quick little touch-up?'

The lawyer's head wriggled. Feeney assumed that was a no.

Feeney didn't move his face, even though Wilson was trying to get away. 'That is sensible. I would not be gentle. You'd be in terrible pain. You'd be distressed and upset,' he whispered. Corbett's head moved in a tiny gesture of agreement.

Feeney continued. 'You're getting the idea. You know the law? Good. I know a bloody common law. Lawyers understand that, don't they?'

Wilson's head moved.

Feeney knew what was going to happen when he got to the lawyer's office and deliberately hadn't cleaned his teeth. That'd add to the revulsion and confusion. Ah ha! At last! The lawyer's eyes were flashing rage. So there was a bit of spirit in the man?

'Corbett, I have a man visiting your colleague, Mr Johnston,' Feeney said. 'He is there now. No, you can't ring him to check. He is asking Mr Johnston to tell him whatever it is you have hidden away. If it does not match whatever you are about to give me, there will be a long look at some land deals in the Hutt Valley. There will also be, and this is quite separate, the statement of a fifteen-year-old girl living in Island Bay. He will not want either of these matters to proceed. I suspect Mr Johnston will provide very precise details.'

Wilson nodded.

'Now, if whatever you give me falls short in any way, Mr Johnston is in deep shit. If Mr Johnston has anything on you he will get a chance to trade his way out – him for you. What you need to decide is whether Mr Johnston has anything on you that he might consider tradeable.' Wilson's head moved in what looked like agreement. Feeney kept silent. Make him doubly and triply nervous.

'I'll prosecute whichever one of you I end up with, and not give it a moment's thought.'

He released his grip a little.

'Inspector Feeney,' Wilson snivelled. 'There is something. It . . . ah . . . could be significant in the . . . er . . . wrong hands.'

'Now we are getting somewhere. I'm the wrong hands. Get it!'

Feeney let him up. Wilson rubbed his neck as he crossed to a small sideboard and eased it aside. He pushed some carpet out of the way and knelt over a safe.

'I thought your safe was in the outer office.'

'There are things that need to be kept . . . safer.'

Wilson reached in and found a brown envelope. He stood up and gave it to Feeney. Then he flopped down behind his desk, still massaging his neck.

'Welcome to the world, Inspector Feeney. You've got what you want and it's going to force you into a few decisions. The very best of fucking luck to you.'

He waved his hands in a gesture of farewell to the envelope.

'Are there copies of this?' Feeney asked.

'Of course there are copies,' Wilson snapped back.

'I want them too.'

Wilson smiled.

'You'll be travelling then – to Melbourne and the Vatican City. That's where the copies are. Go and get them. Here's a bit of free advice. Be prepared for a lot of sitting around and waiting.'

Wilson's eyes were dark and angry. 'You know about Oscar Wilde, don't you, Pat? He said there are two ways to destroy a man. One is to keep him from getting what he wants. The other is to give it to him. Well, Pat, you've got what you want, and good luck to you.'

His smile was a cold knife slash.

'Oh, Inspector, trust in the Lord, and be trusting in something else. You can destroy Johnston. Any of us could. But will you? If he goes, others go. Don't forget, people are watching – more of us than you know. Everyone gets a turn in this game, and you've just had yours.'

Feeney stopped. Something was surging up in him: the temptation to smash a fist straight into that smug face. He bit it back. It was time to be on his way. Corbett Wilson's words were chilling in their truth. From this moment on he couldn't afford to get it wrong or the Furies would come for him, with Wilson leading them.

On the way out he closed the door a little too hard behind

him. He glanced into the envelope. He'd been right. It looked like the ledgers of the late John Augustine O'Malley.

Feeney had spent four long hours slogging through O'Malley's lists and he was dog-tired. His eyes hurt and he'd given up trying to rub the soreness from his neck. Everything in him howled for bed and sleep. But he couldn't just wander off and leave O'Malley's lists. They'd hypnotised him, taunting him into a world circling around and past him. When he'd marched into Wilson's office he'd been an avenging angel, a righteous policeman on the hunt for wicked criminals. Now he felt like a small, innocent child in the sight of a cynical, worldly wise and all-knowing Lord.

O'Malley's grip had reached right across Wellington. Money and influence slopped and slid back and forth between him and the city's publicans, lawyers, MPs, city council inspectors and clerks, and into the police. At least six policemen were involved. O'Malley didn't need more. He had the ear of the ones who decided which gambling investigations went ahead and which were left to die on the vine. He would know which pubs were to be targeted. A 'cleanskin' would be running the book when the police arrived. As first offenders they'd get a small fine, and O'Malley would pay it. The police had their conviction, the public were reassured that the war on gambling went relentlessly onwards. Everyone was happy.

And Murray McCarthy was in the middle of it. The big policeman was the contact man, who removed any obstacles between O'Malley and whatever he wanted or needed. That had lasted until two coppers from Christchurch who couldn't care less about his power and his money had walked in at one in the morning, beaten O'Malley and searched his office, probably for these same records. Since O'Malley could identify them, he'd got a belt on the jaw and had gone out the window. They hadn't wanted to waste a lot of time making it complicated. They needed their sleep so they would be bright and fresh to help in the hunt for Marie West's murderer.

Wilson had been right. The moment Feeney had taken the ledgers and lists, he'd thrust his hand into the fire. Would it have been better not to know? Probably. But he did know now.

Not that it was necessarily all bad news. O'Malley had not discriminated on the grounds of faith. He'd given money to some who famously hated Catholics. Feeney went cold at seeing their names. They'd pay for that. God, they would pay.

His guess was that some had refused O'Malley. Then he'd quietly probed and felt his way along their family's faultline until he found what he wanted: a problem with booze or infidelity, a brother with a failing business, money hidden from the Inland Revenue Department. From then on they ceased to refuse him. Others hoped gambling would free them from Wellington's boredom. Need a loan to keep playing? No problem. Eventually the conversation turned to repayment. Sex was an acceptable coin of the realm. A woman in debt would be sent to service a man, or men, and at least once, another woman. The value of each act was recorded here. Men did the same. Their names were here too.

What surprised Feeney was how little violence had been required. But when someone was hurt, it was vicious, cruel and often deadly. Only one or two people a year needed to be savaged to keep the light flashing out through the dark that O'Malley was not to be crossed or denied. Frank Wilkins's smashed body would have served as a warning to others.

He offered a quick little prayer at Jimmy Byrne's name not being there, although two other detectives on the West case were. Jimmy's next job was a look through their lives.

This could get very nasty – there would be people who would want it stopped, including the two Christchurch coppers. There were limits to how much a baton and a pair of handcuffs would protect the investigators. He'd get Jimmy a gun, and one for himself. Before he set Jimmy loose he'd be offered a little advice of his own, and it wouldn't be from lawyers, whether Catholic or from any other church or God.

There was someone better.

chapter thirty-four

Wellington, 1972

Fred Lashing would have loved to give Maher a round of applause for his latest briefing but he didn't dare. That would not be cool. This Maher guy enjoyed the work, was good at it and said what he thought. He was also much faster with words than Lashing: he seemed to always have the right one aimed, loaded and ready to fire. Trouble was, Maher was using all that to march things in a direction Lashing didn't like.

'So, she stops her car outside the Miramar Fire Station to have a little break in the long dark journey back to Newtown or God knows where. And what's this? Up rolls Bresnahan in his little Austin. He outs with a tyre lever and starts smashing her car windows. If he'd kept going and made a start on her we'd have had to jump in and stop it. That would have been the end of it. Surveillance over. Case in the rubbish tin. Resources wasted. Children back to the classroom. There would have been unhappiness all throughout the Magic Kingdom.'

Maher looked around. No one said anything.

'So do we have the world's dumbest lawyer? That's not an easy title to win. She decides getting her – or rather the rental car company's – car trashed is not a strong enough message. She pays to get the windows fixed herself. Then the tall but stupid one marches up and knocks on the bastard's front door, sits at his frigging table like Lady Muck, and drinks tea with her little finger stuck out.'

Lashing had nothing to say. Better not say anything anyway. Maher did not seem to be noticing him at all.

'So, we've got poor Arthur here, clambering around peeking

through their windows, reminding himself he's an on-duty policeman heroically doing his bit to keep the peace in the community and not some seedy peeping tom. Now, Arthur, you may well be a wanker, but that isn't germane to the, pardon the pun, work at hand. However, moving on, Arthur does tell us he did find it in himself to get past the clothesline without stealing a pair of Bresnahan's Y-front jocks, the ones with the skid marks. For this, Arthur, we thank you.'

One of the policemen nodded his gratitude.

'It wasn't a compliment,' Maher said.

'What did he see?' Lashing asked.

'Not much, by all accounts. Now, if she was on the floor with five axes sticking out of her head that would have been great. Not for her, of course, because she would be dead, but it would give us a proper crime.'

Lashing had been waiting for this. Maher was scaling down and moving on. Helen was being shoved on the backburner.

'Let's look at it,' Lashing protested.

Maher shrugged. 'Fine, let's look at it. She arrives in the parish. She legs it around to Births, Deaths and Marriages and traces Bresnahan's family tree. She goes up there to Nevay Road and hangs around. She knocks on his door. She buggers off. Then he smacks her car around, which might or might not be him doing a Greta Garbo "I vant to be alone!" She's not happy with that. She gets the motor patched up and goes for a cup of tea with him. The only thing keeping us even remotely interested is that the private detective who lately became deceased was doing the exact same search.'

'Surely that's enough to keep going!' Lashing protested.

'It is, but not at this level. Ye gods, we don't have this many people on an actual, genuine murder.'

Maher's tone softened slightly, a small deference to Lashing's disappointment. 'Until something, anything, comes up beyond having two people checking out the family history of a council labourer . . . that's more or less it.'

'I want to stay on it.'

'Fine,' said Maher. 'You keep the car and use the records and the station, but that's it. We're under the gun to provide some staff for another investigation – into the Crewe murders in bloody Pukekawa, more or less your territory.'

That stung. The best and the brightest were being pulled into the Crewe case and Lashing wasn't one of them. So far as anyone in Auckland was concerned he was off the books. Charming. Well, that still left Helen Murphy. He'd come this far and he would see it out.

He wanted to stay near her.

Wellington's Public Library wasn't doing what libraries are supposed to do. Helen had hoped it would offer a bit of quiet, a refuge, and let the world slip away for a while. Instead, its quiet was closing tighter and tighter on her. The seething and churning would not stop.

She'd told Bresnahan she could reach right to the heart of his life, in the same way he'd done to both Jennifer and her. So what? Bresnahan was an animal before, and he was still one now. Would making him angry and defensive push him into making a mistake? She didn't honestly know.

She'd been able to have a good look at the house and the property it was built on. Had it been worth it? Had she made things better or worse?

A book was open on the library table in front of her. This time it was something non-technical, which was unusual for her. It was a novel about Georgian England. Helen had barely looked at the words as she'd turned the pages. A woman had gone to live at a castle to marry someone, or not, she'd been ravished or she hadn't, or she'd ravished someone else. Someone had been ravished. A man was falling in love with her, or he wasn't. Helen didn't care.

Christ!

The lights were being flicked on and off. The place was going to close. A librarian moved quietly through the desks and tables towards her, picking up books as she went.

'Are you going to borrow this one?' she said.

Helen forced a half smile on her face and shook her head.

'We're closing shortly – about another ten minutes.'

The librarian continued on her way, picking up the books left by the people forced out to whatever they called home. Helen walked out to stand in the library's foyer, looking out across to Wakefield Street. It was dark. There was a bright full moon but it was behind some cloud. For the moment it was a perfect night for someone to strike at her. Her car was just over there. She had the key in her hand. Was there a bomb in it? How would she know? Where did you look for a car bomb?

She put the key in the door and got in.

So far so good. She was in the car. But was she safe? Bombs didn't go off when you got in the car; they went off when you turned on the ignition. What was she going to do? She didn't know where to go, but she couldn't stay here either.

Her heart was a bass drum blasting along at double time. If it kept going like this it'd be blasting out through her ribs. Bresnahan wouldn't have to do anything. She'd give herself a heart attack and do the job for him. Breathe in and out. Slowly. Try to get control.

Her hand was shaking too much to put the key in the ignition.

Lashing had no idea where Helen was. He knew about Bresnahan, though. He was in his little car, chugging and smoking his way down Adelaide Road to the Basin Reserve and the Mt Victoria tunnel. Lashing's guess was that he'd turn right and be back to that dark little shithole of a house up on Nevay Road. That wasn't the problem. It was where he had been. He must have waltzed past Lashing and into the Hollywood Motel while he was dozing in his car over on the other side of the road. Lashing had been lucky to see him as he came out.

Lashing started the police car to follow. Then he turned it off. He thought about it. Bresnahan would be going home; Helen was the wild card.

He didn't know if Bresnahan had come here for something else. The Hollywood Motel was the sort of dump where he could get a leg over a prostitute. Pig's bloody ear! Bresnahan wasn't the sort who'd pay for it – he'd just take it. Besides, by the time he got himself drunk most nights, and reluctantly threw what money was left to the family, he couldn't afford it.

He'd been in Helen's room.

Christ, if he'd missed Bresnahan he might have missed Helen too. Lashing's heart was hitting boundaries all around the inside of his chest. Had Bresnahan been in there finishing the job? Was she chopped up or full of bullets? He hadn't heard anything, but that didn't mean a thing. There were silencers and pillows. He got out of the car and began running across the road.

If he didn't see any sign of life in her unit he'd break in. Still, and he felt slightly sick for even thinking of it, he wouldn't mind a quick look at her bed sheets. He flicked a glance up to the sky. His dad! He'd never escape him sending messages like that down to his boy.

He quietly edged himself into the motel entrance. There was no one in the office. Good. Once past those windows he could go all the way along to the end of the block without being seen. He wasn't too worried about the guests. Life at the Hollywood Motel ran by just two commandments: 'Thou shalt pay in cash for thy room and not even consider offering a cheque' and 'Thou shalt see and hear nothing'.

Most of the lightbulbs at the back of the units were either missing or blown. The eerie shadows left just enough light to get him down the pathway without ripping or hurting himself.

He couldn't see into Helen's unit. It was in darkness and the door was locked. He could knock. That might get someone who hadn't had the commandments explained to them poking their head out, seeing him and if they didn't like his story, ringing the police. Having Maher turning up and laughing at him wasn't his idea of fun. There was another way. He'd seen these locks before. All they needed to spring them was a little bit of plastic, just like the one he'd once taken off a burglar and which he happened to have in his wallet at all times. Slip it in between the jamb and the lock, a little downward pressure and *click*!

He took a second to glance both ways. No one. The door opened and he was inside. Well, she wasn't lying on the kitchen floor, or on any of the floors. Flick up the bedspread and make absolutely sure. Leave the sheets alone. Anything in the bathroom? No. Good. Have a quick look in the closet. Empty. Lashing stopped. There was a pile of books on the table. He had a look. They were all about electrical circuits and engineering and quarrying. She was studying bomb-making. The table was a mess, but he saw a parcel.

What the hell was that? Then he heard steps and a key in the unit's other door.

Time to go, and right bloody now!

Helen had needed both hands to get the key into the ignition. She took a deep breath, thought of a little prayer and turned it. There was nothing – no huge explosion, no smoke or flames. It was all right. The car wasn't in pieces across the roadway and she wasn't sprayed all over the wall. She was just a woman sitting in a car. No one was taking any notice.

She'd driven through Courtenay Place, around the Basin Reserve and into her parking space at the Hollywood. So far so good. But she was still in Wellington, and still in this godforsaken motel.

There was only one way back to whatever was going to be a normal life, and she knew exactly what it was. This had to be finished once and for all, and soon, so she could get back to a world without murderers, police, seedy motels and rental cars. She'd never complain about being bored again. Doing fried chicken franchise agreements for the rest of her life would be just fine.

She glanced up at her unit. Was something moving up there? She peered through the car's windscreen. Take your time. Be careful. Make sure. You're already upset, so don't go getting paranoid or anything. There's no one to help you so you have to get it right. Get scared and you'll freeze up. You've told yourself that before. Tell yourself again.

Even so, she stood in the shadows watching her window for a good five minutes. It looked all right – she hadn't seen any more movement. A door closed somewhere up on the same level as her unit, but then people came and went all the time. She didn't hear any 'goodbyes' or conversations, but that was par for the course. The place was a hovel and not many people wanted to advertise the fact that they were here.

Well, she couldn't sit in her car all night. So what was she going to do? Run because she might or mightn't have seen a half-shadow? Now she was scaring herself witless. And she hadn't eaten anything all day. No wonder she was going off the wall. She had to gather some courage, go into the unit and turn on the light.

For the second time tonight she needed both hands to get the key into the keyhole and turn it. Now shove the door open, snap on as many lights as you can and make a noise. If someone's in there they'll run for it.

No one. She went over to the other door. The hair she had stuck across it was gone. Someone had been here.

It was sitting on the little Formica table, in front of the books. Christ! He might be dangerous but he didn't have much imagination. Helen pulled up a chair and looked at it. The height and width were the same as the Auckland bomb. The packaging was better – no wires poking out the side. She stopped for a moment. Leaving another bomb was a bit of dull, oafish contempt. Did he think she wouldn't be watching for something like this? Perhaps he thought all women were stupid and only good for having kids and cooking his dinner.

Still, he had got it in here and that was frightening enough. He could do it again.

Could a life get lower than this? Sitting in a cheap, creepy room, with the sounds of sex coming through the walls, staring at someone's second attempt to kill her?

It felt like an age but it was actually only a couple of minutes before she decided on a plan. He'd forced her hand, that was all. He'd attacked her; now she attacked him. And no more mistakes. From now on she really, really couldn't afford them.

There was a lot to do and time was suddenly a hell of a problem. She picked up the telephone receiver.

chapter thirty-five

Wellington, 1947

The bloody scum, the lot of them, were lined up along the balcony rail laughing at him. Him! Murray McCarthy! They were the audience and he was the show, out here on the lawn scrambling around trying to find his clothes, hopping around on one leg trying to pull his pants up. He was eaten up with humiliation and glared up at them with all the hate he'd ever felt in his life. The more he glowered, the louder the laughing and jeering and pointing. Moira, that bitch who'd bought the dope from Weir's and then bucked and jumped the black, was right there in front.

'We'd love you to stay, Mr McCarthy, but we're getting warmed up and you've already had your little bit of fun. We're sorry it wasn't more, but we do what we can,' she yelled down at him.

The taunting bitch! His fists balled, ready to punch out anything or anyone near him. But even this angry he could see it was hopeless. About eight men were working their way to the front. None of them looked like much, but together they could do anything they liked.

One was sneering at him. 'Come on. Give it a go. Try something. Be a tough guy. You've got your pants on. We'll get them off for you and we'll give you a real surprise!'

McCarthy swallowed. He looked up at Moira.

'I'll get you, you piece of shit bloody arsehole.'

'No you won't. You're going to be praying I don't do anything about you.'

She had something in her hand and was holding it up.

Probably a camera of some sort. Any trouble and the photos would turn up . . . Christ knows where. They'd planned this. Right from the moment she'd seen him out at Weir's she'd known she'd wanted revenge – and for something he couldn't even remember.

One of the bastards was shining a powerful torch down on him as he ferreted around trying to find his shoes and socks. He'd managed to get his shirt on, although it was buttoned up wrong. He'd got one leg in his pants and was trying to get into the other leg, and he was in this spotlight, like a clown in the ring at the circus.

'Make sure you've got your undies on the right way around, so you can get your little cock out in case you need to stop for a pull on the way to Mass,' came from somewhere in the middle of them. It got a big laugh.

He managed to get more or less dressed, except for one sock. It was in the shrubs somewhere. Leave the freaking thing! He pulled his shoe on over his bare foot. His car was parked at the end of the line of cars. As he strode off to it he slid his car key out of his pocket and gouged their cars on the way past.

Shit.

The bastards had realised what he was doing and were after him. If they got hold of him he was dog meat. He jump-started his car, then realised he was in a dead end street, and they were between him and the exit. Fuck them! He got the car turned around. He dropped his head down low over the steering wheel and floored the accelerator.

'Right, you bastards!'

They were throwing stuff at his car. Who cared? The car roared and screamed, begging for him to change a gear and let the pressure off. They'd seen he wasn't stopping and were jumping out of the way.

As he wrenched the car around a corner he heard the grating, sliding shriek of metal on metal as he sideswiped a parked car. Too bloody bad: he wasn't stopping. Not now, not for that lot and not frigging ever.

He looked in the rear-vision mirror. They were slipping back in the distance. No one was following him. Just to make sure, he'd drive around the Karori streets for a while. No, he wouldn't. He'd get the hell out of it. They'd all be on the phone to the coppers. Radio messages would be going out: McCarthy's in Karori. Find him now! He'd go around through Brooklyn. It was time to get somewhere quiet, and hide out until the family has all headed out in the morning.

What the hell else was he going to do? Was this when he called it quits? He'd lost count of the number of offences and crimes he'd committed. Should he walk into the harbour now? No he wouldn't. He was going to make a run for it. If they caught him they could only hang him once, and if the poof was dead it didn't matter what else he'd done.

He'd get out to Miramar and have done with it.

chapter thirty-six

Wellington, 1972

Fred Lashing didn't care what Helen Murphy did, so long as she did something. Being stuck in the bushes outside her unit, right beside the Hollywood Motel's stinking, disgusting rubbish bins, wasn't his idea of a good time. The bin nearest him was half open and he could see a pair of men's underpants with blood on them. They were on top of a pile of rotten food and a couple of used French letters. A rat's long tail flicked out from under them. He had two tries at moving away to somewhere safer, but each time Helen had looked out the window. She might not have seen him but the rat had. It went sharp and tense as it decided whether to run or strike. So far it hadn't done either. It was still foraging in the bin.

The glimpses he had got of Helen told him she was worried.

At least it wasn't raining. She hadn't looked out for a while. Maybe he could have another try at escaping. He couldn't see the rat's tail now. Had it gone? He'd better make sure. Upset a rat and you'd be fighting something far faster, tougher and meaner than you. If it bit you it had about thirty different diseases to pass on to you. That was enough to scare anyone into being certain. He slipped silently along, letting the leaves and branches brush against his face. He didn't want to push them away in case they make a slapping sound.

Then he stopped, frozen.

The bloody rat was still there and it was watching him. Its eyes were unblinking and its gaze cut right through him. He swallowed. This thing was big. He remembered that rats had teeth able to cut through concrete. Anything they fought had better have a loaded gun or it was rat food. He stood still. The rat was in control. He barely breathed. A lifetime went by. Finally, the rat jumped down off the tin and disappeared into the bushes. Lashing nearly collapsed with relief.

He was about to take another step when he froze again.

Helen had come out of the unit and he was damn near in the open. He stood without moving a muscle – if he was lucky she wouldn't look back. She was carrying something which she put in the back seat of her car, draping a rug or something over it. She was going around to the driver's door and getting in. Get ready to move. You can't afford to lose her, not now.

Where in the name of God was she going now?

Helen's car turned out into Adelaide Road and back up towards the hospital. Lashing sprinted for his car. Something snagged at his jacket and tore it. It didn't matter. He got her back in sight just as she was going past the hospital. She turned left, over the hill to Kilbirnie, dropping down the hill and out towards the airport, turning left to the Miramar Cutting. Oh no, not Bresnahan's place again.

Did he call for extra hands? What did he say: that he was following this woman on a drive out to the eastern suburbs but didn't really know why? Maher would laugh him out of town.

There was this other strange feeling, the one he'd had the moment he'd first seen her. Sure, he might be on the trail of a crime. But she was tall, elegant and had middle class written all over her – what was that all about? Was it sex? Was it envy? Look at her. On her own, free and dangerous and fighting back without any help from anyone. And look at him: safe and secure and mouldering away in the police. She was doing something. He was not. He was existing and not much more.

Ah, she was not turning left to head up to Nevay Road. She was turning right. That would take her out to Strathmore and Seatoun. What the hell was this? She hadn't been there before.

He was trying to convince himself that his reason for following her was purely professional. He needed to score a big case. Up in Auckland everyone who was any good had been put on the Crewe murders and his name hadn't come up. Winners were going out to Pukekawa and he was one of the losers being left behind to take stolen bicycle reports.

Lashing waited until the tail-lights of Helen's car had snapped out of sight as she drove around the corner from Scorching Bay. From here she could only go around the Miramar peninsula and through the Shelley Bay Air Force Base to end up back at the Miramar Cutting. For God's sake, that meant she'd gone in a circle.

Hang on a minute. She had parked her car and got out. What had she dumped out here on the rocks at the end of Scorching Bay beach?

This was going to be dangerous. It was cold, dark and wet and the rocks were sharp. Little waves were breaking over his feet, soaking his shoes and socks. Thank God there was a halfway decent moon or he'd have missed this. He'd seen her throw something into the sea, only it had landed short.

It was cardboard, a box of some sort. He carefully picked it up and nearly fell backwards. It had looked as if it was going to be heavy but it wasn't. It was empty. What the hell was going on? He looked at it. This was the box he'd seen beside the books piled up on her table.

Now he knew.

Bresnahan had been there.

There'd been a bloody bomb in this box and she'd figured it out. So did she now have the bloody thing with her? He had to be sure. If he called up and said there was a car with a bomb in it it would be all on. There'd be suburbs cordoned off, the army Bomb Squad would be yanked into action. Then if it turned out there wasn't a bomb he'd have really buggered up. He could see the look on Maher's face.

He had to get after her and find a way to make bloody sure.

He grabbed the box, picked his way back to the car and threw it in the back seat. She had got a hell of a start – she'd be at Shelley Bay by now. The full moon meant he didn't have to use his headlights, because there wasn't any other traffic. It was just him and Helen, and maybe someone from the air force parked up and trying to get his leg over.

He could see the air force base with the public road running through the middle of it. He'd get through quickly because it was well lit. Where the bloody hell was she? He couldn't see anything up ahead. In a couple of minutes she'd be at the Miramar wharf. From there she could go back through the cutting into Miramar or around Evans Bay to Kilbirnie, or anywhere.

Damn. Damn, damn, damn.

Lashing peered out the side windows, then straight ahead. He couldn't turn back now. Unless she'd stopped at the base she was still somewhere ahead. If he went back and checked the base and found she wasn't there he'd have lost her. If that happened, and it was a pretty good bet, he'd have to take a punt she was heading for Bresnahan's and go there.

Helen was parked behind one of the air force sheds, watching for the car that had followed her all the way from the Seatoun tunnel. She'd had to be quick, almost flinging that wretched box out the car window in case whoever was following her saw what she was doing. If it was Bresnahan she was in such deep shit it didn't matter.

But it wasn't Bresnahan's car. It was too new. Who was it? Could it be the police? If it was, they'd be waiting at the Miramar Cutting. Let them. She turned back towards Scorching Bay.

Helen looked across at Bresnahan's house. Her mouth felt raw and dry and she bit her bottom lip. This was it. This was the moment for a bit of courage. If she couldn't find any and let this chance go past he'd keep coming after her until he got her.

Her car was well hidden. Anyone not specifically looking for it would miss her. Did Bresnahan have a dog? Think, Helen. You've been at the house. God, you've been inside the place and looked out the kitchen window. Think! If there is a dog you need a new plan and you need it now.

The rest was all right. She'd grown up around here. There was no mystery about the little track through the scrub. It might have been a while ago but she'd criss-crossed it a hundred times.

The bomb was on the back seat of her car. Christ Almighty.

This used to be home. Now she hated the corner of Nevay and Fortification roads. Too many memories.

So did he have a dog?

There was no one around. Of course there was no one around – it was nearly midnight. She summoned her mental pictures of the Bresnahan house and back garden. She'd seen the two sheds at the back, by the fence, and the clothesline, but was there a kennel?

The entrance to the little track through the bush and down to Miramar North was over there. The bomb was heavy but she was sure she could carry it as far as she needed. The worst part would be the bush track. It was uneven going and she didn't even dare think about using a torch. Her blouse was damp with fear's sweat.

chapter thirty-seven

Wellington, 1947

Pat Feeney and Jimmy Byrne were tired and hungry but they knew they could forget sleep. Food? All they'd be getting was the ripped-open packet of biscuits in front of them. The rest of Feeney's dining-room table was covered with O'Malley's records.

Feeney's family had given up hope of having breakfast on the table and taken their porridge off to the living-room. Even now, after spending most of the night checking and double-checking O'Malley's records, they still weren't sure they had everything completely right. A long time back, around four in the morning, they'd realised they'd have to do their best and settle for that.

Feeney shook his head. 'Look at it. Just about everything we've had go wrong in the last five years goes straight back to that prick O'Malley. He's had the whole frigging place jumping. You wonder if they've been taking it out on the rest of us Catholics because they're too scared to take them on.'

'Them' was two names, all through the ledgers as EHC and MM: Eric Henry Compton and Murray McCarthy.

Feeney stretched. Please God, give me something good. Marie West's investigation was close to being declared dead in the water. Now there was Compton. What was he going to do about him? He could hardly march into his office, tell him he was a crook and a disgrace and rip the medals off his dress uniform. Compton was not likely to drop his resignation on a desk and walk silently away. There had to be something so overwhelming in front of him that he had no choice but to go. Organising that was going to take more care, skill and talent than any murder investigation.

'Now for the good part,' Jimmy said.

He was crossing out the Catholic names on one of the copies they'd made. It still left a long list. Byrne's eyes shone with anger and anticipation. Finally, after years of slights and insults, he had something he could use against the Anglicans, Protestants and Freemasons, in and out of the police, who had slighted him. Feeney couldn't help shuddering at the prospect. He wouldn't want Jimmy Byrne after him. Threatening him would be futile, negotiation hopeless, mercy out of the question. If they managed to keep themselves out of prison or in one piece it wouldn't be because Byrne didn't try.

'There's something else.'

'Yeah?' said Feeney.

'What about these two arseholes who threw Johnny out the window? Compton'll be protecting them. The longer he's around the harder it'll be to get at them.'

Feeney nodded. 'As soon as Compton's gone we go at them, one hundred miles a frigging hour. They'll be mulched and spread over the roses.' He hoped he sounded more confident than he felt.

Jimmy Byrne smiled. He didn't know what Feeney was talking about, but he liked the sound of 'mulched'. Feeney was looking into space. They had no choice now. There had to be an attack on Compton. Once he kicked that off, he'd need a hell of a lot of gods with him. Compton was fast, evil, dangerous and hugely experienced. If anyone ever wanted a worthy adversary he'd do just fine.

His entire adult life had been spent in places like this. Would priests have to do this? Feeney sighed as he looked around the muster room. It didn't matter where they were – they always looked and smelled the same. There were the teapots of stale tea, the piles of fresh paper, typewriter ribbons, the sweat and shoe polish. He'd never been in one that was properly lit. Probably the police were saving on lightbulbs, Feeney thought.

Under that was the air of desperation, of reports running late, of details missed, the fear of stupid or sadistic seniors, of making some public mistake.

Feeney had stood in front of the dispirited detectives. 'All I can say is keep going. Someone killed Marie and he's out there. Never forget that. Keep at it. Demand more. Push harder. Spare nothing and no one.' They hadn't said anything, just nodded, managed to put an encouraging look on their faces and trudged dully off to their cars.

Great, just bloody great. Feeney felt like they'd looked.

Now it was just him, his fear and the briefcase full of O'Malley's records. He heard Corbett Wilson's taunting: 'Are you up to it? Are you?' Was he? Wilson didn't think so. Who knew what the Bishop thought? Feeney let a long breath slide from him. But then who the fricking hell cared? They weren't going to be there when he moved against Compton. If they weren't at his side they didn't get a say. He felt isolated and friendless. Was this going to turn into some sort of Calvary and trial by fire rolled into one?

He closed the briefcase. There was one thing he had to admit. In all of this mess there was at least one person who knew what he was doing and who had done a good job of it. John Augustine O'Malley had kept excellent records.

But they were not quite as good as they had been. He had the list Jimmy Byrne had edited to weigh heavily against the Protestants. He'd been enthusiastic about it, too. Any policeman famously tough on Catholics and taking O'Malley's money was right there at the top of the list.

He walked out of the muster room. Of the cops who'd been taking the money, the dumber ones would be thinking O'Malley's death was the end of their problems. The smart ones would know that this was the most dangerous moment. O'Malley's control was gone, but what was going to happen next? There had been another burglary at O'Malley's office, an expert and professional one. Feeney's guess was that it was policemen. Too late, boys! The lads from Christchurch had been there first and they'd missed out too. Wilson had got there before them. God knows how the information had fallen into his hands. If Feeney had to guess, he'd have a shilling or two on McCarthy.

He picked up his briefcase and left the muster room.

Feeney stood in Waring Taylor Street and looked up at Compton's office. Some of the men named in O'Malley's files were up there, keeping the paperwork moving and doing their best for the police. They hadn't taken anything for years and assumed it was all behind them now. It wasn't. A snake from their past might be about to strike out at them. Feeney liked the image of a vengeful serpent. He tightened his grip on the briefcase.

It was all very Catholic, very original sin. As he crossed the road Feeney risked a quick Sign of the Cross. It was either him or Compton now. They wouldn't both pull through this. He wondered if this was how the gladiators had felt as they walked out onto the Coliseum's sandy floor to stand in front of the howling mob and yell their salute: 'Those who are about to die salute you.'

He looked straight ahead. He had to admit he was frightened.

A few minutes later Eric Compton looked up from Feeney's list. Feeney sat waiting. Compton had studied the material, almost idly, without any particular show of interest or emotion. Finally, he spoke.

'So?' he said quietly.

That surprised Feeney. He'd expected anger, denials, threats – almost anything other than this calm blankness.

'Sir, there are real problems here. It looks like O'Malley has been paying off almost everyone who's got anything to do with chasing up the bookmakers.'

'Yes, so it would seem.'

Feeney had no choice. He had to keep going now even if every word felt like handing Compton the pistol and the bullets he'd use to shoot him. He had to try to shake him out of this sneering calm. Christ, some of them had taken big money. They'd been ruthless about hunting Catholics and if the evidence had dropped short before, here it was.

'Hmmm. I could be wrong but there don't seem to be any

tykes anywhere on this list,' Compton muttered. 'Perhaps they really do listen to the priests and nuns and behave like good little boys and girls. Perhaps they don't. We'll see what we shall see.'

He kept a slowly widening smirk in place as he leaned across to a drawer, opened it and dropped a manila folder on his desk.

Feeney felt the coldness of a fear sweat run down his ankles and into his shoes.

Oh Jesus Lord, he had the original list, before he and Byrne went to work on it.

Feeney managed to keep a straight face and hold Compton's gaze. It was not easy. Compton was all but laughing at him. Those Christchurch cops hadn't been after O'Malley. They'd gone looking for files, and found them. O'Malley had happened to be there. He was a bonus. Sorry, pal. You made a mistake. You should have been home listening to quiz shows on the radio with the wife and kids. So, a Chinese and a sexo had seen them? Let them. This was New Zealand. There were no women on juries, never mind chinks and queers. You want a conviction? Read the Good Book and choose to live a good life. That's the closest you'll get to a conviction over this.

Compton was enjoying this.

'You might be right, Pat. You just might be right. It's definitely time for a hard cull. We do have a few bad ones and we can't have that. They have to go.'

'Absolutely, sir. Murray McCarthy's name's there, right at the top.'

Compton couldn't hold back the grin.

'Yeah, that's good, Pat. I like that, putting the police ahead of religion. There just isn't enough of that, what with the Protestants and Masons and the tykes all either going after each other or taking care of each other.' He shook his head in mock sadness. Now it was taunting, Feeney knew it, and there was nothing to be done.

'Tell you what, Pat. You keep going on the West case. As soon as that's under control and we've got someone safely locked up we'll really move on this stuff. You and me, Pat, all right? Good. Don't worry. This won't be buried. We'll really take it places.

Hitler and Stalin won't have a thing on the purge we'll run through Wellington. It'll be like a dose of the salts. We'll shit the bastards out and flush them away forever. That's a guarantee.'

But Compton's smirk was telling him it was dead and buried. All Feeney could feel now was cold, flat failure. He nodded. What else could he do? Argue? It'd be hopeless. Compton would run him ragged. The only thing to do was get out of there as fast as he could. Check to see whether those two had turned up back in Christchurch. If they hadn't, they were here somewhere. He'd get Jimmy to find them, and bloody do something to them.

Except he wouldn't, and he knew it. That'd make him the same as them. Christ, he wished he didn't have a few morals.

Compton was on his feet and walking to the door. The meeting was over. So much for Compton panicking. He didn't say a word. As soon as Feeney had stepped into the corridor the door closed behind him.

chapter thirty-eight

Wellington, 1947

Now that he was on the Miramar side of the Mt Victoria tunnel Murray McCarthy was feeling safer. This was Mum, Dad and the kids country. The police didn't do too much hard patrolling. The chances of someone springing him had dropped by about one hundred per cent compared to the city side of the tunnel. Even so, there was still a good three hours before he could go anywhere near home to get his stuff. Until then he was going to have to keep out of sight.

He drove up a little road and past a sign telling him the Hataitai Park athletic track and women's basketball courts were under construction. So bloody what? They could build anything they frigging well liked. He'd never be anywhere near it again.

Christ, he was stuffed. The tension of sneaking his way around the back streets from Karori, slithering across Te Aro and the top of Taranaki Street and then praying no one would see him as he drove around the Basin Reserve, on top of everything else, had been enough to finish him.

He had to stop and sleep or he'd be a road statistic as well.

He thought about Worser Bay and topping himself. But he hadn't done it when he was there, so he probably wasn't going to now.

No, he was going to be running. He'd stopped at a phone box to ring his brother. The response from down country had been a bit surly but it was all right. Yeah, he could stay there till it cooled down. Then he'd be on his way out of the country. He'd take some of the money he'd stashed away and leave the rest for the family. That was being bloody generous. Some of them would be only too happy to see the back of him.

It was four o' clock in the morning. Wasn't that the Hour of the Fox, or the Wolf or something, when people got low or weak and if they were going to die that's when it happened? If he snuffed it now he'd be doing it in the car. That wasn't going to be pretty.

He struggled with his suit, getting it buttoned more or less properly. Huh. If he'd done the right thing it wouldn't matter. He and his would be out in the harbour. The queer would be alive, and those bastards up in Karori would be looking for someone else to humiliate.

Was he ever going to stop thinking about death and suicide?

That lot up in Karori would pay for what they'd done. Except they wouldn't. They'd pay for nothing. They'd got clean away with it and he might as well get used to it. Murray McCarthy wasn't a problem to them and they all knew it. He'd be outnumbered in a fight. They'd have lawyers for anything else.

Well, he knew one thing. This might be a crisis but he wasn't going to be doing what he usually did – rush out to see Xavier Weir.

He had two hours before anyone would be out and about. He'd get the car backed up and out of sight. It wasn't completely safe from a really nosy patrol but it was the best he could do.

As sleep pushed his eyelids down he found himself thinking about how he'd jumped at a chance to get out from being a cadet in the Ministry of Works accounts department to being a copper. It'd taken a while of obeying orders and doing what he was told to get himself up to being what he'd really wanted, a one-man army, conquering anything and anyone and frightening the lot of them. A word from him could ruin a career. He was God, and straight out of the Old Testament. None of this forgiving Love Thy Neighbour shit.

Hell! That was the first happy thought he'd had all night.

Now he could let himself coast into sleep. But he snapped awake. That was his whole life going in front of him. Wasn't that what happened when you died?

He hadn't slept long. All the twisting and turning to get comfortable had put paid to any of that. Now his body was turning against him. It complained and ached and yelled for decent sleep in a proper bed and to be washed clean. But he just couldn't escape the thick smell of booze, sweat, coal and blood. What time was it? Six in the morning! God help him – he'd only been out for a couple of hours. He gazed through the rain at the piles of dirt, the big earth-moving machines and the silence. It looked dark and frightening, and the workers would be here soon. The last damned thing he needed was for one of them to go all public-spirited and ring the police.

His teeth felt clogged. God knows what his breath smelt like. He'd love to sneak back up to Ararua Road and beat the shit out of anyone he found there. Leave them in the gutter with a few broken bones and having trouble getting their brain to work properly. That'd be the perfect finish. But he wasn't going back to Karori. He was going to Miramar, and then he'd never see Wellington again.

At a quarter to seven McCarthy sat on a low concrete wall at the corner of Nevay and Totara roads, looking out through the trees to the harbour. He was so sick of people telling him it was one of the world's most spectacular harbours. It was supposed to look like San Fransisco's. He couldn't care less. What he did care about was his wife and kids not seeing him on their way to school. Not many kids went by car – they walked or they got the bus, but not his. There were too many sexos around. He'd beaten up most of them but you never knew when another one would turn up. Safer to take them by car.

A woman in a dressing gown walked down her path to get her milk and paper. She looked more than a little alarmed at seeing McCarthy sitting there. He glanced back at her. You try going around all night covered in coal dust. You kick a bloody poof to death. You get half rooted by frigging aristocrats and you tell me how you'd bloody look. He bit it all back, said nothing.

'Are you all right?' the woman asked.

Of course I'm not bloody all right. If I get caught now I get hanged. If I'm lucky it's ten years inside, with no one to talk to, because I was a copper. Anyone talked to him they'd get smacked over. And that's not all.

'Yeah, I'm fine,' McCarthy snarled.

She bristled at his tone, turned and sped back up the path. McCarthy shook his head. That was a mistake. It'd be just his luck for her to be the only one along here with a phone connected. Ten seconds after she got in the door she'd be on to the Miramar police station and telling anyone who answered that, 'One of your policemen, that Murray McCarthy, has just been quite rude to me.' Word would pick up voltage as it went through Central. McCarthy's out in Miramar! Get out there and get him in here!

They'd have found the poof's body by now. They'd be spinning the rest of them for witnesses. They'll find one, too. Someone will have seen or heard something. They always did. It was just a question of finding them – or having them find you.

Christ!

The next half-hour was going to be a frigging long time. As soon as he got his clothes and money it was off to Jack's. His brother had a farm just out of Te Kuiti. It'd be okay there because Jack was a bit on the strange side. The locals left him alone. It hadn't been that long since Stan Graham had gone nuts down on the West Coast and started shooting everyone he could see. He was a farmer who'd decided the neighbours were against him. Jack was a bit like that, and the neighbours mostly didn't want to take a chance. He wanted to be alone? Leave him alone!

That suited McCarthy down to the ground. Besides, he'd found out when he'd rung Jack that he had expanded the horticultural side of the farm. These days his visitors arrived at night, coming and going quickly. If Jack hadn't been supplying Weir with his marijuana McCarthy would be amazed.

He drove around into Napier Street to get himself away from the old woman's death-white face glaring down from her window. Imagine being the poor sod having to hoist a leg over that. Maybe no one did. Was that why she was so starchy?

He parked the car where he could see the house but they couldn't see him. He got out of the car, leaned against it and lit a cigarette. He smiled. Thank God he had a plainclothes police car. All he'd done that night and the police had provided the transport!

One day he'd dine out on that. But not yet.

The harbour's water was steel grey. Behind it the hills south of Eastbourne were hard green and cold looking. That was mean country. Get caught out there in the winter and you were history. He looked over to his house. He swallowed. There was a heaviness in his stomach knowing that he was actually leaving it. Most of his adult life had been spent in that house, and now he was going on to something else. That house had been permanent, but life for him now was only going to be as far ahead as the next feed and the next sleep.

He'd done a lot for Wellington, being the line between the citizens and the thieves, the poofs and the rest. Was he going to get any gratitude? No, of course he wasn't. Guys like him never did. They did the dirty work so others could make their money and wander about all dreamy and safe. Well, someone else could do it now.

He flicked his cigarette butt away. If it started a fire then so what? No one cared about him, and he didn't bloody care about them.

chapter thirty-nine

Wellington, 1972

There couldn't be a dog. There just couldn't be. It was the early hours of the morning. Helen was the only thing moving for miles around and she was getting close to Bresnahan's house. In the crispness of the night there was nothing to confuse a scent or stop it travelling on the cool night air. No dog could resist barking and there'd been nothing, just silence.

The moon was behind a cloud now, and losing its light made carrying the bomb across the rough ground even more dangerous. It had been hard enough before, when the light was good, to keep moving. Twice now she'd had to stop and rest the bomb on a tree branch. She couldn't afford to exhaust herself. She'd need her energy. Getting there was only half the job.

It had taken nearly a quarter of an hour to go the ten yards to the fork in the track. In daylight she'd have done it in about two minutes. Going left would bring her out at the bottom of the hill near the terminal where the Miramar buses turned around for the return trip into Wellington. Turn right and the track skirted along the boundaries of the houses facing out on Nevay Road. The second one along was Mack Bresnahan's.

Helen could feel the sweat on her face. What if she'd been completely wrong and Bresnahan hadn't sent the bomb? Come on! Stop that! She'd checked twice and three times and double-checked again. He had. The real worry was whether Archie Fallon would be able to do everything she'd asked when she'd rung from the motel. There had been a lot for him to do and she could have done without him reminding her about cops being deep in the mix. She knew that, thank you very much.

She had to concentrate on the bomb. Make a mistake, and nothing else would matter. She'd be in small pieces and Bresnahan could relax. His crusade would be over. She tried to get her breathing under control and not panic. There'd never be another chance like this. The man was mad, dangerous and stupid. He'd given her a weapon she could use. Next time he might get things right.

She stopped and rested the bomb on the fence behind Bresnahan's house.

She'd been right when she'd taken that quick glance out his kitchen window. There were two sheds in the backyard, one up close to the house and the other one down here by the fence.

The fence was pretty rickety – getting through it wouldn't be a problem. Lucky she didn't have to climb over it.

Now, this was her last chance to make sure there wasn't a dog! If there was, once she was through the fence she'd be trapped in there with it. She stood very still and waited for a moment. Nothing. Good. The grass hadn't been mown lately but the ground looked reasonably level. Keep your eye on that house. Watch that back door. If Bresnahan is awake and catches you out in the open you won't have a chance.

Helen inched up to the shed closest to the fence. Its curtains were closed but there were tiny gaps. She peered in. The workbench was covered in wires. No explosives or detonators, but they'd be somewhere else, probably hidden in the bush behind her. Everything else he needed to make a bomb was there. It was a bomb factory all right. Please, Lord, let Archie Fallon have done his job.

She was on her hands and knees now, keeping the shed between her and the house, easing the bomb along with one arm and steadying herself with the other. It was wet, slow and hard going but it was as close to being safe as she could get.

Shit! Was that Bresnahan at the kitchen window? Had he heard anything? The face wasn't moving. At least she knew he was in the house and not out here somewhere. The face turned away and was gone. If her heart didn't stop thumping like this she'd have a heart attack. Of course it was thumping – she was going to kill a man!

The two wires she'd carefully cut from the bomb when she'd opened the package from the bottom were hanging down. They weren't long enough! Christ! Hang on. There was a carpenter's sawhorse over there – she could sit the bomb on that. Only, it was right beside the house. She crawled along the fence towards it. It was too heavy to drag along the ground. She'd have to run and grab it. Do it fast!

Okay. Now to balance the bomb on it, and wrap the wires around the shed's door handle. So far, so good.

Now, to get Bresnahan out here . . .

One of Fallon's jobs was to get in touch with a mate who had contacts in the hospital system, who would organise Bresnahan's wife's sister to get her and the kids out to the sister's house. Some terrible gynaecological emergency! Helen's bet, and prayer, was that Bresnahan wouldn't want any part of that.

She hadn't missed the cheerily cynical note in Fallon's voice as he'd poured himself another gin and told her, 'You know, don't you, that generous provision can be made for those finding themselves widowed and orphaned by unexplained circumstances? All it needs is a person of good standing to vouch for them.'

He'd chortled at the idea of Helen killing their husband and father, and then speaking for them to make sure they got money. Fallon had roared down the phone, 'Oh yes, the wonders of the quality of mercy and the power of justice. The Lord and the lawyers taketh away, and the Lord and the lawyers giveth.'

Back to the matter in hand. So far there'd been no sign of the wife or the children – that was hopeful. Now she had to get Bresnahan outside. Her guess was that the first thing he'd check would be his bomb factory. If he did, that would be the end of him.

She stopped still. From where she stood she could see between the house and the bush, up to the road.

Oh no. Please, God, no!

Someone was up on the road looking down at Bresnahan's house. Shit! It looked like Lashing! How had he got here? By bloody car, of course. But why? What did he know? Go away! Lashing was pacing up and down outside Bresnahan's house. Then suddenly he was out of sight. Where the hell was he? Please, God, keep him up there on the road.

Thwack.

Forget about Lashing – Bresnahan was standing on his back steps and he was shooting at her.

Thwack. Thwack.

He had an air gun – a powerful one, too. A pellet smacked into a tree branch just above her, making a deep mark. It'd do the same to her.

'What's going on? Who's that?' It was Lashing, yelling from the road.

Thwack.

He was not a great shot, and he was shooting blind. But if the moon came back out she'd have had it. It wouldn't be long – there wasn't much cloud up there. Helen scratched around and found a piece of a child's bike. She jumped up, swung it back and broke one of the bomb shed's windows.

'What the fuck?' Bresnahan.

Thwack.

Run for the fence!

'What's going on?' Lashing was still up on the road.

'I'll fucking get you! Fuck you!' Bresnahan was running down the steps now

'You fuckin' bitch! You want it? You'll fuckin' get it!'

His powerful arm swung out and his fist hit her just above the cheekbone. Then he grabbed her with his other arm. She lunged at him, trying to bite. He pulled back.

'What the fuck are you doing here? Eh?'

He punched her again. She felt her knees go soft. This was it . . .

'What the fuck are you doing here, eh?' Bresnahan repeated.

No sign of the kids or the wife. There were no witnesses. Bresnahan could do anything he liked to her. The face glaring down at her was all white rage. She could smell peanut butter and beer on his breath. He was going to kill her. He was going to kill her, right here and now. Who'd stop him?

Point at the shed! Point at the shed! Bresnahan looked around. Then swung his arm back and punched her in the stomach. He let her go and turned back to the shed. She wasn't going far.

Helen began to crawl. Bresnahan was at the shed. He had a key. He was opening the door. She had to get away, just get away. She could feel the pain screaming through her to stop, but if she did, she'd die.

Boom!

A bright sheet of yellow and red flashed above and behind her. Pieces of wood, roof and glass flew up and sprayed out above her. There was a great roar, like a thousand animals simultaneously raging in pain. A blast of hot air rolled her over and pushed her against the fence as she heard Bresnahan scream. A cloud of smoke forced itself up at the sky, leaving a dull pinkness on the ground where the shed had been.

After that, all Helen could hear was her own voice yelling, 'Get away! Get away!'

Her mind was saying, 'Move, move, go, go!' but her body was refusing. What was wrong? Helen heard herself scream, almost in the distance, 'Pleeeaaasee!'

Then there was nothing, just a slow, deep and warm silence.

chapter forty

Wellington, 1947

Was it actually his house any more? Technically it was, but it wouldn't be for much longer. Yes, the name Murray McCarthy was on the title, but he was about to take off. His wife would report him missing. In a few years she would have him declared dead and the house would be hers. She'd never know it had become hers at the exact second the poof from the Taj had stopped breathing. Would a suicide note help? No, that wouldn't hold up – not when it was discovered he'd taken a suitcase full of clothes.

He still didn't like the idea of running. Murray McCarthy didn't run from anyone. Well, he did now, and it was because he'd just become one of the scum he'd always kept under control. Perhaps he should have been nicer to some of them. Then he'd have someone to talk to.

Okay. It was time. There was his wife bustling the kids out to the car. It'd only be a couple of minutes now.

'Vincent!' she snapped. 'If you are going to get the bus, just you make sure you don't miss it.'

It hurt, watching and listening to them chattering as they climbed into the car. She did what she always did – missed the gear change from first to second. The screeching made McCarthy's teeth grind. It always had.

The car was out of sight now. That was it. All their lives were changed forever, but he was the only one who knew it.

He lit another cigarette. He had a few moments and he might as well take them. Once he went back down the hill that was it.

What would his wife say when she realised he was gone? Would she care? He didn't know. Her attention was always on the children, always the bloody kids. He wasn't jealous of them. It wasn't their fault, the poor little buggers. He'd had his chance to be there with them and he hadn't taken it. He couldn't go blaming anyone else. It was his fault, no one else's.

If she was smart she wouldn't tell anyone until she'd been into his locker at Wellington Central and got the little briefcase full of money he'd told her about. She was smart. She'd do it. There was an inspector there who knew where the rest of the money was and he'd help her.

He threw away the butt and took a last look out at Wellington Harbour. He crossed the road to the house. Ye gods! His stupid wife had left the garage door half open. He could see the crane he used for lifting engines out of cars and keeping them raised while he fixed whatever was wrong. Those long, slow Sunday afternoons that were gone now. He'd miss them. There was a lot he'd miss. His shoulders slumped. The world was such shit. It'd be so easy just to go in there, shut the door and hang himself. Hell, he could still go down to the harbour and walk in.

Suddenly he realised he wasn't alone.

That cheeky bloody Murphy girl, the older one – what was her name? Jennifer – was standing there, all bright and scrubbed in her school uniform. Huh! From what he'd heard she ought to be in a cycle outfit because she and her sister were a couple of real bikes. Everyone rode them. She was looking at his battered, creased suit, trying to keep a straight face. The little bitch was bloody laughing at him. Standing there, with her pink cheeks, freshly washed blouse and perky little tits and trying not to giggle!

Those stinking bloody Murphies couldn't laugh at anyone. They were bloody losers, the lot of them. They were lucky to be walking around free. She thought she could just stand there and snigger. Well, no one, no one, did that to him, and especially not this morning.

A two-word phrase pumped up and up and through him as he looked at Jennifer Murphy. Why not? Yeah, why not? Why the hell not! He was finished here and wasn't coming back.

She wanted to snigger at him, there'd be a price. He took a couple of steps towards her. She saw trouble and turned to run but he was too quick. He had her – one hand around her mouth, the other around her waist, and he was dragging her into the garage. She kicked and fought but he was too strong. He'd bloody teach her to laugh at him. He slapped her hard across the face. She reeled. He grabbed at her, reached under her dress and pulled her panties down to her ankles. Then pushed her down on the floor, holding her face with one hand and loosening his belt and flicking the buttons of his fly open with the other.

A voice inside him screamed, Go on, go on. It doesn't matter now. They can't do anything else to you. Let's see what the boys around here have been into!

'Please stop it. Don't. Please. Please leave me alone. I'm a virgin. I've never done it. Please!'

Yeah, sure.

She was fighting back hard, and it was an effort to keep control of her. Neither of them noticed Helen coming up behind him. She'd seen something moving in the garage, looked in and taken a few seconds to register what was happening. It was too late to run and get help. The panic in Jennifer's eyes was terrible.

There was the answer: the machine that pulled engines out of cars. She'd been in here; she knew how it worked. You folded that piece of wire through that one, and you pushed a button, and the engine went into the air.

McCarthy had his pants down around his knees. He had one hand down between him and Jennifer, trying to shove himself into her.

'No, please stop. Please.'

Suddenly Helen appeared, reached down and grabbed his balls. She squeezed as hard as she could, then squeezed again. McCarthy howled, and Jennifer wriggled out from underneath him.

'Do it again!' Jennifer gasped.

Helen tightened her grip. The muscles on her forearm were

sharply defined. McCarthy was bent over, sobbing and gasping against the pain. Then Jennifer grabbed the wire and pulled it across. Together they fitted the noose around his neck. Helen pushed the button.

McCarthy tried to punch at them but the pain was too much. The wire tightened around his neck. His feet lashed out. His hands pulled at the wire, trying to ease its choking grip. One hand grabbed out, trying to find support from something, anything. His legs were kicking and jerking, lashing out, but they could not travel far, trapped by the trousers around his ankles. Helen stood out of range, horrified and fascinated. This was a man dying! It was ghastly! Gradually McCarthy's fight slowed to a shuddering twitch. His tongue poked out from the corner of his mouth. His eyes were wide and staring across at the far corner of the ceiling.

'Come on,' Jennifer snapped to her sister. 'Help me.'

She was pulling McCarthy's underpants up from around his shoes. She closed her eyes as she pushed his soft manhood safely inside them. Jennifer lifted his pants back up and they buttoned the fly. Helen used her shoe to spread the dust on the garage's earth floor, to cover any traces. Then Helen brushed the dirt from the back of Jennifer's uniform.

They didn't have much time if they were to get down Totara Road to Darlington Road and the tram to school. They peeked out of the garage. No one in sight. All the way down the hill Helen kept brushing at Jennifer's uniform. The dirt was gone. Ahead was a day of the nuns teaching them maths, science, French, Latin and how they must respect other people and themselves. The latter was code for 'Don't have sex until you have a wedding ring on your finger.'

On the tram Helen and Jennifer agreed. They might be Catholic girls and believe in the power of confession, but they weren't going near a confession box with this, ever. This was going into the past and staying there.

Vincent McCarthy didn't like school and wasn't going. Once the bus had gone without him he'd walked back towards home and seen the Murphy sisters walking, almost running, away from his garage. Now he stood there, quietly looking up at the body suspended from the engine-lifting machine. His father's face was awful. The eyes were open, staring but not seeing anything. The tongue sticking out the mouth was turning blue. Any life in that big, strong body was gone now. He didn't know much about dying but he did know one thing: his father was gone.

He also knew he didn't want him back – not if this was the end of being hit and stripped down by sarcasm. There'd been many, many nights when he'd prayed for something like this. Now his prayers had been answered but he didn't feel the way he'd expect to. It felt bad. He wasn't happy or even close to it.

What should he do?

Leave him there. If he did anything else he'd bring too many questions down on himself. He reached up and touched his father on the forehead. That was goodbye and as close as he'd get to the last rites. Vincent needed to get out of here, now. It wouldn't be long before his mother found the body. In fact he was on the track down to the bus terminus when he heard his mother's scream, and then silence.

Vincent didn't think his father would be left hanging there for long, but he was wrong. His body would swing until three-thirty that afternoon, like a side of beef at the butcher's shop. His mother had rushed into Wellington Central, looking for the hidden money. He would never forget that. His father might have been a bully, but no one deserved that.

Six years later Vincent hadn't forgotten what his father looked like. Now it was time for his own brother to hang. He'd discovered that hanging doesn't let people stride nobly to their death. Their knees are strapped together, enough to allow them to walk but not enough to kick out. The official witnesses had to be spared appalling images of legs flailing about.

The priest had led the way up the corridor muttering his prayers. The guards whispered to his brother, 'Take a breath, don't fight and it'll be over quickly.'

He struggled down the long, cold, stone corridor and through the door into the little courtyard by the kitchen, where they'd assembled the gallows. The door was open and a prison warder stood beside it. He had thought there would be stairs. Instead, he walked straight out onto the wooden platform. He caught a glimpse of the noose before the black hood went over his face and a pair of surprisingly gentle hands fitted the rope around his neck.

A voice behind him said, 'James David Savage' – the name he'd taken by deedpoll when he'd discovered what people thought of his father – 'you've been convicted of murder and sentenced to death. Do you have anything to say before the sentence of execution is carried out?'

'I'm sorry!'

It seemed useless and stupid – and nothing. But he couldn't think of anything else. Suddenly there was nothing under his feet, and his stomach muscles tensed as he dropped. He felt the rope cut into his neck. His legs moved in their straps. His last thought was a bitter 'Like father, like son!' Then his feet were still, a silhouette against the damp stone. The superintendent glanced over. The witnesses were trying to keep control.

About ten minutes later the doctor took his stethoscope off his chest and nodded.

They lowered him to an ambulance-style stretcher on the floor, out of sight of the witnesses, undid the rope and dropped it. The body would be offered to the family. If they didn't want him he'd be buried in the prison grounds.

The witnesses would wait the required one hour and leave, signing the book to record their presence and going off to think whatever they thought. None of them had touched the tea and biscuits.

It was all over. The hangman nodded to the superintendent, put on his large hat to prevent the prisoners recognising him, and went back to his other life, running a menswear store less than five miles from the prison. The superintendent noted the time on his clipboard for the official record. Ten past nine. The prison would be edgy and unsettled for a few days but would gradually return to normal.

In a house in Wellington his mother looked at the clock. Eight o'clock. The phone was quiet. No one had called to say the execution had been postponed or delayed. That meant her son was dying, right now, in Auckland's Mt Eden prison. Her head fell back, her terrible banshee wail smashed off the walls. Her small, wrinkled hands beat on the battered dining-room table.

'Aaaaaagggghhhhhh!'

It was loud and uncontrolled, and it seemed as if it would never stop. Her head rocked back and forth as the grief and anger rolled inside her. The child she had carried, borne, loved and nursed was no more. The next time she saw him would be in his coffin. She had lost a husband, and now a son to hanging. The horror of every mother – that she will outlive her child – had come real.

The women wrapped her up in a deep, warm embrace. The men stood awkward and unsure, muttering consoling words. She let herself be gently swayed, like a baby. In the background the children watched, not sure what to do, so they kept still as her scream gave way to sobbing. The women held her and looked over her shoulder, their eyes telling the men to go, and take the children with them. One of her little boys wriggled away, to stand in the living-room looking at his mother and the women. He didn't know what to do. The adult world was too dark and complicated for a nine-year-old, even one as sharp as him. He remembered what his father had always said: 'Never forget, and never forget to wait.'

Vincent knew the Murphy sisters had been there when his dad died. Ever since that day, his older brother had never been quite right. He had hated everything and everyone. Now he was dead too.

'Come on, son.'

A kind old man was taking him by the shoulder. This wasn't a time to fight. Besides, he liked Mr Bresnahan. He lived a few houses away and he always let them take shortcuts to the beach across his property and play soccer against his garage door. Years later, in Western Australia, when he'd needed a name quickly, he'd choked back 'Vincent McCarthy' and blurted out 'Mack Bresnahan'.

Vincent McCarthy was wanted in New Zealand but the

system had never heard of anyone by the name of Mack Bresnahan. The police let him go and he went back to the Kalgoorlie mines, learning all about blasting and explosives, earning his ticket and making a nice living, until he'd blown up a safe – and his fellow burglar with it. He'd come back to New Zealand.

When his mother died she still hadn't recovered from the shock of losing her husband. Her son vowed he'd never forget, and he would wait. The Murphy girls had done something that had ended with his father, brother and mother being dead. Then he'd seen a story in the *New Zealand Woman's Weekly* about Helen Murphy getting a law degree. He'd decided it was time for revenge.

chapter forty-one

Wellington, 1947

Pat Feeney looked up. Jimmy Byrne wasn't waiting to be invited in.

'We can't find McCarthy. We just bloody can't. He didn't get on the Christchurch ferry. There's a cop at Petone and another one at the top of the Ngauranga Gorge. He hasn't been up to Paraparaumu airport, and we've been watching the railway station. We've been checking his house. Nothing. Either he's slipped us or he's hiding out somewhere in Wellington. But Christ knows where.'

Feeney nodded. Okay. That wasn't too bad. McCarthy would turn up. The look on Byrne's face said there was more, and judging by his frown, it was bad. Feeney waited while Bryne checked the corridor and shut the door. Whatever was on his mind, it couldn't get much worse. They were no closer to Marie's killer. The Wests had a lawyer. (Want to talk to the parents? Do it through me, and I'll be attending all interviews.) O'Malley was dead. Compton had finessed him and the bloody Bishop had summoned him again. Go on, Jimmy, see if you can add to that . . .

'They're applying for a warrant for McCarthy's house . . . and another for Gerry Gregan's. They've already been around to Jack Finch's place.'

Feeney let out a long breath. So, he'd been wrong. It could get worse. That was Compton moving against the Catholics. If he was quick enough and the carnage was bad enough there would be political pressure to stop it, right now. Confidence had to be maintained in the police. It would also stop the

Catholics moving. If it was fast enough and deadly enough the Freemasons would be left in control.

'Two of them were at my brother's place, asking whether he'd been declaring all his taxes, and if I was earning anything from his business,' Byrne said.

It was against police regulations for officers to have a second source of income.

'They're coming at us with anything they can get, Pat . . . Mr Feeney.'

'Pat's fine.'

Feeney leaned back in his chair. He had to make up his mind. Was he loyal to the Catholics or to the police? He couldn't be both. That time was gone. Feeney remembered something someone said about Nazi Germany: 'They came for the Jews and I didn't speak up because I was not a Jew . . . then they came for the Catholics and I was a Protestant so I didn't speak up. Then they came for me . . . by that time there was no one to speak up for anyone.'

'Leave it with me, Jimmy.'

Byrne did not move.

'Look, Jimmy, I'll do something, I promise.'

Byrne looked unconvinced but stood up.

'It's going to be bad,' he said. 'They're after all of us.' Feeney knew what that meant. 'All of us' included him.

The detective checked the corridor again before he stepped out of the office, then walked quickly away. So what was Feeney going to do? He could do nothing. They weren't coming for him and probably never would. He had O'Malley's list: that gave him a good chip to play. He could let the bullets fly past, and fight back later. But then if he didn't fight now, there might not be a later. That would mean attacking the one outfit that had given him a job when others were turning him away for being Catholic. In the police he had risen to power and influence. Was this how he repaid the debt?

All but one of the policemen Byrne had mentioned was in O'Malley's original records, so maybe they deserved what was coming to them. Perhaps it wasn't a matter of Protestants and Catholics at all. Was it the corrupt and the innocent? But there was Jimmy Bryne. He'd done nothing. His name wasn't on O'Malley's list but they'd taken a blowtorch to him. No, this was Protestants and Freemasons versus Catholics. Simple as that.

He had no choice. The moment he'd shown Compton the doctored list he'd taken sides. The middle ground had melted away like ice. This must be what it felt like being Jewish and looking out the window as the soldiers jumped out of their trucks and ran at your front door.

Judas would have been early too. And he'd have been as tense as Feeney was now. Meet the soldiers, hand over your bit of information, grab the money and get the hell out of there. Except it turned out to be more than he thought. Just after Jesus had sprung him he'd found a rope and a tree and called it quits.

Feeney wasn't doing that – it wasn't in him. People like him were born to keep going, plodding and ploughing their way on and on, until nature decided to end it for them in old age. They were solid workhorses.

He tapped his fingers on the side of the beer glass. Why couldn't people just get along instead of fighting to the death because they went to different churches? There must be somewhere where they didn't fight over religion, but if there was, he couldn't think of it. If it wasn't religion it was skin colour. Or money. There was always something to keep the bodies piling up.

Was he talking himself into becoming a priest? Had his mother finally won?

He was sitting in the back room of Mick Mahoney's pub, waiting for Hubert Jefferson. The *Truth* journalist's columns happily lashed out at anyone and everyone. For the last three months he'd been scorching Wellington's Catholics, police and bookmakers as the 'Unholy Trinity'. Jefferson's column was tagged 'by the most feared writer in New Zealand', and it was probably true.

Was Feeney meeting him to feed him more trouble – a priest's work? Of course he was. He'd been raised on the stories of Ignatius Loyola and his Jesuits, finding their ways to the centre of power and altering the course of history to favour the Vatican. Loyola would have sat swapping information with more than one devil.

Jefferson was on time. His smile was cool and professional, the bow tie crisp and neat and the outstretched hand firm, cool and dry.

'Pat, it's good to be seeing you.'

Feeney looked up, surprised at the warmth of the welcome.

'Oh Pat, for God's sake, I've been waiting for weeks for you – or one of yours – to turn up. You have no idea how sick I am of these crowing, keening Prods lording it over you. Now, busy, busy, busy. There's work to be done. It might not be pleasant but it needs doing, so what say we step right along. I'd stop and chat but deadlines press.'

Feeney reached into his pocket and dropped O'Malley's list down on the table. Jefferson looked at it. He smiled, carefully moved the list to one side, swung his briefcase up and took out an exact copy, putting it down beside Feeney's.

'I do believe the correct word on these occasions is "snap",' Jefferson said.

'You knew, and you knew about the Prods?'

Jefferson nodded. 'Oh, Pat. Look, the lists are good, perhaps even great, but they're not enough. I need guideposts to go along with them. Trust me, the Masons and the Prods have been lining up to steer me on the road to be merrily mowing down the Catholics. They make sure I don't stray either. I am phoned every damn day. Now, Pat, we can't be dilly-dallying. Unfortunately you're new to this and it's your virtue you're losing. I'll be gentle but it's better if it's quick.'

'You could have done something about the bloody Prods, with or without a "guidepost",' Feeney managed.

Jefferson sat silent for a moment. 'Yes, I suppose I could.'

'You did nothing!'

'Not a thing!'

'Is this a trap?' Feeney asked.

'It could be,' Jefferson answered.

Feeney looked at him quietly and coldly.

'You could hand me over to the Protestants,' Feeney said.

'It'd ruin me, but one night there'd be someone come at you out of the dark. You wouldn't ever be quite the same again.' He said it quietly and with as much menace as he had in him.

Jefferson sighed and slapped his hand on the table.

'Christ, with the Protestants it was a threat to be finding reefers in my house or car or on my sons!' He was smiling.

'God help us, Pat, do you think that if I worked like that I'd be able to get anyone to talk to me ever again? It'd be bad for business. That's what is important to me. Lord, you're a wonderful tenacious policeman. You've got all the thieves and the sexos scared shitless of you, but this is a new world, so can we be moving on with it?'

Feeney glared at him. Jefferson sighed.

'Understand something very clearly. The church has had it. Gone. Kaput. It just doesn't know it yet. This is the new priesthood – reporters. The new churches are the radio and the papers. We're the pulpits now.'

Feeney waited. If Jefferson was in a mood to talk, let him.

'I don't think there's any point going after individual policemen. Well, except one, and we'll get to that bastard. If I do, it'll come straight back to yourself. They all know you've been up at the Bishop's house, and consorting with the likes of Corbett Wilson. Even the Prods aren't so stupid that they won't put that together.'

'Meanwhile mine are getting the swords run through them,' said Feeney bitterly.

'I'm thinking we might have to wait a little bit.'

Feeney folded his arms across his chest. Jefferson continued.

'I've a little something that fell into my hands, a link between McCarthy and Compton, one going straight to O'Malley. The next time we meet, and we will be meeting, I'll be finding ways to confirm it. Compton's the man. He's the target. In a couple of years he'll have the top job and be strutting around with the leaf on his cap and the black leather gloves and the swagger stick.'

He smiled.

'That's when we move – when he's a big soft, juicy target nicely laid out on the plate for consuming. Ambitious men will be all around him, wanting the job. He'll get no help from them. It'll be easy enough. A few hints in the column, a couple of news stories and we're away.'

Jefferson was enjoying Feeney seeing it open up in front of him.

'Get Compton's name out there. Make him deny it. We examine the denial. Others pick it up. The politicians sniff at it. Our friend Corbett whispers his way through Parliament Buildings, encouraging a royal commission, to be clearing the stain from the police once and for all. By then, Compton's being fed to the dogs. The rats will be running down the ropes and away.'

Jefferson rested a hand on Feeney's forearm.

'The police'll be yours for the taking – you'll have the job for the next thirty years. But you have to wait. Can you do it, Pat? Have you got it in you? Because, my friend, those bastards are making the rope I'll use to hang them. And don't go screaming corruption until you're sure your own henhouse doesn't have any shit on its floor.'

Feeney nodded. Jefferson was right. God, he was an innocent. Please let him never change.

'We'll have to meet again,' Jefferson muttered, almost embarrassed at cutting across Feeney's moment. Feeney nodded. It had been too much to hope that he'd get away with one meeting. He'd never been corrupt, but so help him, this felt like corruption. It was certainly treachery. He didn't know why but suddenly he felt like a bath.

'Okay,' Feeney muttered. 'Call me when you are ready to move.' He got up, shook Jefferson's hand and left.

Jefferson watched him go. He'd get over it. Once they'd been blooded they were always a little more realistic next time, and more the next, and the next. One day they realised they weren't any different to him at all. He shook his head as he gathered up O'Malley's lists. Was this God's work? How would he know?

Maybe his mother was right. He should have been a priest after all.

chapter forty-two

Wellington, 1972

Helen was being moved slowly, until she could feel the ambulance walls surround her. Through the mist she could see people standing around – police and firemen. A white sheet lay near where the shed used to be. Bresnahan was dead.

Half an hour later she was in Wellington Hospital's accident and emergency department with a policeman standing at the door. A nurse had found phone numbers for Archie Fallon and Felicity Castles-O'Brien in Helen's purse. She'd got Felicity first. No, Felicity was not a relative, but she would take care of everything. Later that morning she arrived at Wellington Hospital. Yes, she was Helen Murphy's friend and also her lawyer. Helen would not be talking to anyone until the doctors decided she was fully capable.

Lashing was furious when he heard that.

'The bloody bitch is going to sail away from it, the murdering hoooer!'

Maher asked a uniformed officer to get Lashing under control as Felicity came around the corner.

'Your client's a bloody murderer!' Lashing yelled. 'I'm going after her and I'll prove it!'

'I'll mention that when I am talking to the papers,' Felicity replied.

'She's going to spend the next ten years getting felt up by tattooed bloody lesbians in the shower, and no bloody slippery lawyer's going to stop that either!' Lashing yelled.

'This conversation is over,' Felicity said.

'You're a bloody interfering bitch. That client of yours bloody near got me blown up too. Did you know that? What the hell was she doing there in the middle of the frigging night?'

'If you touch me again, Detective, you'll face assault charges.'

There was a discussion back at Wellington Central about Lashing. Had the blast affected him, or was he just stupid? No one was wasting time finding out which. He'd be writing his report in Auckland – his plane was leaving in about an hour. They'd been to the hotel and packed his stuff. It was all in the car.

Beverley Martinelli arrived about an hour later. She said a quick hello to Helen, squeezed her hand, and went off to chat with the registrar who'd decide on Helen's fitness to be interviewed by the police. It was not a long chat, and very little of it was about Helen. Most of it was about the registrar's sister, also a doctor, who was applying for a big job in Auckland. Beverley had good contacts in the Auckland hospital system. It was wrong that she could influence two of the men making the final decision as to who was and wasn't hired. Of course it was wrong. Careers were at stake. But what was Beverley to do? Go friendless and without sex?

The registrar listened carefully and agreed wholeheartedly that Beverley needed a social life. Beverley was pleased the registrar understood, and offered to be a supportive presence when she talked to the police about Helen's condition.

Unfortunately, the police were told, Helen Murphy was still in no condition to be talking to them – not for some time. How much time? Two days, perhaps three. Could they have a second opinion? Of course. This is Dr Martinelli. I'm sorry but the registrar is absolutely correct.

Felicity was picking up a feeling, now that Lashing had gone, that Bresnahan had been his own victim and that this wasn't shaping up as a case for anyone to be busting a gut over. However, there was the question of what Helen had been doing at the house.

Felicity let it be known, in strict confidence, that Helen had enlisted Fallon to get the wife and the children away, and that Helen and Bresnahan were lovers. Bizarre, yes, but sadly true. Helen's history did include some rough trade. Look where she had chosen to stay – at the Hollywood Motel, for God's sake, when she could afford anything she liked! And hadn't the police seen her at the house only the day before? Yes, they had. Helen had seemed uncomfortable – but wouldn't you be if you had been planning a quickie and the wife and kids had turned out to be there?

The bombs? Well, once Helen had found about Bresnahan's 'hobby' she'd gone right off him. Des Laughlan was on the same case. Bresnahan might have found out.

The owner of the Hollywood Motel hadn't seen any bomb being delivered. Management respected the privacy of its guests.

Lashing's cardboard box had been in water long enough to make it useless for forensics. Lashing was a worry, going on and on about her being a murderer. Christ. If he kept going he'd end up blaming Helen for killing President Kennedy. He'd really lost it.

Through it all Helen said nothing.

Had it been Bresnahan who'd sent the bomb to Helen and Jennifer? Possibly, but then all the evidence was in the shed and it'd take years to reassemble it all. Was it worth it? Technically yes, but if something bigger came along it would be pushed back, until it was forgotten.

Two days later Helen was free to go back to Auckland. The investigation would go on, but unless something spectacular turned up Felicity had picked up the feeling it could quietly wither. Why not? Bresnahan made bombs. Something went wrong. He was not here any more. Tough shit. Judging by how quickly Gwen had dried her tears it didn't look as if he was going to be missed.

Helen, Felicity and Beverley sat in a small Wellington coffee bar.

Helen didn't like the atmosphere. No one seemed to want to celebrate. She was free. The bomber was gone. It didn't look as if the police were going to push too hard – where was the problem?

'If the police contact you, ring me or Fallon immediately,'

Felicity was saying. 'Say nothing until I'm there. Unless something goes really, really badly they don't have enough to charge you with anything. But they'll keep at it. They do.'

Helen looked at the other two.

'Thank you. Thank you so much for everything. It's been wonderful. No it hasn't. It's been horrible. But you have been terrific.'

They both nodded. There was something not quite right. Neither of them was keen to meet her gaze. Beverley was pointedly looking at her watch.

'Will I catch up with you in Auckland?' Helen asked, hopefully, as Beverley picked up her bag.

'Of course. I am pretty busy, though. What say I give you a ring?'

Beverley bit her bottom lip.

'Look, um, it's okay really, but, um, I had to do quite a lot to keep the police away from you till Felicity could get going. Look, I don't want to know if you did something – if you killed him or anything.'

Helen looked at her. How could she be saying this? Did Beverley think she was a murderer? Is this why her friend was looking so uncomfortable?

'Beverley!' Helen said.

But Beverley still couldn't meet her eye. She gave Felicity a hug and a kiss on the cheek; Helen got a handshake. The message rang bright and clear. Beverley didn't like what she'd had to do for her friend, and wanted space and distance – plenty of both. That hurt. Now she was walking away.

Helen looked at Felicity, who reassumed her chilled professional gaze.

'Perhaps it'd be better if we kept things on a professional basis for a while,' Felicity said. 'If anything comes up, definitely call me, all right?'

Helen knew her mouth had fallen open. Beverley had just made it clear that she had done what friends did – help each other through a crisis – but that Helen had asked too much. Felicity obviously felt the same way.

'Thank you,' Helen managed to say.

Felicity nodded and was gone. There was no handshake, never mind a kiss on the cheek or a hug.

Helen watched her go. She turned the corner at the end of the building and was gone. So this was what it was like when people found out you were a murderer and they knew you were going to get away with it.

It wasn't a great feeling. Those were her two best friends, and they were gone. She felt hollow. Yes, she was free, but she was also on her own. What was she going to do? How far could she get without friends?

The waitress came back. Yes, Helen would have another coffee. She'd get back to Auckland and ring that man from the public service. Yes, the police were looking into a case, but it wasn't going to be a problem – there'd be no stain on her character. Look, she was extremely keen about those royal commissions he mentioned. The coffee arrived and it hit the spot. Things were looking up. A life with no skeletons in the closet might turn out to be a good one.

Postscript

In 1955 *Truth* ran a series of articles exposing Eric Henry Compton for owning radio receiving equipment not available to the general public. A Commission of Inquiry was announced and Compton took early retirement.

The disappearance of Wendy Mayes was treated as a murder. It is unsolved.

The murders of Francis Roy Wilkins, Marie West and Herbert Ratcliffe, a homosexual man found kicked and beaten to death near Courtenay Place, remain in New Zealand police files as unsolved crimes.